THE AVENGING
SAINT

FOREWORD BY
JEAN-MARC LOFFICIER

THE ADVENTURES OF THE SAINT

Enter the Saint (1930), *The Saint Closes the Case* (1930),
The Avenging Saint (1930), *Featuring the Saint* (1931),
Alias the Saint (1931), *The Saint Meets His Match* (1931),
The Saint Versus Scotland Yard (1932), *The Saint's Getaway* (1932),
The Saint and Mr Teal (1933), *The Brighter Buccaneer* (1933),
The Saint in London (1934), *The Saint Intervenes* (1934),
The Saint Goes On (1934), *The Saint in New York* (1935),
Saint Overboard (1936), *The Saint in Action* (1937),
The Saint Bids Diamonds (1937), *The Saint Plays with Fire* (1938),
Follow the Saint (1938), *The Happy Highwayman* (1939),
The Saint in Miami (1940), *The Saint Goes West* (1942),
The Saint Steps In (1943), *The Saint on Guard* (1944),
The Saint Sees It Through (1946), *Call for the Saint* (1948),
Saint Errant (1948), *The Saint in Europe* (1953),
The Saint on the Spanish Main (1955), *The Saint Around the World* (1956),
Thanks to the Saint (1957), *Señor Saint* (1958), *Saint to the Rescue* (1959),
Trust the Saint (1962), *The Saint in the Sun* (1963),
Vendetta for the Saint (1964), *The Saint on TV* (1968),
The Saint Returns (1968), *The Saint and the Fiction Makers* (1968),
The Saint Abroad (1969), *The Saint in Pursuit* (1970),
The Saint and the People Importers (1971), *Catch the Saint* (1975),
The Saint and the Hapsburg Necklace (1976), *Send for the Saint* (1977),
The Saint in Trouble (1978), *The Saint and the Templar Treasure* (1978),
Count On the Saint (1980), *Salvage for the Saint* (1983)

THE AVENGING SAINT

LESLIE CHARTERIS

SERIES EDITOR: IAN DICKERSON

Text copyright © 2014 Interfund (London) Ltd.
Foreword © 2014 Jean-Marc Lofficier
Preface first published in *The Avenging Saint,* Fiction Publishing edition, 1964
Publication History and Author Biography © 2014 Ian Dickerson
All rights reserved.

Published by Thomas & Mercer, Seattle

www.apub.com

ISBN-13: 9781477842638
ISBN-10:1477842632

Cover design by David Drummond, www.salamanderhill.com

Printed in the United States of America.

To Raymond Savage

London, May 1930

PUBLISHER'S NOTE

FOREWORD TO THE
NEW EDITION

The book you hold in your hands changed my life.

I know that sounds rather overblown, but it's still true. Without it, I might never have become a writer. Maybe I would have been a teacher, a lawyer, or (Heaven forbid!) a banker, but not a writer.

Because I owe it all to Leslie Charteris—and the Saint. But not quite in the way you may think.

A bit of context is necessary before I go any further. Please bear with me while I acquaint you with the basics of the publication of the Saint in France.

Simon made his first appearance in a mystery imprint put out by publisher Gallimard in 1935, but it was the competing Editions Fayard which, from 1938 to 1968, popularized the character in France. Since I wasn't born until 1954, you might well ask how this is relevant. It's like this:

Due to contractual obligations, Gallimard had reserved the rights to the two novels it published, *Meet—the Tiger!* and *The Saint Closes the Case*, so Fayard was obliged to start their own Saint imprint with *The Saint in New York* as No. 1, then *The Avenging Saint* as No. 2. The latter was released under the title *The Heroic Adventure*.

When I discovered, and began collecting, Saint books in 1967, at age thirteen, they were one of the cheapest and most entertaining series of paperbacks available on the market, endlessly reprinted since the 1940s.

They were virtually everywhere, on the newsstands and in the bookstores, given a boost by Roger Moore's television series, which was then playing on our small screens.

Graced by colorful, high-design covers by the gifted Regino Bernad, most of the later volumes were loose adaptations of the American radio-plays or *The New York Herald Tribune* comic strips, ably rendered into French by Madeleine Michel-Tyl, whose husband, Edmond (who passed away in 1949), was himself an author of popular novels. Edmond had not only translated the first Saint books, but also Rex Stout's Nero Wolfe mysteries for Fayard.

For the record, my very first Saint books were No. 48, *Le Saint exige la tête*, and No. 18, *La Marque du Saint*, which contained such Charteris classics as "The Man Who Was Clever" and "The Logical Adventure."

Being the kind of person I am, I immediately decided to collect them all, and read them in what I thought was their proper, numbered order. Unfortunately, as is often the case with series, No. 1 (*The Saint in New York*) was hard to find. In fact, I never found a Fayard edition until much, much later, and I eventually had to satisfy myself with a Livre de Poche reprint.

So I began the series with No. 2, *The Avenging Saint*.

The problem was—one couldn't very well follow *The Avenging Saint* without having first read *The Saint Closes the Case*!

There was no internet back then, no Wikipedia, no books or articles where I could have looked up a complete bibliography of Leslie Charteris. And Fayard wasn't obliging enough to list *The Saint Closes the Case* (and *Meet the Tiger!*) in their back pages, since they had been published by one of their competitors. In fact, Fayard didn't get to publish *The Last Hero* in its own imprint until No. 72!

So, there I was, stuck with *Knight Templar*, without a copy of *The Last Hero*. While I could plainly see that something was being kept hidden from me, I couldn't tell what. I had no clue that *The Saint Closes the Case* existed, only hints about the fairly cataclysmic events that had pitted Simon against Rayt Marius ("Marus" in the French edition because the name "Marius" is associated with the happy-go-lucky popular character in Marseilles fiction), Prince Rudolf, and Professor Vargan, and that it had resulted in the death of the Saint's dearest friend, Norman Kent.

You might say that's really all one needs to know to tackle *The Avenging Saint*, but it was still a very annoying feeling to realize that half of the story had somehow already occurred before I turned the first page.

Feeling very frustrated over that state of things, I did what any teenager in my place would have done. No, I didn't discard the book; I decided to write my own prequel.

I promptly embarked upon writing my own version of *The Saint Closes the Case*, and, with the touching hubris that only a fourteen-year-old can muster, I grabbed first credit by signing it "by Jean-Marc Lofficier & Leslie Charteris."

As William Goldman discovered when he abridged S. Morgenstern's immortal classic *The Princess Bride*, the problem with prose fiction is that one spends a lot of time with descriptions and other boring background stuff, and that we don't get quickly enough to the "best bits."

So, after a couple of pages, I switched to doing it in the comic book format, using an avant-garde artistic technique referred to by ignoramuses as "stick figures." If there is one character, after all, whose story can be told through stick figures, isn't it the Saint?

Story-wise, that worked rather well. In the space of a couple of months, I filled well over a hundred notebook-sized pages with small panels telling my own version of the Saint's adventure. If I recall correctly, in my version, Marius and Vargan belonged to a secret organization called "Shadow" led by a villain named Doctor (or was it Professor?) Skull. The story involved thuggees and idols made of a strange kind of unmelting ice and daggers that spat electron fire, and all kinds of outlandish elements.

Through it all, the little stick figure of Simon fought bravely through countless perils, dispatching villains with his unique brand of wit and determination.

When I was eventually lucky enough to talk to Mr. Charteris himself, in 1974, an experience which was not unlike that of a small village priest meeting the Pope, I conspicuously refrained from mentioning *The Last Hero* or Doctor Skull.

But for all its faults, its naiveté and outrageous pulpishness, its shameless "borrowings" from other sources and over-melodramatic plot, this was my first long-distance narrative, with proper dialogue and plot. It was an invaluable teaching tool that later enabled me to tackle more serious works, and eventually write real books and real comics.

If I had read *The Saint Closes the Case* before *The Avenging Saint*, would have I embarked upon such a quixotic task? Who can tell? But I can't help feel that, if I became a writer, I owe it all to this odd case of the two books being published out of order.

Understandably, in light of what I've just written, *The Avenging Saint* remains, to this day, my favorite Saint book—in fact, the only one which I have in both its French and English editions. I would argue it may well be the best Saint novel of all. There are so many things to like about it, from Simon's ground-breaking triangular relationship with Sonia and Pat, with the shadow of Norman Kent's death looming over his head, to the return of Inspector Carn, from the callous villainy of Marius (a proto-Bondian villain who surely must have inspired Fleming!), to the smooth deadliness of Prince Rudolf, and, of course, the best ending ever!

But before you embark upon reading this thrilling novel, let me offer a word of caution:

Make sure you read *The Saint Closes the Case* first.

Because, otherwise, who knows, you might become a writer too.

—Jean-Marc Lofficier

THE AVENGING
SAINT

PREFACE

This book is an almost immediate sequel to *The Saint Closes the Case*, and was in fact written only a year later. Unfortunately for its vulnerability to some radical and justifiable criticisms from modern readers, that was still only 1930, and a lot of notions were then current, which I shared with many of my contemporaries, which seem rather naive and outmoded today.

The belief that unscrupulously ambitious rulers were manipulated like chessmen by shadowy international billionaires to wage wars that would only enrich the armaments industry was held by not a few reasonably intelligent people, nor was it, perhaps, without some interesting facets of truth. But in the context of today's primarily ideological conflicts, and the steady dwindling of the prospects of realizable profit from a shooting war (as against a cold war, which is still great for "defense" industries), it starts to look somewhat tired and frail.

So also does the facility of the engineered casus belli. When this novel was written, the last of a lengthy historical series of specious pretext for launching hostilities which were politically predestined anyway was the assassination of an Austrian Archduke in 1914, which embroiled one nation after another in the "Armageddon" which has since been demoted to merely World War I. In this decade, when even the assassination of a President of the United States by an ex-Marxist and Cuban sympathiser did not even trigger a general mobilization, half of this story's plot must seem, to a jaundiced eye, pathetically thin.

Therefore, since the Saint is still alive and active in a contemporary world astronautically removed from the one in which this episode was laid, I feel that I again need to point out that this is really a kind of historical novel, just as a novel of the aftermath of the American Civil War might be, in a background encompassed by some living memories, but no less valid because it pre-dates the personal experience of most readers.

You may stub your toes on other oddities. Such as the handling of an airplane towards the end, which would give any jet pilot hysterics. But flying, in those days, was like that: I can vouch for the fact, with my own pilot's licence which I earned in 1929, which in the sublime confidence of the future which characterized those days authorized me to fly "all types" of aircraft. One day I hope to show it to the captain of a supersonic Concorde and ask if I may play around a bit . . .

The "Russia" referred to in this story, I must also remind you, was not only pre-Khrushchev but pre-Stalin, at least as the world menace which he later became. So, please, by-pass the anachronisms, and enjoy what I still think was one of the Saint's best outright adventures.

—Leslie Charteris (1964)

CHAPTER ONE:

HOW SIMON TEMPLAR SANG
A SONG AND FOUND SOME OF
IT TRUE

1

The Saint sang:

> *"Strange adventure! Maiden wedded*
> *To a groom she'd never seen—*
> *Never, never, never seen!*
> *Groom about to be beheaded,*
> *In an hour on Tower Green!*
> *Tower, Tower, Tower Green!*
> *Groom in dreary dungeon lying—"*

"'Ere," said an arm of the Law. "Not so much noise!"

The Saint stopped, facing round, tall and smiling and debonair.

"Good evening—or morning—as the case may be," said the Saint politely.

"And what d'you think you're doing?" demanded the Law.

"Riding on a camel in the desert," said the Saint happily.

The Law peered at him suspiciously. But the Saint looked very respectable. The Saint always looked so respectable that he could at any time have walked into an ecclesiastical conference without even being asked for his ticket. Dressed in rags, he could have made a bishop look like two cents at a bad rate of exchange. And in the costume that he had donned for that night's occasion his air of virtue was overpowering. His shirt-front was of a pure and beautiful white that should have argued a pure and beautiful soul. His tuxedo, even under the poor illumination of a street lamp, was cut with such a dazzling perfection, and worn moreover with such a staggering elegance, that no tailor with a pride in his profession could have gazed unmoved upon such a stupendous apotheosis of his art. The Saint, as he stood there, might have been taken for an unemployed archangel—if he had remembered to wear his soft black felt a little less rakishly, and to lean a little less rakishly on his gold-mounted stick. As it was, he looked like a modern pugilist, the heir to a dukedom, a successful confidence man, or an advertisement for Wuggo. And the odour of sanctity about him could have been scented a hundred yards upwind by a man with a severe cold in the head and no sense of smell.

The Law, slightly dazed by its scrutiny, pulled itself together with a visible effort.

"You can't," said the Law, "go bawling about the streets like that at two o'clock in the morning."

"I wasn't bawling," said the Saint aggrievedly. "I was singing."

"Bawling, I call it," said the Law obstinately.

The Saint took out his cigarette-case; it was a very special case, and the Saint was very proud of it, and would as soon have thought of travelling without it as he would have thought of walking down Piccadilly in his pyjamas. Into that cigarette-case had been concentrated an enthusiastic ingenuity that was typical of the Saint's flair for detail—a flair that had already enabled him to live about twenty-nine years longer than a good many people thought he ought to have. There was much more in that case than met the eye. Much more. But it wasn't

8

in action at that particular moment. The cigarette which the Law was prevailed upon to accept was innocent of deception, as also was the one which the Saint selected for himself.

"Anyway," said the Saint, "wouldn't you bawl, as you call it, if you knew that a man with a name like Heinrich Dussel had recently received into his house an invalid who wasn't ill?"

The Law blinked, bovinely meditative. "Sounds fishy to me," conceded the Law.

"And to me," said the Saint. "And queer fish are my hobby. I'd travel a thousand miles any day to investigate a kipper that was the least bit queer on the kip—and it wouldn't be for the first time. There was a smear of bloater paste, once, that fetched me from the Malay Peninsula via Chicago to a very wild bit of Devonshire . . . But this is more than bloater paste. This is real red herring."

"Are you drunk?" inquired the Law, kindly.

"No," said the Saint. "British Constitution. Truly rural. The Leith police dismisseth us . . . No, I'm not drunk. But I'm thinking of possible accidents. So would you just note that I'm going into that house up there—number ninety—perfectly sound and sane? And I shan't stay more than half an hour at the outside—voluntarily. So if I'm not out here again at two-thirty, you can walk right in and demand the body. *Au revoir*, sweetheart."

And the Saint smiled beatifically, hitched himself off his gold-mounted stick, adjusted the rakish tilt of his hat, and calmly resumed his stroll and his song, while the Law stared blankly after him.

> *"Groom in dreary dungeon lying,*
> *Groom as good as dead, or dying*
> *For a pretty maiden sighing—*
> *Pretty maid of seventeen!*
> *Seven—seven—seventeen!"*

"Blimey," said the Law, blankly.

But the Saint neither heard nor cared what the Law said. He passed on, swinging his stick, into his adventure.

2

Meet the Saint.

His godfathers and his godmothers, at his baptism, had bestowed upon him the name of Simon Templar, but the coincidence of initials was not the only reason for the nickname by which he was far more widely known. One day, the story of how he came by that nickname may be told: it is a good story, in its way, though it goes back to the days when the Saint was nineteen, and almost as respectable as he looked. But the name had stuck. It was inevitable that it should stick, for obviously it had been destined to him from the beginning. And in the ten years that had followed his second and less godly baptism, he had done his very best to live up to that second name—according to his lights. But you may have heard the story of the very big man whose friends called him Tiny.

He looked very Saintly indeed as he sauntered up Park Lane that night.

Saintly . . . you understand . . . with the capital S. That was how Roger Conway always liked to spell the adjective, and that pleasant conceit may very well be carried on here. There was something about the way Simon wore the name, as there was about the way he wore his clothes, that naturally suggested capital letters in every context.

Of course, he was all wrong. He ought never to have been let loose upon this twentieth century. He was upsetting. Far too often, when he spoke, his voice struck disturbing chords in the mind. When you saw him, you looked, instinctively and exasperatedly, for a sword at his side, a feather in his hat, and spurs at his heels. There was a queer keenness in the chiselling of his tanned face, seen in profile—something that can only be described as a swiftness of line about the nose and lips and chin, a swiftness as well set off by the slick sweep of patent-leather hair as by the brim of a filibustering felt hat—a laughing dancing devil of mischief that was never far from the very clear blue eyes, a magnificently medieval flamboyance of manner, an extraordinary vividness and vital challenge about every movement he made, that too clearly had no place in the organization of the century that was afflicted with him. If he had been anyone else, you would have felt that the organization was likely to make life very difficult for him. But he was Simon Templar, the Saint, and so you could only feel that he was likely to make life very difficult for the organization. Wherefore, as a respectable member of the organization, you were liable to object . . .

And, in fact, objections had been made in due season—to such effect that, if anything was needed to complete the Saint's own private entertainment at that moment, it could have been provided by the reflection that he had no business to be in England at all that night. Or any other night. For the name of the Saint was not known only to his personal friends and enemies. It was something like a legend, a public institution; not many months ago, it had been headlined over every newspaper in Europe, and the Saint's trade-mark—a childish sketch of a little man with straight-line body and limbs, and a round blank head under an absurd halo—had been held in almost superstitious awe throughout the length and breadth of England. And there still reposed, in the desk of Chief Inspector Teal, at New Scotland Yard, warrants for the arrest of Simon Templar and the other two who had been with him in all his misdeeds— Roger Conway and Patricia Holm. Why the Saint had come back to England was nobody's business. He hadn't yet advertised his return, and, if he had advertised it, nothing is more certain than that Chief Inspector Claud Eustace Teal would have been combing London for him within the hour—with a gun behind each ear, and an official address of welcome according to the Indictable Offences Act, 1848, in his pocket . . .

Wherefore it was very good and amusing to be back in London, and very good and amusing to be on the trail of an invalid who was not ill, though sheltering in the house of a man with a name like Heinrich Dussel . . .

The Saint knew that the invalid was still there, because it was two o'clock on Sunday morning, and near the policeman a melancholy-looking individual was selling very early editions of the Sunday papers, apparently hoping to catch returning Saturday-night revellers on the rebound, and the melancholy-looking individual hadn't batted an eyelid as the Saint passed. If anything interesting had happened since the melancholy-looking individual had made his last report, Roger Conway would have batted one eyelid, and Simon would have bought a paper and found a note therein. And if the invalid who was not ill had left the house, Roger wouldn't have been there at all. Nor would the low-bodied long-nosed Hirondel parked close by. On the face of it, there was no connection between Roger Conway and the Hirondel, but that was part of the deception . . .

> *"Strange adventure that we're trolling*
> *Modest maid and gallant groom—*
> *Gallant, gallant, gallant groom!*

> *While the funeral bell is tolling,*
> *Tolling, tolling—"*

Gently the Saint embarked upon the second verse of his song. And through his manifest cheerfulness he felt a faint electric tingle of expectation.

For he knew that it was true. He, of all men living, should have known that the age of strange adventures was not past. There were adventures all around, then, as there had been since the beginning of the world; it was a matter for the adventurer, to go out and challenge them. And adventure had never failed Simon Templar—perhaps because he had never doubted it. It might have been luck, or it might have been his own uncanny genius, but at least he knew, whatever it was he had to thank, that whenever and wherever anything was happening, he was there. He had been born to it, the spoilt child of a wild tempestuous Destiny—born for nothing else, it seemed, but to find all the fun in the world.

And he was on the old trail again.

But this time it was no fluke. His worst enemy couldn't have said that Simon Templar hadn't worked for all the trouble he was going to find that night. For weeks past he had been hunting two men across Europe—a slim and very elegant man, and a huge and very ugly man— and one of them at least he had sworn to kill. Neither of them went by the name of Heinrich Dussel, even in his spare time, but Heinrich Dussel had conferred with them the night before in the slim and very elegant man's suite at the Ritz, and accordingly the Saint had become interested in Heinrich Dussel. And then, less than two hours before the Saint's brief conversation with the Law, had commenced the Incident of the Invalid who was not.

> *"Modest maiden will not tarry;*
> *Though but sixteen year she carry,*

> *She must marry, she must marry,*
> *Though the altar be a tomb—*
> *Tower, Tower, Tower tomb!"*

Thus the Saint brought both his psalm and his promenade to a triumphant conclusion, for the song stopped as the Saint stopped, which was at the foot of a short flight of steps leading to a door—the door of the house of Heinrich Dussel.

And then, as Simon Templar paused there, a window was smashed directly above his head, so that chips of splintered glass showered on to the pavement all around him. And there followed a man's sudden sharp yelp of agony, clear and shrill in the silence of the street.

"'Ere," said a familiar voice, "is this the 'ouse you said you were going into?"

The Saint turned.

The Law stood beside him, its hands in its belt, having followed him all the way on noiseless rubber soles.

And Simon beamed beatifically upon the Law.

"That's so, Algernon," he murmured, and mounted the steps.

The door opened almost as soon as he had touched the bell. And the Law was still beside him.

"What's wrong 'ere?" demanded the Law.

"It is nothing."

Dussel himself had answered the bell, suave and self-possessed— exactly as the Saint would have expected him to be.

"We have a patient here who is—not right in the head. Sometimes he is violent. But he is being attended to."

"That's right," said the Saint calmly. "I got your telephone message, and came right round."

He turned to the Law with a smile.

"I am the doctor in charge of the case," he said, "so you may quite safely leave things in my hands."

His manner would have disarmed the Chief Commissioner himself. And before either of the other two could say a word, the Saint had stepped over the threshold as if he owned the house.

"Good night, officer," he said sweetly, and closed the door.

3

Now, the unkind critic may say that the Saint had opened his break with something like the most fantastic fluke that ever fell out of the blue, but the unkind critic would be wrong, and his judgement would merely indicate his abysmal ignorance of the Saint and all Saintly methods. It cannot be too clearly understood that, having determined to enter the house of Heinrich Dussel and dissect the mystery of the invalid who was not, Simon Templar had walked up Park Lane with the firm intention of ringing the bell, walking in while the butler was still asking him his business, closing the door firmly behind him, and leaving the rest to Providence. The broken window, and the cry that came through it, had not been allowed for in such nebulous calculations as he had made—admitted, but in fact they made hardly any difference to the general plan of campaign. It would be far more true to say that the Saint refused to put off his stroke by the circumstances, than to say that the circumstances helped him. All that happened was that an unforeseen accident intervened in the smooth course of the Saint's progress, and the Saint, with the inspired audacity that lifted him so high above all ordinary adventurers, had flicked the accident into the accommodating machinery of his stratagem, and passed on . . . And the final result was unaltered, for the Saint simply arrived where he had meant to arrive, anyway—with his back to the inside of the door of Heinrich Dussel's house, and all the fun before him . . .

And Simon Templar smiled at Heinrich Dussel, a rather thoughtful and reckless smile, for Heinrich Dussel was the kind of man for whom the Saint would always have a rather thoughtful and reckless smile. He was short, heavily built, tremendously broad of shoulder, thin-lipped, with a high bald dome of a forehead, and greenish eyes that gleamed like glazed pebbles behind thick gold-rimmed spectacles.

"May I ask what you mean by this?" Dussel was blustering furiously. The Saint threw out his hands in a wide gesture.

"I wanted to talk to you, dear heart."

"And what do you imagine I can do for you?"

"On the contrary," said the Saint genially, "the point is—what can I do for you? Ask, and you shall receive. I'm ready. If you say, 'Go and get the moon,' I'll go right out and get the moon—that's how I feel about you, sweetheart"

Dussel took a step forward.

"Will you stand away from that door?"

"No," said the Saint, courteous but definite.

"Then you will have to be removed by force."

"If you could spare me a moment," began the Saint warily.

But Heinrich Dussel had half turned, drawing breath, his mouth opening for one obvious purpose.

He could hardly have posed himself better.

And before that deep purposeful breath had reached Dussel's vocal cords on the return journey, his mouth closed again abruptly, with a crisp smack, under the persuasive influence of a pile-driving upper-cut.

"Come into my study," invited the Saint, in a very fair imitation of Heinrich Dussel's guttural accent.

"Thank you," said the Saint, in his own voice.

And his arms were already around Heinrich Dussel, holding up the unconscious man, and, as he accepted his own invitation, the Saint stooped swiftly, levered Dussel on to his shoulder, moved up the hall, and passed through the nearest door.

He did not stay.

He dropped his burden unceremoniously on the floor, and passed out again, locking the door behind him and putting the key in his pocket. Then, certainly, luck was with him, for, in spite of the slight disturbance, none of the household staff were in view. The Saint went up the stairs as lightly as a ghost.

The broken window had been on the first floor, and the room to which it belonged was easy to locate. The Saint listened for a couple of seconds at the door, and then opened it and stepped briskly inside.

The room was empty.

"Bother," said the Saint softly.

Then he understood.

"If the cop had insisted on coming in, he'd have wanted to see this room. So they'd have shifted the invalid. One of the gang would have played the part. And the real cripple—further up the stairs, I should think . . ."

And Simon was out of the empty room in an instant, and flashing up the next flight.

As he reached the upper landing, a man—a villainous foreign-looking man, in some sort of livery—emerged from a door.

The Saint never hesitated.

"All right?" he queried briefly.

"Yes," came the automatic answer.

No greater bluff could ever have been put in two words and a stride. It was such a perfect little cameo of the art that the liveried man did not realize how he had been bluffed until three seconds after the

Saint had spoken. And that was about four seconds too late. For by that time the Saint was only a yard away.

"That's fine," said the Saint crisply. "Keep your face shut, and everything will still be all right. Back into that room . . ."

There was a little knife in the Saint's hand. The Saint could do things with that knife that would have made a circus performer blink. But at that moment the Saint wasn't throwing the knife—he was just pricking the liveried man's throat with the point. And the liveried man recoiled instinctively.

The Saint pushed him on, into the room, and kicked the door shut behind him. Then he dropped the knife, and took the man by the throat . . .

He made very little noise. And presently the man slept . . . Then the Saint got to his feet, and looked about him.

The invalid lay on the bed—an old man, it seemed, judging by the thick grey beard. A shabby tweed cap was pulled down over eyes shielded by dark glasses, and his clothes were shapeless and ill-fitting. He wore black gloves, and above these there were ropes, binding his wrists together, and there were ropes also about his ankles.

The Saint picked him up in his arms. He seemed to weigh hardly anything at all.

As swiftly and silently as he had come, the Saint went down the stairs again with his light load.

Even then, it was not all perfectly plain sailing. A hubbub began to arise from below as Simon reached the first floor, and as he turned the corner on to the last flight, he saw a man unlocking the door of the room in which Heinrich Dussel had been locked. And Simon continued calmly downwards.

He reached the hall level in time to meet two automatics—one in the hand of the man who had unlocked the door, and one in the hand of Heinrich Dussel.

"Your move, Heinrich," said the Saint calmly. "May I smoke while you're thinking it over?"

He put the shabby old man carefully down on a convenient chair, and took out his cigarette-case.

"Going to hand me over to the police?" he murmured. "If you are, you'll have to figure out a lot of explanations pretty quickly. The cop outside heard me say I was your doctor, and he'll naturally want to know why you've waited such a long time before denying it. Besides, there's Convalescent Cuthbert here . . ." The Saint indicated the old man in the chair, who was trying ineffectually to say something through a very efficient gag. "Even mental cases aren't trussed up quite like that."

"No," said Dussel deliberately, "you will not be handed over to the police, my friend."

"Well, you can't keep me here," said the Saint, puffing. "You see, I had some words with the cop before I came to your door, and I told him I shouldn't be staying more than half an hour—voluntarily. And after the excitement just before I walked in, I should think he'll still be waiting around to see what happens."

Dussel turned to his servant.

"Go to a window, Luigi, and see if the policeman is still waiting."

"It is a bit awkward for you, Heinrich, old dear, isn't it?" murmured Simon, smoking tranquilly, as the servant disappeared. "I'm so well known to the police. I'd probably turn out to be well known to you, too, if I told you my name. I'm known as the Saint . . ." He grinned at Dussel's sudden start. "Anyway, your pals know me. Ask the Crown Prince—or Dr Marius. And remember to give them my love . . ."

The Saint laughed shortly, and Heinrich Dussel was still staring at him, white-lipped, when the servant returned to report that the constable was watching the house from the opposite pavement, talking to a newspaperman.

"You seem annoyed, Heinrich," remarked the Saint, gently bantering, though the glitter behind Dussel's thick glasses should have told him that he was as near sudden death at that moment as it is healthy for any man to be. "Now, the Crown Prince never looks annoyed. He's much more strong and silent than you are, is Rudolf . . ."

Simon spoke dreamily, almost in a whisper, and his gaze was intent upon his cigarette- end. And, all the while, he smiled . . .

Then—

"I'll show you a conjuring trick," he said suddenly. "Look!"

He threw the cigarette-end on the carpet at their feet, and closed his eyes. But the other two looked.

They heard a faint hiss, and then the cigarette burst into a flare of white-hot eye- aching light that seemed to scorch through their eyeballs and sear their very brains. It only lasted a moment, but that was long enough. Then a dense white smoke filled the hall like a fog. And the Saint, with the old man in his arms again, was at the front door. They heard his mocking voice through their dazed blindness.

"Creates roars of laughter," said the Saint. "Try one at your next party—and invite me . . . So long, souls!"

The plop of a silenced automatic came through the smoke, and a bullet smacked into the door beside the Saint's head. Then he had the door open, and the smoke followed him out.

"Fire!" yelled the Saint wildly. "Help! He rushed down the steps, and the policeman met him on the pavement. "For heaven's sake try to save the others, officer! I've got this old chap all right, but there are more in there—"

He stood by the kerb, shaking with silent laughter, and watched the Law brace itself and plunge valiantly into the smoke. Then the Hirondel purred up beside him, with the melancholy-looking vendor of newspapers at the wheel, and the Saint stepped into the back seat.

"OK, Big Boy," he drawled, and Roger Conway let in the clutch.

4

"Altogether a most satisfactory beginning to the Sabbath," the Saint remarked, as the big car switched into a side street. "I won't say it was dead easy, but you can't have everything. The only real trouble came at the very end, and then the old magnesium cigarette was just what the doctor ordered . . . Have a nice chat with the police?"

"Mostly about you," said Roger. "The ideas that man had about the Saint were too weird and wonderful for words. I steered him on to the subject, and spent the rest of the time wishing I hadn't—it hurt so much trying not to laugh."

Simon chuckled.

"And now," he said, "I'm wondering what story dear Heinrich is trying to put over. That man won't get any beauty sleep tonight. Oh, it's a glorious thought! Dear Heinrich . . ."

He subsided into a corner, weak with merriment, and felt for his cigarette-case. Then he observed the ancient invalid, writhing helplessly on the cushions beside him, and grinned.

"Sorry, beautiful," he murmured, "but I'm afraid you'll have to stay like that till we get home. We can't have you making a fuss now. But as soon as we arrive we'll untie you and give you a large glass of milk, and you shall tell us the story of your life."

The patriarch shook his head violently; then, finding that his protest was ignored, he relapsed into apathetic resignation.

A few minutes later the Hirondel turned into the mews where Simon Templar had established his headquarters in a pair of luxuriously converted garages. As the car stopped, Simon picked up the old man again and stepped out. Roger Conway opened the front door for him, and the Saint passed through the tiny hall into the sitting-room, while Roger went to put the car away. Simon deposited the ancient in a chair and drew the blinds; not until after he had assured himself that no one could look in from outside did he switch on the lights and turn to regard his souvenir of the night's entertainment.

"Now you shall say your piece, uncle," he remarked, and went to untie the gag. "Roger will make your Glaxo hot for you in a minute, and—Holy Moses!"

The Saint drew a deep breath.

For, as he removed the gag, the long grey beard had come away with it. For a moment he was too amazed to move. Then he snatched off the dark glasses and the shabby tweed cap, and a mass of rich brown hair tumbled about the face of one of the loveliest girls he had ever seen.

CHAPTER TWO:
HOW SIMON TEMPLAR
ENTERTAINED A GUEST AND
SPOKE OF TWO OLD FRIENDS

1

"That hand-brake's still a bit feeble, old boy." Roger Conway came in, unfastening the gaudy choker which he had donned for his character part. "You ought to get—"

His voice trailed away, and he stood staring.

The Saint was on his knees, his little throwing-knife in his hand, swiftly cutting ropes away from wrists and ankles.

"I'll have it seen to on Monday," said the Saint coolly.

Roger swallowed.

"Damn it, Saint—"

Simon looked round with a grin.

"Yes, I know, sonny boy," he said. "It is our evening, isn't it?" He stood up and looked down at the girl.

"How are you feeling, old thing?"

She had her hands clasped to her forehead.

"I'll be all right in a minute," she said. "My head—hurts . . ."

"That dope they gave you," murmured the Saint. "And the crack you got afterwards. Rotten, isn't it? But we'll put that right in a brace of shakes. Roger, you beetle off to the kitchen and start some tea, and I'll officiate with the dispensary."

Roger departed obediently, and Simon went over to a cupboard, and took therefrom a bottle and a glass. From the bottle he shook two pink tablets into the glass. Then he fizzed soda-water on to them from the siphon, and thoughtfully watched them dissolve.

"Here you are, old dear." He touched the girl lightly on the shoulder, with the foaming drink in his other hand. "Just shoot this down, and in about five minutes, when you've lowered a cup of tea on top of it, you'll be prancing about like a canary on a hot pancake."

She looked up at him a little doubtfully, as if she was wondering whether her present headache might not be so bad as the one she might get from the glass he was offering. But the Saint's smile was reassuring.

"Good girl . . . And it wasn't so very foul, was it?"

Simon smiled approval as she handed him back the empty glass.

"Thank you—so much . . ."

"Not at all," said the Saint "Any little thing like that . . . Now, all you've got to do, lass, is just to lie back and rest and wait for that cup of tea."

He lighted a cigarette and leaned against the table, surveying her in silence.

Under her tousled hair he saw a face that must have been modelled by happy angels. Her eyes were closed then, but he had already seen them open—deep pools of hazel, shaded by soft lashes. Her mouth was proud and imperious, yet with laughter lurking in the curves of the red lips. And a little colour was starting to ebb back into the faultless cheeks. If he had ever seen real beauty in a woman, it was there. There was a serene dignity in the forehead, a fineness of line about the small, straight nose, a wealth of character in the moulding of the chin, that would have singled her out in any company. And the Saint was not surprised, for it was dawning upon him that he knew who she was.

The latest *Bystander* was on the table beside him. He picked it up and turned the pages . . . She was there. He knew he could not have been mistaken, for he had been studying the picture only the previous afternoon. He had thought she was lovely then, but now he knew that the photograph did her no justice.

He was still gazing at her when Roger entered with a tray.

"Good man." Simon removed his gaze from the girl for one second, with an effort, and then allowed it to return. He shifted off the table. "Come along, lass."

She opened her eyes, smiling.

"I feel ever so much better now," she said.

"Nothing to what you'll feel like when you've inhaled this Château Lipton," said the Saint cheerfully. "One or two lumps? Or three?"

"Only two." She spoke with the slightest of American accents, soft and utterly fascinating.

Simon handed her the cup.

"Thank you," she said, and then, suddenly: "Oh, tell me how you found me . . ."

"Well, that's part of a long story," said the Saint. "The short part of it is that we were interested in Heinrich Dussel—the owner of the house where I found you—and Roger here was watching him. About midnight Roger saw an old man arrive in a car—drugged . . ."

"How did you know I was drugged?"

"They brought a wheelchair out of the house for you," Roger explained. "They seemed to be in rather a hurry, and as they lifted you out of the car they caught your head a frightful crack on the door. Now, even a paralysed old man doesn't take a bang on the head like that without making some movement or saying something, but you took it like a corpse, and no one even apologized."

The Saint laughed.

"It was a really bright scheme," he said. "A perfect disguise, perfectly thought out—right down to those gloves they put on you in case anyone noticed your hands. And they'd have brought it off if it hadn't been for that one slip—and Roger's eagle eye. But after that, the only thing for us to do was to interview Heinrich . . ."

He grinned reminiscently, and retailed the entire episode for Roger Conway's benefit. The latter half of it the girl already knew, but they laughed again together over the thought of the curtain to the scene—the Law ploughing heroically in to rescue other greybeards from the flames, and finding Mr Dussel . . .

"The only thing I haven't figured out," said the Saint, "is how it was a man I heard cry out, when the window was smashed in the frolic before I came in."

"I bit him in the hand," said the girl simply. Simon held up his hands in admiring horror.

"I get you . . . You came to, and tried to make a fight of it—and you—you—bit a man in the hand?"

She nodded.

"Do you know who I am?"

"I do," said the Saint helplessly. "That's what makes it so perfect"

2

Simon Templar picked up the *Bystander*.

"I recognized you from your picture in here," he said, and handed the paper to Roger. "See if you can find it, sonny boy."

The girl passed him her cup, and he took and replenished it.

"I was at a ball at the Embassy," she said. "We're staying there . . . It was very dull. About half-past eleven I slipped away to my room to rest—it was so hot in the ballroom. I'm very fond of chocolates"—she smiled whimsically—"and there was a lovely new box on my dressing-table. I didn't stop to think how they came there—I supposed the Ambassador's wife must have put them in my room, because she knows my weakness—and I just naturally took one. I remember it had a funny bitter taste, and I didn't like it, and then I don't remember anything until I woke up in that house."

She shuddered; then she laughed a little.

"And then you came in," she said.

The Saint smiled, and glanced across at Roger Conway, who had put down the *Bystander* and was staring at the girl. And she laughed again, merrily, at Roger's consternation.

"I may be a millionaire's daughter," she said, "but I enjoyed your tea like anyone else."

Simon offered his cigarette-case.

"Those are the ones that don't explode," he said, pointing, and helped himself after her. Then he said, "Have you started wondering who was responsible?"

"I haven't had much time—"

"But now—can you think of anyone? Anyone who could do a thing like that in an Embassy, and smuggle you out in those clothes?"

She shook her head.

"It seems so fantastic—"

"And yet I could name the man who could have done it—and did it."

"But who?"

"You probably danced with him during the evening."

"I danced with so many."

"But he would be one of the first to be presented."

"I can't think—"

"But you can!" said the Saint. "A man of medium height—slim—small moustache—very elegant—" He watched the awakening comprehension in her eyes, and forestalled it. "The Crown Prince Rudolf of—"

"But that's impossible!"

"It is—but it's true. I can give you proof . . . And it's just his mark. It's worthy of him. It's one of the biggest things that have ever been done!"

The Saint was striding up and down the room in his excitement, with a light kindling in his face, and a fire in his eyes, that Roger Conway knew of old. Simon Templar's thoughts, inspired, had leapt on leagues beyond his spoken words, as they often did when those queer flashes of genius broke upon him. Roger knew that the Saint would come back to earth in a few moments, and condescend to make his argument plain to less vivid minds; Roger was used to these moods, and had learnt to wait patiently upon them, but bewildered puzzlement showed on the girl's face.

"I knew it!" Simon stopped pacing the room suddenly, and met the girl's smiling perplexity with a laugh. "Why, it's as plain as the nose on your—on—on Roger's face! Listen . . ."

He swung on to the table, discarded a half-smoked cigarette, and lighted a fresh one. "You heard me tell Dussel that I was—the Saint?"

"Yes."

"Hadn't you heard that name before?"

"Of course, I'd seen it in the newspapers. You were the leader of a gang—"

"And yet," said the Saint, "you haven't looked really frightened since you've been here."

"You weren't criminals."

"But we committed crimes."

"Just ones—against men who deserved it."

"We have killed men."

She was silent.

"Three months ago," said the Saint, "we killed a man. It was our last crime, and the best of all. His name was Professor K. B. Vargan. He had invented a weapon of war which we decided that the world would be better without. He was given every chance—we risked everything to offer him his life if he would forget his diabolical invention. But he was mad. He wouldn't listen. And he had to die. Did you read that story?"

"I remember it very well."

"Other men—agents of another country—were also after Vargan, for their own ends," said the Saint. "That part of the story never came out in the papers. It was hushed up. Since they failed, it was better to hush up the story than to create an international situation. There was a plot to make war in Europe, for the benefit of a group of financiers. At the head of this group was a man who's called the Mystery Millionaire and the Millionaire Without a Country—one of the richest men in the world—Dr Rayt Marius. Do you know that name?"

She nodded. "Everyone knows it."

"The name of the greatest private war-maker in modern history," said Simon grimly. "But this plot was his biggest up to date. And he was using, for his purpose, Prince Rudolf. It was one of those two men who killed one of my dearest friends, in my bungalow up the river, where we had taken Vargan. You may remember reading that one of our little band was found there. Norman Kent—one of the whitest men that ever walked this earth . . ."

"I remember."

The Saint was gazing into the fireplace, and there was something in his face that forbade anyone to break the short silence which followed.

Then he pulled himself together.

"The rest of us got away, out of England," he went on quietly. "You see, Norman had stayed behind to cover our retreat. We didn't know then that he'd done it deliberately, knowing he hadn't a hope of getting away himself. And when we found out, it was too late to do anything. It was then that I swore to—pay my debt to those two men . . ."

"I understand," said the girl softly.

"I've been after them ever since, and Roger with me. It hasn't been easy, with a price on our heads, but we've had a lot of luck. And we've found out—many things. One of them is that the work that Norman died to accomplish isn't finished yet. When we put Vargan out of Marius's reach we thought we'd knocked the foundations from under his plot. I believe Marius himself thought so, too. But now he seems to have discovered another line of attack. We haven't been able to find out anything definite, but we've felt—reactions. And Marius and Prince Rudolf are hand in glove again. Marius is still hoping to make his war.

That is why Marius must die very soon—but not before we're sure that his intrigue will fall to pieces with his death."

The Saint looked at the girl.

"Now do you see where you come in?" he asked. She passed a hand across her eyes.

"You're terribly convincing." Her eyes had not left his face all the time he had been talking. "You don't seem like a man who'd make things like that up . . . or dream them . . . But—"

"Your left hand," said the Saint.

She glanced down. The ring on the third finger caught the light, and flung it back in a blaze of brilliance. And was he mistaken, or did he see the faintest shadow of fear touch a proud face that should never have looked afraid?

But her voice, when she spoke, told him nothing. "What has that to do with it?"

"Everything," answered Simon. "It came to me when I first mentioned Prince Rudolf's name to you. But I'd already got the key to the whole works in the song I was singing just before I barged into Heinrich Dussel's house—and I didn't know it . . ."

The girl wrinkled her brow.

"What do you mean?"

"I told you that Marius was working for a group of financiers— men who hoped to make millions out of the war he was engineering for them," said the Saint. "Now, what kind of financier do you think would make the most out of another great war?"

She did not answer, and Simon took another cigarette. But he did not light it at once. He turned it between his fingers with a savage gentleness, as if the immensity of his inspiration cried aloud for some physical expression.

He went on, in the same dispassionate tone:

"In the story I've just told you, Vargan wasn't the whole of the plot. He was the key piece—but the general idea went deeper and wider. Before he came into the story, there'd been an organized attempt to create distrust between this country and others in Europe. You must see how easy that would be to wealthy and unscrupulous men. A man alleged to be, say, a French spy is arrested—here. A man alleged to be a spy of ours is arrested—in France. And it goes on. Spies aren't shot in time of peace. They merely go to prison. If I can afford to send for a number of English crooks, say, and tell them, 'I want you to go to such and such a place, with certain things which I will give you. You will behave in such and such a manner, you will be arrested and convicted as a spy, and you will be imprisoned for five years. If you take your sentence and keep your mouth shut, I will pay you ten thousand pounds.'—aren't there dozens of old lags in England who'd tumble over each other for the chance? And it would be the same with men from other countries. Of course, their respective governments would disown them, but governments always disown their spies. That wouldn't cut any ice. And as it went on, the distrust would grow . . . That isn't romance. It's been done before, on a smaller scale. Marius was doing it before we intervened, in June last. What they call 'situations' were coming to dangerous heads. When Marius fell down over Vargan, the snake was scotched. We thought we'd killed it, but we were wrong. Do you remember the German who was caught trying to set fire to our newest airship, the R103?"

"Yes."

"Marius employed him—for fifteen thousand pounds. I happened to know that. In fact, it was intended that the R103 should actually be destroyed. The plot only failed because I sent information to Scotland Yard. But even that couldn't avert the public outcry that followed . . . Then, perhaps, you remember the Englishman who was caught trying to photograph a French naval base from the air?"

"The man there was so much fuss about a month ago?"

The Saint nodded.

"Another of Marius's men. I know, because I was hiding in Marius's wardrobe at the Hotel Edouard VII, in Paris, when that man received his instructions . . . And the secret treaty that was stolen from our Foreign Office messenger between Folkestone and Boulogne—"

"I know."

"Marius again."

The Saint stood up, and again he began to pace the room.

"The world's full of Peace Pacts and Disarmament Conferences," he said, "but where do those things go to when there's distrust between nations? No one may want war—those who saw the last war through would do anything to prevent another—but if a man steals your chickens, and throws mud at your wife when she goes for a walk, and calls you names over the garden wall, you just naturally have to push his teeth through the back of his neck. You can be as long-suffering as you like, but presently he carefully lays on the last straw just where he knows it'll hurt most, and then you either have to turn round and refashion his face or earn the just contempt of all your neighbours. Do you begin to understand?"

"I do . . . But I still don't see what I've got to do with it."

"But I told you!"

She shook her head, blankly.

"When?"

"Didn't you see? When I was talking about financiers—after I'd recognized you? Isn't your father Hiram Delmar, the Steel King? And aren't you engaged to marry Sir Isaac Lessing, the man who controls a quarter of the world's oil? And isn't Lessing, with his Balkan concessions, practically the unofficial dictator of south-eastern Europe? And hasn't he been trying for years to smash ROP? . . . Suppose, almost on the eve of your wedding, you disappear—and then you're found—on the other side—in Russia . . ."

The Saint's eyes were blazing.

"Why, it's an open book!" he cried. "It's easy enough to stir up distrust among the big nations, but it's not so easy to get them moving—there's a hell of a big coefficient of inertia to overcome when you're dealing with solid old nations like England and France and Germany. But the Balkans are the booster charge—they've been that dozens of times before—and you and Lessing make up the detonator . . . It's worthy of Marius's brain! He's got Lessing's psychology weighed up to the last lonely milligram. He knows that Lessing's notorious for being the worst man to cross in all the world of high finance. Lessing's gone out of his way to break men for nothing more than an argument over the bridge table, before now . . . And with you for a lever, Marius could engineer Lessing into the scheme—Lessing could set fire to the Balkans—and there might be war in Europe within the week!"

3

Once, months before, when Simon Templar had expounded a similar theory, Roger Conway had looked at him incredulously, as if he thought the Saint must have taken leave of his senses. But now there was no incredulity in Roger's face. The girl looked at him, and saw that he was as grave as his leader.

She shook her head helplessly.

"It's like a story-book," she said, "and yet you make it sound so convincing. You do . . ."

She put her hand to her sweet head, and then, only then, Simon struck a match for his mauled cigarette, and laughed gently.

"Poor kid! It has been a thick night, hasn't it? . . . But you'll feel heaps better in the morning, and I guess our council of war won't grow mould if it stands over till breakfast. I'll show you your room now, and Roger shall wade out into the wide world first thing tomorrow, and borrow some reasonable clothes for you off a married friend of mine."

She stood up, staring at him.

"Do you mean that—you're going to keep me here?"

The Saint nodded.

"For tonight, anyway."

"But the Embassy—"

"They'll certainly be excited, won't they?"

She took a step backwards. "Then—after all—you're—"

"No, we aren't. And you know it."

Simon put his hands on her shoulders, smiling down at her. And the Saint's smile, when he wished, could be a thing no mortal woman could resist.

"We're playing a big game, Roger and I," he said. "I've told you a little of it tonight. One day I may be able to tell you more. But already I've told you enough to show you that we're out after something more than pure soft roe and elephant's eggs. You've said it yourself."

Again he smiled.

"There'll be no war if you don't go back to the Embassy tonight," he said. "Not even if you disappear for twenty-four hours—or even forty-eight. I admit it's a ticklish game. It's rather more ticklish than trying to walk a tight-rope over the crater of Vesuvius with two sprained ankles and a quart of bootleg hooch inside you. But, at the moment, it's the only thing I can see for us—for Roger and me—to take Marius's own especial battle-axe and hang it over his own ugly head. I can't tell you yet how the game will be played. I don't know myself. But I shall think something out overnight . . . And meanwhile—I'm sorry—but you can't go home."

"You want to keep me a prisoner?"

"No. That's the last thing I want. I just want your parole—for twelve hours."

In its way the half-minute's silence that followed was perhaps as tense a thirty seconds as Simon Templar had ever endured.

Since he started talking he had been giving out every volt of personality he could command. He knew his power to a fraction—every inflection of voice and gesture, every flicker of expression, every perfectly timed pause. On the stage or the screen he could have made a fortune. When he chose he could play upon men and women with a sure and unfaltering touch. And in the last half-hour he had thrown all his genius into the scale.

If it failed . . . He wondered what the penalty was for holding a millionaire's daughter prisoner by force. Whatever it was, he had every intention of risking it. The game, as he had told her, was very big. Far too big for any half-hearted player . . .

But none of this showed on his face. Poised, quiet, magnificently confident, with that ghost of a swashbuckling smile on his lips, he bore her calm and steady scrutiny. And, looking deep into her eyes, he thought his own thoughts, so that a faint strange tremor moved him inwardly, in a way that he would not have thought possible.

But the girl could see none of this, and the hands that rested on her shoulders were as cool and firm as a surgeon's. She saw only the Saint's smile, the fineness of the clear blue eyes, the swift swaggering lines of the lean brown face. And perhaps because she was what she was, she recognized the quality of the man . . .

"I'll give you my parole," she said. "Thank you," said the Saint.

4

Then Simon showed her to his own room.

"You'll find a very good selection of silk pyjamas in the wardrobe," he remarked lightly. "If they aren't big enough for you, wear two suits. That door leads into the bathroom . . ." Then he touched her hand. "One day," he said, "I'll try to apologize for all this."

She smiled.

"One day," she said, "I'll try to forgive you."

"Good night, Sonia."

He kissed her hand quickly and turned and went down the stairs again.

"Just one swift one, Roger, my lad," he murmured, picking up a tankard and steering towards the barrel in the corner, "and then we also will retire. Something accomplished, something done, 'as earned a k-night's repose . . . Bung-ho!"

Roger Conway reached morosely for the decanter.

"You have all the luck, you big stiff," he complained. "She only spoke to me once, and I couldn't get a word in edge-ways. And then I heard you call her Sonia."

"Why not?" drawled the Saint. "It's her name."

"You don't call a Steel Princess by her first name—when you haven't even been introduced."

"Don't I!"

Simon raised his tankard with a flourish, and quaffed. Then he set it down on the table, and clapped Roger on the shoulder.

"Cheer up," he said. "It's a great life."

"It may be for you," said Roger dolefully. "But what about me? If you'd taken the girl straight back to the Embassy I might have taken a few easy grands off papa for my share in the rescue."

"Whereas all you're likely to get now is fifteen years—or a bullet in the stomach from Marius." Simon grinned, then his face sobered again. "By this time both Marius and Rudolf know that we're back. And how much the police know will depend on how much Heinrich has told them. I don't think he'll say much about us without consulting the Prince and Marius—"

"Well, you can bet Marius will spread the alarm."

"I'm not so sure. As long as he knows that we've got Sonia, I think he'd prefer to come down after us with his own gang. And he'll find out tomorrow that she hasn't been sent back to the loving arms of the Embassy."

Roger Conway flicked some ash from his cigarette. Those who had known him in the old days, before his name, after the death of K. B. Vargan, became almost as notorious as the Saint's, would have been surprised at his stern seriousness. Fair-haired and handsome (though less beautiful now on account of the make-up that went with his costume) and as true to a type as the Saint was true to none, he had led a flippant and singularly useless life until the Saint enlisted him and trained him on into the perfect lieutenant. And in the strenuous perils of his new life, strange to say, Roger Conway was happier than he had ever been before . . .

Roger said, "How much foundation had you got for that theory you put up to Sonia?"

"Sweet damn all," confessed the Saint. "It was just the only one I could see that fitted. There may be a dozen others, but if there are, I've missed them. And that's why we've got to find out a heap more before we restore that girl to the bosom of the Ambassador's wife. But it was a good theory—a damned good theory—and I have hunches about theories. That one rang a distinct bell. And I can't see any reason why it shouldn't be the right one."

"Nor do I. But what beats me is how you're going to use Sonia."

"And that same question beats me, too, Roger, at the moment I know that for us to hold her is rather less cautious than standing pat on a bob-tail straight when the man opposite has drawn two. And yet I can't get away from the hunch that she's heavy artillery, Roger, if we can only find a way to fire the guns . . ."

And the Saint relapsed into a reverie.

Certainly, it was difficult. It would have been difficult enough at the best of times—in the old days, for instance, when only a few select people knew that Simon Templar, gentleman of leisure, and the Saint, of doubtful fame, were one and the same person, and he had four able lieutenants at his call. Now his identity was known, and he had only Roger—though Roger was worth a dozen. The Saint was not the kind of man to have any half-witted Watson gaping at his Sherlock—any futile Bunny balling up his Raffles. But, even so, with the stakes as high as they were, he would have given anything to be able to put back the clock of publicity by some fourteen weeks.

An unprofitable daydream . . . of a kind in which the Saint rarely indulged. And with a short laugh he got to his feet, drained his tankard, and stretched himself.

"Bed, my Roger," he murmured decisively. "That's where I solve all my problems."

And it was so.

CHAPTER THREE:
HOW SONIA DELMAR ATE BACON
AND EGGS AND SIMON TEMPLAR
SPOKE ON THE TELEPHONE

1

A silver coffee machine was chortling cheerfully to itself when Sonia Delmar came down to the sitting-room at about ten o'clock, and the fragrance of grilling bacon, to the accompaniment of a sizzling noise of frying eggs, was distilling into the atmosphere. The room had been newly swept and garnished, and bright September sunshine was pouring through the open windows.

Almost immediately Roger Conway entered by another door bearing a frying-pan in one hand and a chafing-dish in the other.

"Excuse the primitive arrangements," he remarked. "I'm afraid we don't employ a staff of servants—they're liable to see too much."

She seemed surprised to see him, and it was not until then that he realized that she had had some excuse for ignoring him earlier in the day, when his face and hands had been villainously grimed for his role of unsuccessful street news-agent.

She was wearing one of the Saint's multifarious dressing-gowns—a jade-green one—with the sleeves turned up and the skirt of the gown trailing the floor, but Roger wondered if any woman could have looked more superbly robed. In the circumstances, she could have used no artificial aids to beauty, yet she had lost none of her fresh loveliness. And if Roger's enslavement had not already been complete, it would have been completed by the smile with which she rewarded his efforts in the kitchen.

"Bacon and eggs!" she said. "My favourite breakfast."

"They're my favourite, too," said Roger, and thus a friendship was sealed.

But it was not without a certain rueful humility that he noticed that she seemed to be looking for someone else. He supplied the information unasked.

"The Saint went off to get you some clothes himself. He shouldn't be long now."

"Saint . . . Hasn't he any other name?"

"Most people call him the Saint," said Roger. "His real name is Simon Templar."

"'Simon'?" She made enchantment of the name, so that Roger wished she would change the subject. And, in a way, she did. She said, "I remembered a lot more after I left you last night. There were three of you who escaped, weren't there? There was a girl—"

"Patricia Holm?"

"That's right—"

Roger nodded, impaling another rasher of bacon.

"She isn't here," he said. "As a matter of fact, she's somewhere in the Mediterranean. The Saint wouldn't let her come back with us. She's been with him in most things, but he put his foot down when it came to running the risk of a long term in prison—if not worse. He roped in an old friend who has a private yacht, and sent her off on a long cruise. And just we two came back."

"Has she been with him a long time?"

"About three years. He picked her up in another adventure, and they've stuck together ever since."

"Were they—married?"

"No."

Even then, when Roger was reflecting miserably within him upon the ease with which conquests came to some men who didn't deserve them, he couldn't be guilty of even an implied disloyalty to his leader.

He added, with simple sincerity, "You see, the question never really arose. We're outlaws. We've put ourselves outside the pale—and ordinary standards don't apply. One day, perhaps—"

"You'll win back your place inside the pale?"

"If we could, everything would be different."

"Would you like to go back?"

"For myself? I don't know . . ." She smiled.

"Somehow," she said, "I can't picture your friend handing round cakes at tea-parties, and giving his duty dances to gushing hostesses . . ."

"The Saint?" Roger laughed. "He'd probably start throwing knives at the orchestra, just to wake things up. And here he is."

A car hummed down the mews and stopped outside. A moment later, a bent old man, with grey beard, smoked glasses, and shabby hat, entered the sitting-room. He leaned on a stick, with an untidy brown-paper parcel in his other hand.

"Such a lovely morning," he wheezed, in a quavering voice. "And two such lovely young people having breakfast together. Well, well, well!" He straightened up. "Roger, have you left anything for me, you four-flushing son of a wall-eyed horse-thief?"

He heaved parcel and stick into a corner—sent beard, glasses, and hat to join them—and smoothed his coat. By some magic he shed all the illusion of shabbiness from his clothes without further movement, and it was the Saint himself who stood there, adjusting his tie with the aid of the mirror over the mantelpiece—trim, immaculate, debonair.

"Getting younger and more beautiful every day," he murmured complacently, then he turned with a laugh. "Forgive the amateur theatricals, Sonia. I had an idea there might be several policemen out looking for me this morning—and I was right. I recognized three in Piccadilly alone, and I stopped to ask one of them the time. Anyway, I raised you an outfit. You needn't be shy about wearing it, because it belongs to a lady who married a real live lord—though I did my best to save him."

He sank into a chair with a sigh, and surveyed the plate which Roger set before him.

"What—only one egg? Have the hens gone on strike, or something?"

"If you want another," said Roger offensively, "you'll have to lay it yourself. There were only four in the house and our guest had two."

Simon turned to the girl with a smile.

"Well," he said, "it's something to hear you were fit enough to cope with them."

"I feel perfectly all right this morning," she said. "It must have been that drink you gave me last night."

"Wonderful stuff," said the Saint. "I'll give you the prescription before you go, so that you can have some ready for the next time you're doped. It's also an infallible preventative of the morning after—if that's any use to you."

He picked up his knife and fork.

"Did I hear you say you saw some detectives?" asked Roger.

"I saw several. All in very plain clothes, and all flat-footed. A most distressing sight for an old man on his way home from church. And they weren't just out for constitutionals—sniffing the balmy breezes and thinking about their dinners. They weren't keeping holy the Sabbath Day. They were doing all manner of work. Rarely have I run such a gauntlet of frosty stares. It was quite upsetting." The Saint grinned gently. "But what it most certainly means is that the cat has leapt from the portmanteau with some agility. Enough beans have been spilt to keep Heinz busy for a year. The gaff has been blown from here to Honolulu. You know, I had an idea Heinrich would rise to the occasion."

2

It was the girl who spoke first.

"The police are after you?"

"They've been after me for years," said the Saint cheerfully. "In a general sort of way . . . But just recently the hunt's been getting a bit fierce. Yes, I think I can claim that this morning I'm at the height of my unpopularity, so far as Scotland Yard's concerned."

"After all," said Roger, "you can't go round kidnapping Steel Princesses without something happening."

Simon helped himself to marmalade.

"True, O King," he murmured. "Though that's hardly likely to be the charge. If Heinrich had sung a song about a stolen Steel Princess they'd have wanted to know what she was doing in his house . . . Curse Sunday! On any other day I could have bought an evening paper and found out exactly what psalm he warbled. As it is, I shall have to go round and inquire in person."

"You'll have to what?" spluttered Roger.

"Make personal inquiries," said the Saint. "Disguised as a gentleman, I shall interview Prince Rudolf at the Ritz Hotel, and hear all the news."

He pushed back his chair and reached for the cigarette-box.

"It may not have occurred to your mildewed intellect," he remarked pleasantly, "that the problems of international intrigue can usually be reduced to quite simple terms. Let's reduce Rudolf, A, wishing to look important, desires to smite B on the nose. But B, unfortunately, is a bigger man than A. C comes along and offers A a gun, wherewith B can be potted from a safe distance. But we destroyed that gun. C then suggests a means of wangling an alliance between A and D, whereby the disgusting superiority of B may be overcome. C, of course, is sitting on the fence, waiting to take them into his very expensive nursing-home when they've all half-killed each other. Is that clear?"

"Like mud," said Roger.

"Well," said the Saint, unmoved, "if you wanted to find out exactly how the alliance was to be wangled, mightn't it be helpful to ask A?"

"And, naturally, he'd tell you at once." Simon shook his head sadly.

"There are subtleties in this game," he said, "which are lost upon you, Roger. But they may be explained to you later. Meanwhile . . ."

The Saint leaned back, with a glance at his watch, and looked across the table at the girl. The bantering manner which he wore with such an ease slipped from his shoulders like a cloak, and he studied her face soberly, reading what he could in the deep brown eyes.

She had been watching him ever since he came into the room, and he knew that the fate of his plan was already sealed—one way or the other.

"Your parole has still more than four hours to run," he said, "but I give it back to you now."

She could thank him coldly, and go. She could thank him nicely, rather puzzledly—and go. And if she had made the least move to do either of those things, he would not have said another word. It would be no use, unless she delayed of her own free will. And only one thing could so bend her will—a thing that he hardly dared to contemplate . . .

"Why do you do that?" she asked simply.

3

"Why do you do that? . . . I'll give you my parole." . . . He turned over those forthright sentences in his mind. And the way in which they had been spoken. The way in which everything he had heard her say had been spoken. Her superb simplicity . . .

"America's Loveliest Lady," the *Bystander* caption had called her, and the Saint reflected how little meaning was left in that last word. And yet it was the only word for her. There was something about her that one had to meet to understand. If he had had to describe it, he could only have done so in flowery phrases—and a flowery phrase would have robbed the thing of its fresh naturalness, would have tarnished it, might even have made it seem pretentious. And it was the most unpretending thing he had ever known. It was so innocent that it awed him, and yet it made his heart leap with a fantastic hope.

"I did my thinking last night, as I said I would," he answered her quietly.

Still she did not move.

She prompted him: "And you made your plan?"

"Yes."

"I wonder if it was the same as mine?"

Simon raised his eyebrows.

"The same as yours?"

She smiled.

"I can think, too, Mr—Saint," she said. "I've been taught to. And last night I thought a lot. I thought of everything you'd said, and everything I'd heard about you. And I believed what you'd told me. So—I knew there was only one thing to do."

"Namely?"

"Didn't you call me—Marius's battle-axe? . . . I think you were right. And that's something for us to know. But there's so much else that we don't know—how the axe is to be used, and what other weapons there are to reinforce it. You've taken the axe away, but that's all. Marius still means to bring down the tree. Once before you've thought he was beaten, but you were wrong. This time, if you just take away his axe, you'll know he isn't beaten. He's already undermined the tree. Even now it may fall before the next natural storm. It may be hard enough to prop it up now, until the roots grow down again, without leaving Marius free to strike at it again. And to make sure that he won't strike again, you've got to break his arm."

"Or his neck," said the Saint grimly.

Again she smiled.

"Haven't I read your thoughts?"

"Perfectly."

"And what was your plan?" Simon met her eyes.

"I meant," he said deliberately, "to ask you to go back—to Heinrich Dussel."

"That was what I meant to suggest."

In that moment Roger Conway felt utterly off the map. The Saint had told him nothing. The Saint had merely sung continuously in his bath—which, with the Saint, was a sure sign of peace of mind. And, in the circumstances, Roger Conway had wondered . . . But Simon had donned his disguise and departed in the car without a word in explanation of his high spirits, and Roger had been left to wonder . . . And then—this. He saw the long deliberate glance which the other two exchanged, and felt that they were moving and speaking in another world—a world to which he could never aspire. And like a man in a dream he heard them discussing the impossible thing.

He knew the Saint, and the thunder-bolts of dazzling audacity which the Saint could launch, as no other man could have claimed to know them, and yet this detonation alone would have reeled him momentarily off his balance. But it didn't stand alone. It was matched—without a second's pause. They were of the same breed, those two. Though their feet were set on different roads, they walked in the same country—a country that ordinary people could never reach. And it was then that Roger Conway, who had always believed that no one in all the world could walk shoulder to shoulder with the Saint in that country, began to understand many things.

He heard them, in his dream—level question and answer, the quiet, crisp words. He would have been less at sea if either of them had said any of the things that he might have expected, in any way that he might have expected, but there was none of that. Those things did not exist in their language. Their calm, staccato utterances plunged into his brain like clear-cut gems falling through an infinite darkness.

"You've considered the dangers?"

"To myself?"

"Yes."

"I'm never safe—at any time."

"The destinies we're playing with, then. I might fail you. That would mean we'd given Marius the game."

"You might not fail."

"Have we the right?" asked the Saint.

And then Roger saw him again—the new Saint to whom he had still to grow accustomed. Simon Templar, with the old careless swashbuckling days behind him, more stern and sober, playing bigger games than he had ever touched before—yet with the light of all the old ideals in blue eyes that would never grow old, and all the old laughing hell-for-leather recklessness waiting for his need.

"Have we the right to risk failure?" Simon asked.

"Have you the right to turn back?" the girl answered him. "Have you the right to turn back and start all over again—when you might go forward?"

The Saint nodded.

"I just meant to ask you, Sonia. And you've given your answer. More—you've taken the words out of my mouth, and the objections I'm making are the ones you ought to have made."

"I've thought of them all."

"Then—we go forward."

The Saint spoke evenly, quite softly, yet Roger seemed to hear a blast of bugles. And the Saint went on.

"We've had enough of war. Fighting is for the strong—for those who know what they're fighting for, and love the fight for its own sake. We were like that, my friends and I—and yet we swore that it should not happen again. Not this new fighting—not this cold-blooded scientific maiming and slaughter of schoolboys and poor grown-up fools herded to squalid death to make money for a bunch of slimy financiers. We saw it coming again. The flags flying, and the bands playing, and the politicians yaddering about a land fit for heroes to live in, and the poor fools cheering and being cheered, and another madness, worse than the last. Just another war to end war . . . But we know that you can't end war by war. You can't end war by any means at all, thank God, while men believe in right and wrong, and some of them have the courage to fight for their belief. It has always been so. And it's my own creed.

I hope I never live to see the day when the miserable quibbling hair-splitters have won the earth, and there's no more black and white, but everything's just a dreary relative grey, and everyone has a right to his own damned heresies, and it's more noble to be broad-minded about your disgusting neighbours than to push their faces in as a preliminary to yanking them back into the straight and narrow way . . . But this is different. There's no crusading about it. It's just mass murder—for the benefit of the men with the big bank balances. That's what we saw— and we were three blistered outlaws who'd made scrap-iron of every law in Europe, on one quixotic excuse or another, just to make life tolerable for ourselves in this half-hearted civilization. And when we saw that, we knew that we'd come to the end of our quest. We'd found the thing worth fighting for—really worth fighting for—so much more worth fighting for than any of the little things we'd fought for before. One of us has already died for it. But the work will go on . . ."

And suddenly the Saint stood up.

And all at once, in that swift movement, with the old gay devil-may-care smile awakening again on his lips, Simon Templar seemed to sweep the room clear of all doubts and shadows, leaving only the sunlight and the smile and the far cry of impossible fanfares.

"Let's go!"

"Where?" demanded Roger helplessly, and the Saint laughed.

"On the job, sweetheart," he said, "on the job! Here—shunt yourself, and let me get at that telephone."

Roger shunted dazedly, and watched the Saint dial a number. The Saint's face was alight with a new laughter, and, as he waited, he began to hum a little tune. For the wondering and wavering was over, the speculating and the scheming, the space for physical inaction and sober counsel—those negative things at which the Saint's flaming vitality would always fret impatiently. And once again he was on the move—swift, smiling, cavalier, with a laugh and a flourish for battle and sudden death and all good things, playing the old game with all the magnificent zest that only he could bring to it.

"Hullo. Can I speak to Dr Marius, please? . . . Templar—Simon Templar . . . Thank you."

Roger Conway said, suddenly, sharply, "Saint—you're crazy! You can't do it! The game's too big—"

"Who wants to play for brick-dust and bird-seed?" Simon required to know.

And then, before Roger could think of an adequate retort to such an arrogance, he had lost any audience he might have had. For the Saint was speaking to the man he hated more than anyone else in the world.

"Is that you, Marius, my little lamb?" Genially, almost caressingly, the Saint spoke. "And how's Heinrich? . . . Yes, I thought you'd have heard I was back. I'd have rung you up before, only I've been so busy. As a medical man, I can't call my time my own. Only last night I had an extraordinary case. Did Heinrich tell you? . . . Yes, I expected he would. I think he was very struck with my methods. Quite—er—dazzled, in fact . . . No, nothing in particular. It just occurred to me to soothe my ears with the sound of your sweet voice. It's such a long time since we had our last heart-to-heart talk . . . The invalid? . . . Oh, getting on as well as can be expected. She ought to be fit to go back to the Embassy tomorrow . . . No, not today. That dope you used on her seems to have a pretty potent follow-through, and I never send my patients home till they've got a bounce on them that's a free advertisement for the cure . . . Well, you can remember me to Rudolf. I may drop in at the Ritz and have a cocktail with him before lunch. Bye-bye, Angel Face . . ." He hung up the receiver.

"Beautiful," he murmured ecstatically. "Too, too beautiful! When it comes to low cunning, I guess that little cameo makes anything Machiavelli ever did look like a lame hippopotamus with in-growing toenails trying to impersonate Douglas Fairbanks. Angel Face was great—he kept his end up right through the round—but I heard him take the bait. Distinctly. It fairly whistled through his epiglottis . . . D'you get the idea, my Roger?"

"I don't," Conway admitted. Simon looked at the girl. "Do you, Sonia?"

She also shook her head, and the Saint laughed, and helped himself to another cigarette.

"Marius knows I've got you," he said. "He thinks he knows that you're still laid out by this dope. And he knows that I wouldn't tell the world I've got you—things being as they are. On that reckoning, then, he's got a new lease of life. He's got a day in which to find me and take you away. And he thinks I haven't realized that—and he's wrong!"

"Very lucid," observed Roger sarcastically. "But I gather he's supposed to find out where we are."

"I've told him."

"How?"

"At this moment, he's finding out my telephone number from the Exchange."

"What good will that do him? The Exchange won't give him your address."

The Saint grinned.

"Roger," he remarked dispassionately, "you have fully half as much brain as a small boll- weevil. A very small boll-weevil. Your genius for intrigue would probably make you one of the most successful glue-boilers that ever lived."

"Possibly. But if you'd condescend to explain—"

"But it's so easy!" cried the Saint. "I had to do it tactfully, of course. I couldn't say anything that would let him smell the hook. Thanks to our recent encounter, he knows we're not solid bone from the gargle upwards, and if I'd dropped a truck-load of bricks on his Waukeezis, he'd've stopped and thought for a long time before he picked one up. But I didn't. I only dropped that one little bricklet—just big enough for him to feel the impact, and just small enough for him to be able to believe I hadn't seen it go. And Angel Face is so clever . . . What d'you think he's doing now?"

"Boiling glue," suggested Roger.

"He's got his whole general staff skidding through the telephone directory like so many hungry stockbrokers humming down the latest Wall Street prices during a slump. The Exchange will have told him that the call didn't come from a public call-box, and that alone will have made him shift his ears back two inches. The only other thing that could put salt horse in his soufflé would be if the call turned out to have been put through from a hotel or a restaurant, but he'd have to take his chance on that. And he'd know there was a shade of odds in his favour. No, Roger—you can bet your last set of Aertex that the entire personnel of the Ungodly is at this moment engaged in whiffling through every telephone number in the book as they've never whiffled before, and in anything from one to thirty minutes from now, according to how they split up the comic *annuaire* between them, one of them will be letting out a shrill squawk of triumph and starting to improvise a carol about 7, Upper Berkeley Mews."

"And how does that help us?" asked Roger.

"Like this," said the Saint, and proceeded to explain thus and thus.

CHAPTER FOUR:

HOW SIMON TEMPLAR DOZED IN GREEN PARK AND DISCOVERED A NEW USE FOR TOOTHPASTE

.

1

To walk from Upper Berkeley Mews to the Ritz Hotel should ordinarily have taken a man with the Saint's stride and the Saint's energy about four minutes. Simon Templar in motion, his friends used to say, was the most violent man that ever fumed through London; all his physical movements were made as if they were tremendously important. Buccaneer he was in fact, and buccaneer of life he always looked— most of all when he strode through London on his strange errands, with his incredibly vivid stride, and a piratical anachronism of a hat canted cavalierly aslant over the face of a fighting troubadour.

But there was nothing of that about the aged greybeard who emerged inconspicuously from a converted garage in Upper Berkeley Mews at half-past eleven that Sunday morning. He did not look as if he had ever been anything in the least like a buccaneer, even fifty years ago, and, if in those decorously wild young days he had once cherished lawless aspirations, he must long since have decently buried all such disturbing thoughts. He walked very slowly, almost apologetically, as if he doubted his own right to be at large, and when he came to Piccadilly he stopped at the edge of the sidewalk and blinked miserably through his dark glasses at the scanty traffic, looking so forlorn and helpless that a plain-clothes man who had been searching for him for hours was moved to offer to help him across the road—an offer which was accepted with plaintive gratitude, and acknowledged with pathetic effusiveness. So an officer of the Criminal Investigation Department did his day's good deed, and the pottering patriarch shuffled into the Green Park by the gate at the side of the Ritz Hotel, found a seat in the shade, sat there, folded his arms, and presently appeared to sleep . . .

He slept for an hour, and then he climbed stiffly to his feet and shambled out of the park by the way he had entered it, turning under the shadow of the Ritz. He pushed through the revolving doors without hesitation, and it says much for the utter respectability of his antique appearance that the flunkey who met him within made no attempt to eject him, but greeted him deferentially, hoping that he would prove to be a millionaire, and certain that he could not turn out to be less than an earl.

"I wish to see Prince Rudolf," said the Saint, and he said it in such a way that the lackey almost grovelled.

"What name, sir?"

"You may send up my card."

The Saint fumbled in his waistcoat pocket; he had a very fine selection of visiting cards, and the ones he had brought with him on this expedition bore the name of Lord Craithness. On the back of one, he wrote, "Maidenhead, June 28."

It was the day on which he had last seen the Prince—the day on which Norman Kent had died.

"Will you take a seat, your lordship?"

His lordship would take a seat. And he waited there only five minutes, a grave and patient old aristocrat, before the man returned to say that the Prince would see him—as Simon had known he would say.

It was a perfect little character study, that performance—the Saint's slow and sober progress down the first-floor corridor, his entrance into the Prince's suite, the austere dignity of his poise in the moment that he waited for the servant to announce him.

"Lord Craithness."

The Saint heard the door close behind him, and smiled in his beard. And yet he could not have told why he smiled, for at that moment there came back to him all that he had to remember of his first and last meeting with the man who now faced him—and those were not pleasant memories. Once again he saw the friendly house by the Thames, the garden cool and fresh beyond the open French windows, the sunlit waters at the end of the lawn, and Norman Kent with a strange peace in his dark eyes, and the nightmare face of Rayt Marius, and the Prince . . . Prince Rudolf, calmest of them all, with a sleek and inhuman calm, like a man of steel and velvet, impeccably groomed, exquisite, impassive—exactly as he stood at that moment, gazing at his visitor with his fine eyebrows raised in faint interrogation . . . not betraying by so much as the flicker of an eyelid the things that must have been in his mind. He could not possibly have forgotten the date that had been written on that card, it could not by any stretch of imagination have omened good news for him, and yet he was utterly master of himself, utterly at his ease . . .

"You're a wonderful man," said the Saint, and the Prince shrugged delicately.

"You have the advantage of me."

"Have you forgotten so quickly?"

"I meet many people."

The Saint put up his hand and removed his grey wig, his glasses, his beard . . . straightened up.

"You should remember me," he said.

"My dear Mr Templar!" The Prince was smiling. "But why such precautions? Or did you wish to make your call an even greater surprise?"

The Saint laughed.

"The precautions were necessary," he said, "as you know. But I'll say you took it well—Highness. I never expected you to bat an eyelash, though—I remembered so well that your self-control was your greatest charm."

"But I am delighted to see you."

"Are you?" asked Simon Templar, gently.

2

The Prince proffered a slim gold case.

"At least," he said, "you will smoke."

"One of my own," said the Saint affably. "I find that these are the only brand I can indulge in with safety—my heart isn't what it was."

The Prince shrugged.

"You have missed your vocation, Mr Templar," he said regretfully. "You should have been a diplomat."

"I could have made a job of it," said Simon modestly.

"I believe I once made you an offer to enter my own service."

"You did."

"And you refused."

"I did."

"Perhaps you have reconsidered your decision."

The Saint smiled.

"Listen," he said. "Suppose I said I had. Suppose I told you I'd forgotten the death of my dearest friend. Suppose I said that all the things I once believed in and fought for—the things that he died for—meant nothing more to me. Would you welcome me?"

"Candidly," said the Prince, "I should not. I admire you. I know your qualities, and I would give much to have them in my service. But that is an ideal—a daydream. If you turned your coat, you would cease to be what you are, and so you would cease to be desirable. But it is a pity . . ."

Simon strolled to a chair. He sat there, watching the Prince through a curling feather of cigarette-smoke. And the Prince, sinking on to the arm of another chair, with a long thin cigarette-holder between his perfect teeth, returned the gaze with a glimmer of amusement on his lips.

Presently the Prince made one of his indescribably elegant gestures.

"As you have not come to enlist with me," he remarked, "I presume you have some other reason. Shall we deal with it?"

"I thought we might have a chat," said the Saint calmly. "I've discovered a number of obscure odours in the wind during the last twenty-four hours, and I had an idea you might have something to say which would clear the air. Of course, for one thing, I was hoping our dear friend Marius would be with you."

The Prince glanced at his watch.

"I am expecting him at any moment. He was responsible for your friend's unfortunate—er—accident, by the way. I fear that Marius has never been of a very even temper."

"That is one thing I've been wanting to know for many weeks," said the Saint quietly, and for a moment something blazed in his eyes like a sear of blue flame.

And then, once again, he was smiling.

"It'll be quite a rally, won't it?" he murmured. "And we shall have such a lot to tell each other . . . But perhaps you'd like to open the palaver yourself—Highness? For instance, how's Heinrich?"

"I believe him to be in good health."

"And what did he tell the police?"

"Ah! I thought you would ask that question."

"I'm certainly curious."

The Prince tapped his cigarette fastidiously against the edge of an ashtray.

"If you wish to know, he said that his uncle—an invalid, and unhappily subject to violent fits—had arrived only yesterday from Munich. You entered the house, pretending to be a doctor, before he could disclaim you, and you immediately threatened him with an automatic. You then informed him that you were the Saint, and abducted his uncle. Dussel, naturally, had no idea why you should have done so—but, just as naturally, he considered that that was a problem for the police to solve."

Simon nodded admiringly.

"I'm taking a distinct shine to Heinrich," he drawled. "You will admit that it was an ingenious explanation."

"I'll tell the world."

"But your own strategy, my dear Mr Templar—that was superb! Even if I had not been told that it was your work, I should have recognized the artist at once."

"We professionals!" sighed the Saint.

"And where did you take the lady?"

The question was thrown off so carelessly, and yet with such a perfect touch, that for an instant the Saint checked his breath. And then he laughed.

"Oh, Rudolf, that wasn't worthy of you!"

"I am merely being natural," said the Prince, without annoyance. "There was something you wanted to know—you asked me—I answered. And then I followed your example."

Simon shook his head, smiling, and sank deeper into his chair, his eyes intent upon an extraordinarily uninteresting ceiling. And he wondered, with a certain reckless inward merriment, what thoughts were sizzling through the brain of the imperturbable hidalgo opposite him.

He wondered . . . but he knew that it would be a waste of time to attempt to read anything in the Prince's face. The Prince was his match, if not more than his match, at any game like that. If Simon had come there to fence—that would have been a duel! Already, in the few words they had exchanged, each had tested afresh the other's mettle, and each had tacitly recognized that time had fostered no illusions about the other: neither had changed. Weave and feint, thrust, parry, and riposte—each movement was perfect, smooth, cool, effortless . . . and futile . . . And neither would yield an inch of ground . . . And now, where cruder and clumsier exponents would still be ineffectually lunging and blundering, they had admitted the impasse. The pause was of mutual consent.

Their eyes met, and there was a momentary twist of humour in each gaze.

"We appear," observed the Prince politely, "to be in the position of two men who are fighting with invisible weapons. We are both equally at a disadvantage."

"Not quite," said the Saint.

The Prince fluttered a graceful hand.

"It is agreed that you are an obstacle in my path which I should be glad to remove. I might hand you over to the police—"

"But then you might have some embarrassing questions to answer."

"Exactly. And as for any private action—"

"Difficult—in the Ritz Hotel."

"Exceedingly difficult. Then, there is reason to believe that you are—or were—temporarily in possession of a property which it is necessary for me to recover."

"Dear old Heinrich's uncle."

"Whereas my property is the knowledge of why it is necessary for me to recover—your property."

"Perhaps."

"And an exchange is out of the question."

"Right out."

"So that the deadlock is complete."

"Not quite," said the Saint again.

The Prince's eyes narrowed a fraction. "Have I forgotten anything?"

"I wonder!"

There was another moment of silence, and, in the stillness, the Saint's amazingly sensitive ears caught the ghost of a sound from the corridor outside the room. And, at that instant, with the breaking of the silence by the perfunctory knock that followed on the door, the grim mirth that had been simmering inside the Saint for minutes past danced mockingly into his eyes.

"Highness "

It was Marius, looming gigantically in the doorway, with a flare of triumph in the face that might have served as a model for some hideous heathen idol, and triumph in his thin rasping voice.

And then he saw the Saint, and stopped dead.

"You see that our enterprising young friend is with us once more, my dear Marius," said the Prince suavely, and Simon Templar rose to his feet with his most seraphic smile.

3

"Marius—my old college chum!"

The Saint stood there in the centre of the room, lean and swift and devil-may-care, his hands swinging back his coat and resting on his hips, and all the old challenging hints of lazy laughter that both the other men remembered were glinting back through the tones of his voice. The reckless eyes swept Marius from head to foot, with the cold steel masked down into their depths by a shimmer of gay disdain.

"Oh, precious!" spoke on that lazy half-laughing voice. "And where have you been all these months? Why haven't you come round to hold my hand and reminisce with me about the good old days, and all the fun we had together? And the songs we used to sing . . . And do you remember how you pointed a gun at me one night, in one of our first little games, and I kicked you in the—er—heretofore?"

"Marius has a good memory," said the Prince dryly.

"And so have I," beamed the Saint, and his smile lightened a little. "Oh, Angel Face, I'm glad to meet you again!"

The giant turned, and spoke harshly in his own language, but the Prince interrupted him.

"Let us speak English," he said. "It will be more interesting for Mr Templar."

"How did he come here?"

"He walked up."

"But the police—"

"Mr Templar and I have already discussed that question, my dear Marius. It is true that Dussel had to make certain charges in order to cover himself, but it might still be inconvenient for us if Mr Templar were arrested."

"It is awkward for you, you know," murmured Simon sympathetically. The Prince selected a fresh cigarette.

"But your own news, my dear Marius? You seemed pleased with yourself when you arrived—"

"I have been successful."

"Our friend will be interested."

Marius looked across at the Saint, and his lips twisted malevolently. And the Saint remembered what lay between them . . .

"Miss Delmar is now in safe hands," said the giant slowly. Simon stood quite still.

"When you rang me up—do you remember?—to boast—I asked the Exchange for your number. Then the directory was searched, and we learned your address. Miss Delmar was alone. We had no difficulty, though I was hoping to find you and some of your friends there as well—"

"Bluff," said the Saint unemotionally.

"I think not, my dear Mr Templar," said the Prince urbanely. "Dr Marius is really a most reliable man. I recollect that the only mistake we have made was my own, and he advised me against it."

Marius came closer.

"Once—when you beat me," he said vindictively. "When you undid years of work—by a trick. But your friend paid the penalty. You also—"

"I also—pay," said the Saint, with bleak eyes.

"You—"

"My dear Marius!" Once again the Prince interrupted. "Let us be practical. You have succeeded. Good. Now, our young friend has elected to interfere in our affairs again, and since he has so kindly delivered himself into our hands—"

Suddenly the Saint laughed.

"What shall we do with the body?" he murmured. "Well, souls, I'll have to give you time to think that out. Meanwhile, I shouldn't like you to think I was getting any grey hairs over Marius's slab of ripe boloney about Miss Delmar. My dear Marius, that line of hooey's got wheels!"

"You still call it a bluff?" sneered the giant "You will find out—"

"I shall," drawled Simon. "Angel Face, don't you think this is a peach of a beard? Makes me look like Abraham in a high wind . . ."

Absent-mindedly the Saint had picked up his disguise, and axed the beard to his chin and the dark glasses to his nose. The hat had fallen to the floor. Moving to pick it up, he kicked it a yard away. The second attempt had a similar result. And it was all done with such a puerile innocence that both Marius and the Prince must have been no more than vaguely wondering what motive the Saint could have in descending to such infantile depths of clowning—when the manoeuvre was completed with a breath-taking casualness.

The pursuit of his hat had brought the Saint within easy reach of the door. Quite calmly and unhurriedly he picked up the hat and clapped it on his head.

"Strong silent man goes out into the night," he said. "But we must get together again some time. Au revoir, sweet cherubs!"

And the Saint passed through the sitting-room door in a flash, and a second later the outer door of the suite banged.

Simon had certainly visited the Prince with intent to obtain information, but he had done so, as he did all such things, practically without a plan in his head. The Saint was an opportunist: he held that the development of complicated plans was generally nothing but a squandering of so much energy, for the best of palavers was liable to rocket on to unexpected rails—and these surprises, Simon maintained, could only be turned to their fullest advantage by a mind untrammelled by any preconceived plan of campaign. And, if the Saint had anticipated anything, he had anticipated that the arrival of Rayt Marius in the role of an angel-faced harbinger of glad tidings would result in a certain amount of more or less informative backchat before the conversation became centred on prospective funerals. And, indeed, the conversazione had worn a very up-and-coming air before the Prince had switched it back into such a very practical channel. But Prince Rudolf had that sort of mind, wherefore the Saint had chased his hat.

4

It had been a slick job, that departure, and it was all over before Marius had started to move. Even then, the Prince had to stop him.

"My dear Marius, it would be useless to cause a disturbance now."

"He could be arrested—"

"But you must see that he could say things about us, if he chose, which might prove even more annoying than his own interference. At large, he can be dealt with by ourselves."

"He has fooled us once, Highness—"

"He will not do so again . . . Sit down, sit down, Marius! You have something to tell me." Impatiently, the giant suffered himself to be soothed into a chair. But the Prince was perfectly unruffled—the cigarette glowed evenly in his long holder, and his sensitive features showed no sign of emotion.

"I took the girl," said Marius curtly. "She has been sent to Saltham. The ship will call there again tonight, and Vassiloff will be on board. They can be married as soon as they are at sea—the captain is my slave."

"You think the provocation will be sufficient?"

"I am more sure of it than ever. I know Lessing. I will see him myself—discreetly—and I guarantee that he will accept my proposition. Within a week you should be able to enter Ukraine . . ."

In the bathroom, the Saint heard every word. He had certainly banged the outer door of the suite, but the bedroom door had been equally convenient for the purposes of his exit. It has been explained that he came to the Ritz Hotel to gather information.

The communicating door between the sitting-room and the bedroom was ajar; so also was that between bedroom and bathroom. And, while he listened, the Saint was amusing himself.

He had found a new tube of Prince Rudolf's beautiful pink toothpaste, and the glazed green tiles of the bathroom offered a tempting surface for artistic experiment. Using his material after the style of a chef applying fancy icing to a cake, the Saint had drawn a perfect six-inch circle upon the bathroom wall; from the lowest point of the circle he drew down a vertical line, which presently bi furcated into two downward lines of equal length, and on either side of his first vertical line he caused two further lines to project diagonally upwards . . .

"And the other arrangements, Marius—they are complete?"

"Absolutely. You have read all the newspapers yourself, Highness — you must see that the strains could not have been more favourably ordered. The mine is ripe for the spark. Today I received a cable from my most trusted agent, in Vienna—I have decoded it—"

The Prince took the form and read it, and then he began to pace the room steadily, in silence.

It was not a restless, fretful pacing—it was a matter of deliberate, leisured strides, as smooth and graceful and eloquent as any of the Prince's gestures. His hands were lightly clasped behind his back; the thin cigarette-holder projected from between his white teeth; his forehead was serene and unwrinkled.

Marius waited his pleasure, sitting hunched up in the chair to which the Prince had led him, like some huge grotesque carving in barbarous stone. He watched the Prince with inscrutable glittering eyes.

And Simon Templar was putting the finishing touches to his little drawing.

He understood everything that was said. Once upon a time, he had felt himself at a disadvantage because he could not speak a word of the Prince's language, but since then he had devoted all his spare time, night and day, to the task of adding that tongue to his already extensive linguistic accomplishments. This fact he had had neither the inclination nor the opportunity to reveal during their brief reunion.

Presently the Prince said, "Our friend Mr Templar—I find it hard to forget that he once saved my life. But when he cheated me, at Maidenhead, I think he cancelled the debt."

"It is more than cancelled, Highness," said Marius malignantly. "But for that treachery, we should have achieved our purpose long ago."

"It seems a pity—I have admitted as much to him. He is such an active and ingenious young man."

"A meddlesome young swine!"

The Prince shook his head.

"One should never allow a personal animosity to colour one's abstract appreciations, my dear Marius," he said dispassionately. "On the other hand, one should not allow an abstract admiration to overrule one's discretion. I have a most sincere regard for our friend— but that is all the more reason why I should encourage you to expedite his removal. He will endeavour to trace Miss Delmar, of course, when he finds that you were telling the truth—"

"I shall take steps to assist him—up to a point."

"And then you will dispose of him in your own way."

"There will be no mistake," said the giant venomously, and the Prince laughed softly.

In the bathroom, Simon Templar, with a very Saintly smile on his lips, was crowning his shapely self-portrait with a symbolical halo—at a rakish angle, and in scrupulously correct perspective.

CHAPTER FIVE:
HOW SIMON TEMPLAR TRAVELLED TO SALTHAM AND ROGER CONWAY PUT UP HIS GUN

1

"A Bulge—a distinct Bulge," opined the Saint, as he shuffled out of the Ritz Hotel, leaving a young cohort of oleaginous serfs in his wake. There was, he thought, a lot to be said for the principle of riding on the spur of the moment. If he had called upon the Crown Prince to absorb information, he had indubitably inhaled the mixture as prescribed—a canful. Most of it, of course, he either knew already or could have guessed without risk of bringing on an attack of cerebral staggers, but it was pleasant to have one's deductions confirmed. Besides, one or two precise and irrefutable details of the enemy's plan of attack had emerged in all their naked glory, and that very much to the good. "Verily—a Bulge," ruminated the Saint . . .

He found his laborious footsteps automatically leading him down St James's Street, and then eastwards along Pall Mall. With an éclat equalled only by that of his recent assault upon the Ritz, he carried the portals of the Royal Automobile Club—of which he was not a member—and required an atlas to be brought to him. With this aid to geographical research, he settled himself in a quiet corner of the smoke-room and proceeded to acquire the dope about Saltham. This

LESLIE CHARTERIS

he discovered to be a village on the Suffolk coast between Southwold and Aldeburgh; a gazetteer which lay on a table conveniently near him added the enlightening news that it boasted a fine sandy beach, cliffs, pleasure grounds, a 16th cent, ch., a coasting trade, and a population of 3,128—it was, said the gazetteer, a wat.-pl.

"And that must be frightfully jolly for it," murmured the Saint, gently depositing the Royal Automobile Club's property in a convenient waste-basket.

He smoked a thoughtful cigarette in his corner, and then, after a glance at his watch, he left the club again, turned down Waterloo Place, and descended the steps that lead down to the Mall. There he stood, blinking at the sunlight, until a grubby infant accosted him.

"Are you Mr Smith, sir?"

"I am," said the Saint benignly.

"Gen'l'man gimme this letter for you."

The Saint took the envelope, slit it open, and read the pencilled lines:

> "No message. Heading N.E. Wire you Waldorf on arrival.—R."

"Thank you, Marmaduke," said the Saint.

He pressed a piece of silver into the urchin's palm, and walked slowly back up the steps, tearing the note into small shreds as he went. At the corner of Waterloo Place and Pall Mall he stopped and glanced around for a taxi.

It seemed a pity that Roger Conway would waste a shilling, but that couldn't be helped. The first bulletin had already meant an unprofitable increase in the overhead. But that, on the other hand, was a good sign. In the Saint's car and a chauffeur's livery Roger Conway had been parked a little distance away from the converted garage, in a position to observe all that happened. If Sonia Delmar had been in a position to drop a note after her abduction she would have done so, and the bones of it would have been passed on to the Saint via the infant they had employed for the occasion; otherwise, Roger was simply detailed to give inconspicuous chase, and he must have shot his human carrier-pigeon overboard as they neared the northeastern outskirts of London. But the note carried by the human telegraph would only have been interesting if anything unforeseen had happened.

So that all things concerned might be assumed to be paddling comfortably along in warm water—unless Roger had subsequently wrapped the automobile round a lamp-post, or taken a tack into the bosom of a tyre. And even that could not now prove wholly disastrous, for the Saint himself knew the destination of the convoy without waiting for further news, and he reckoned that a village with a mere 3,128 souls to call it their home town wasn't anything like an impossible covert to draw, even in the lack of more minute data.

Much, of course, depended on how long a time elapsed before the Prince took it into his head to have a bath . . . Thinking over that touch of melodramatic bravado, Simon was momentarily moved to regret it. For the sight of the work of art which the Saint had left behind him as a souvenir of his visit would be quite enough to send the entire congregation of the ungodly yodelling frantically over the road to Saltham like so many starving rats on the trail of a decrepit Camembert . . . And then that very prospect wiped every sober regret out of the Saint's mind, and flicked a smile on his lips as he beckoned a passing cab.

After all, if an adventurer couldn't have a sense of humour about the palpitations of the ungodly at his time of life—then he might as well hock his artillery forthwith and blue the proceeds on a permanent wave. In any case, the ungodly would have to see the night through. The ship of which Marius had spoken would be stealing in under cover of dark, and the ungodly, unless they were prepared to heave in their hand, would blinkin' well have to wait for it—dealing with any interference as best they could.

"That little old watering-place is surely going to hum tonight," figured the Saint.

The taxi pulled in to the kerb beside him, and, as he opened the door, he glimpsed a mountain of sleepy-looking flesh sauntering along the opposite pavement. The jaws of the perambulating mountain oscillated rhythmically, to the obvious torment of a portion of the sweetmeat which has made the sapodilla tree God's especial favour to Mr Wrigley. Chief Inspector Teal seemed to be enjoying his walk . . .

"Liverpool Street Station," directed the Saint, and climbed into his cab, vividly appreciating another factor in the equation which was liable to make the algebra of the near future a thing of beauty and a joy for Einstein.

2

He had plenty of time to slaughter a sandwich and smoke a quartet of meditative cigarettes at the station before he caught Sunday's second and last train to Saxmundham, which was the nearest effective railhead for Saltham. He would have had time to call in at the Waldorf for Roger's wire on his way if he had chosen, but he did not choose. Simon Templar had a very finely calibrated judgement in the matter of unnecessary risks. At Liverpool Street he felt pretty safe: in the past he had always worked by car, and he fully expected that all the roads out of London were well picketed, but he was anticipating no special vigilance at the railway stations—except, perhaps, on the Continental departure platform at Victoria. He may have been right or wrong; it is only a matter of history that he made the grade and boarded the 4:35 unchallenged.

It was half-past seven when the train decanted him at Saxmundham, and in the three hours of his journey, having a compartment to himself, he had effected a rejuvenation that would have made Dr Voronoff's best experiment look like a piffled porcupine trying to play the Fifth Symphony on a cracked oboe in a pail of molasses. He even contrived to brush and batter a genuine jauntiness into his ancient hat, and he swung off the train with his beard and glasses in his pocket, and an absurdly boyish glitter in his eyes.

He had lost nothing by not bothering to collect Roger Conway's telegram, for he knew his man. In the first bar he entered he discovered his lieutenant attached by the mouth to the open end of a large tankard of ale. A moment later, lowering the tankard in order to draw breath, Roger perceived the Saint smiling down at him, and goggled.

"Hold me up, someone," he muttered, "And get ready to shoo the pink elephants away when I start to gibber . . . And to think I've been complaining that I couldn't see the point of paying seven-pence a pint for brown water with a taste!"

Simon laughed.

"Bear up, old dear," he said cheerfully. "It hasn't come to that yet"

"But how did you get here?"

"Didn't you send for me?" asked the Saint innocently.

"I did not," said Roger. "I looked out the last train, and I knew my message wouldn't reach you in time for you to catch it. I wired you to phone me here, and for the last three hours I've been on the verge of heart failure every time the door opened. I thought Teal must have got after you somehow, and every minute I was expecting the local cop to walk in and invite me outside."

Simon grinned, and sank into a chair. A waiter was hovering in the background, and the Saint hailed him and ordered a fresh consignment of beer.

"I suppose you pinched the first car you saw," Roger was saying, "That'll mean another six months on our sentences. But you might have warned me."

The Saint shook his head.

"As a matter of fact, I never went to the Waldorf. Marius himself put me on to Saltham, and I came right along."

"Good Lord—how?"

"He talked, and I listened. It was dead easy."

"At the Ritz?"

Simon nodded. Briefly he ran over the story of the reunion, with its sequel in the bathroom, and the conversation he had overheard, and Conway stared.

"You picked up all that?"

"I did so . . . The man Marius is the three-star brain of this cockeyed age—I'll say. And by the same token, Roger, you and I are going to have to tune up our grey matter to an extra couple of thousand revs, per if we want to keep Angel Face's tail skid in sight over this course . . . But what's your end of the story?"

"Three of 'em turned up—one in a police-inspector's uniform. When the bell wasn't answered in about thirty seconds they whipped out a jemmy and bust it in. As they marched in, an ambulance pulled into the mews and stopped outside the door. It was a wonderful bit of team work. There were ambulance men in correct uniforms and all. They carried her out on a stretcher, with a sheet over her. All in broad daylight. And slick! It was under five minutes by my watch from the moment they forced the door to the moment when they were all piling into the wagon, and they pulled out before anything like a crowd had collected. They'd doped Sonia, of course . . . the swine . . ."

"Gosh!" said the Saint softly. "She's just great—that girl!"

Roger gazed thoughtfully at the pewter can which the waiter had placed before him.

"She is—just great . . ."

"Sweet on her, son?"

Conway raised his eyes.

"Are you?"

The Saint fished out his cigarette-case and selected a smoke. He tapped it on his thumbnail abstractedly, and there was a silence.

Then he said quietly, "That ambulance gag is big stuff, Note it down, Roger, for our own use one day . . . And what's the battlefield like at Saltham?"

"A sizeable house, standing in its own grounds on the cliffs, away from the village. They're not much, as cliffs go—not more than about fifty feet around there. There are big iron gates at the end of the drive. The ambulance turned in, and I went right on past without looking round—I guessed they were there for keeps. Then I had to come back here to send you that wire. By the way, there was a bird we've met before in the ambulance outfit—your little friend Hermann."

Simon stroked his chin.

"I bust his jaw one time, didn't I?"

"Something like that. And he did his best to bust my ribs and stave my head in."

"It will be pleasant," said the Saint gently, "to meet Hermann again,"

He took a pull at his beer, and frowned at the table.

Roger said, "It seems to me that all we've got to do now is to get on the phone to Claud Eustace and fetch him along. There's Sonia in that house—we couldn't have the gang more red-handed."

"And we troop along to the pen with them, and take our sentences like little heroes?"

"Not necessarily. We could watch the show from a safe distance."

"And Marius?"

"He's stung again."

The Saint sighed.

"Roger, old dear, if you'd got no roof to your mouth, you'd raise your hat every time you hiccoughed," he remarked disparagingly. "Are we going to be content with simply jarring Marius off his trolley and leaving it at that—leaving him to get busy again as soon as he likes? There's no evidence in the wide world to connect him up with

Saltham. All that bright scheme of yours would mean would be that his game would be temporarily on the blink. And there's money in it. Big money. We don't know how much, but we'd be safe enough in putting it in the seven-figure bracket. D'you think he'd give the gate to all that capital and preliminary carving and prospective gravy just because we'd trodden on his toes?"

"He'd have to start all over again—"

"And so should we, Roger—just as it happened a few months back. And that isn't good enough. Not by a mile. Besides," said the Saint dreamily, "Rayt Marius and I have a personal argument to settle, and I think—I think, honeybunch—that that's one of the most important points of all, in this game . . ."

Conway shrugged.

"Then what?"

"I guess we might tool over to Saltham and get ready to beat up this house-party."

Roger fingered an unlighted cigarette.

"I suppose we might," he said.

The Saint laughed, and stood up.

"There seems to be an attack of respectability coming over you, my Roger," he murmured. "First you talk about fetching in the police, and then you have the everlasting crust to sit there in a beer-sodden stupor and suppose we might waltz into as good a scrap as the Lord is ever likely to stage-manage for us. There's only one cure for that disease, sweetheart—and that's what we're going after now. Long before dark Marius himself and a reinforcement of lambs are certain to be steaming into Saltham, all stoked up and sizzling at the safety-valve, and the resulting ballet ought to be a real contribution to the gaiety of nations. So hurry up and shoot the rest of that beer through your face, sonny boy, and let's go!"

3

They went . . .

Not that it was the kind of departure of which Roger Conway approved. In spite of all the training which the Saint had put into him, Roger's remained a cautious and deliberate temperament. He had no peace of mind about haring after trouble with an armoury composed of precious little more than a sublime faith in Providence and a practised agility at socking people under the jaw. He liked to consider. He liked to weigh pro and con. He liked to get his hooks on to a complete detail map of the campaign proposed, with all important landmarks underlined in red ink. He liked all sorts of things that never seemed to come his way when he was in the Saint's company. And he usually seemed to be tottering through the greater part of their diverse adventures in a kind of lobster-supper dream, feeling like a man who is compelled to run a race for his life over a delirious cake-walk on a dark night in a gale of wind and a pea-soup fog. But always in that nightmare the Saint's fantastic optimism led him on, dancing ahead like a will-o'-the wisp, trailing him dizzily behind into hell-for-leather audacities which Roger, in the more leisured days that followed, would remember in a cold sweat.

And yet he suffered it all. The Saint was just that sort of man. There was a glamour, a magnificent recklessness, a medieval splendour about him that no one with red blood in his veins could have resisted. In him there was nothing small, nothing half-hearted: he gave all that he had to everything he did, and made his most casual foolishness heroic.

"Who cares?" drawled the Saint, with his lean brown hands seeming merely to caress the wheel of the Hirondel, and his mad, mocking eyes lazily skimming the road that hurtled towards them at seventy miles an hour. "Who cares if a whole army corps of the heathen comes woofling into Saltham tonight, even with a detachment of some of our old friends in support—the Black Wolves, for instance, or the Snake's Boys, or the Tiger Cubs, or even a brigade of the Crown Prince's own household cavalry—old Uncle Rayt Marius an' all? For it seems years since we had what you might call a one hundred per cent rodeo, Roger, and I feel that unless we get moving again pretty soon we shall be growing barnacles behind the ears."

Roger said nothing. He had nothing to say. And the big car roared out into the east.

The sun had long since set, and now the twilight was closing down with the suddenness of the season. As the dusk became dangerous for their speed, Simon touched a switch, and the tremendous twin headlights slashed a blazing pathway for them through the darkness.

They drove on in silence, and Roger Conway, strangely soothed by the swift rush of wind and the deep-chested drone of the open exhaust, sank into a hazy reverie. And he remembered a brown-eyed slip of a girl, sweet and fresh from her bath, in a jade-green gown, who was called America's loveliest lady, and who had sat in a sunny room with him that morning and eaten bacon and eggs. Also he remembered the way she and the Saint had spoken together, and how far away and unattainable they had seemed in their communion, and how little the Saint would say afterwards. He was quiet . . .

And then, it seemed only a few minutes later Simon was rousing him with a hand on his shoulder, and Roger struggled upright and saw that it was now quite dark, and the sky was brilliant with stars.

"Your cue, son," said the Saint. "The last signpost gave us three miles to Saltham. Where do we go from here?"

"Right on over the next crossroads, old boy . . ." Roger picked up his bearings mechanically. "Carry on . . . and bear left here . . . Sharp right just beyond that gate, and left again almost immediately . . . I should watch this corner—it's a brute . . . Now stand by to fork right in about half a mile, and the house is about another four hundred yards farther on . . ."

The Saint's foot groped across the floor and kicked over the cut-out control, and the thunder of their passage was suddenly hushed to a murmuring whisper that made the figures on the speedometer seem grotesque. The Saint had never been prone to hide any of his lights under a bushel, and in the matter of racing automobiles particularly he had cyclonic tastes, but his saving quality was that of knowing precisely when and where to get off.

"We won't tell the world we're on our way till we've given the lie of the land a brisk double-O," he remarked. "Let's see—where does this comic chemin trail to after it's gone past the baronial hall?"

"It works round the grounds until it comes out on to the cliffs," Roger answered. "Then it runs along by the sea and dips down into the village nearly a mile away."

"Any idea how big these grounds are?"

"Oh, large . . . I could give you a better idea of the size if I knew how much space an acre takes up."

"Park land, or what?"

"Trees all round the edge and gardens round the house—as far as I could see. But part of it's park—you could play a couple of cricket matches on it . . . The gates are just round this bend on your right now."

"OK, Big Boy . . ."

The Saint eased up the accelerator, and glanced at the gates as the Hirondel drifted past. They were tall and broad and massive, fashioned in wrought iron in an antique style; far beyond them, at the end of a long straight drive, he could see the silhouette of a gabled roof against the stars, with one tiny square of window alight in the black shadow . . . Maybe Sonia Delmar was there . . . And he looked the other way, and saw the grim line of Roger's mouth.

"Feeling a bit more set for the stampede, son?" he asked softly.

"I am," Roger met his eyes steadily. "And it might amuse you to know, Saint, that there isn't another living man I'd have allowed to make it a stampede. Even now, I don't quite see why Sonia had to go back."

Simon touched the throttle again, and they swept on.

"D'you think I'd have let Sonia take the risk for nothing myself?" he answered. "I didn't know what I was going to get out of my trip to the Ritz. And even what I did get isn't the whole works. But Sonia— she's right in their camp, and they've no fear of her squealing. It would amuse them to boast to her. Roger—I can see them doing it."

"That Russian they're bringing over—"

"Vassiloff?"

"That's it—"

"I rather think he'll boast more than any of them."

"What's he getting out of it?"

"Power," said the Saint quietly. "That's what they're all playing for— or with. And Rayt Marius most of all, for the power of gold—Marius and the men behind him. But he's the mad dog . . . Did you know that he was once a guttersnipe in the slums of Prague . . . ? Wouldn't it be the greatest thing in his life to sit on the unofficial throne of Europe—to play with kings and presidents for toys—to juggle with great nations as in the past he's juggled with little ones? That's his idea. That's why he's playing Vassiloff with one finger, because Vassiloff hates Lessing, and Prince Rudolf with another finger, because Rudolf fancies himself as a modern Napoleon—and by the Lord, Roger, Rudolf could make that fancy into fact, with Marius behind him . . . ! And God knows how many other people are on his strings, here and there. And Sonia's the pawn that's right inside their lines—that might become a queen in one move, and turn the scales of their tangled chess game to hell or glory."

"While we're—just dancing round the board . . ."

"Not exactly," said the Saint.

They had swung out on to the cliff road, and Simon was braking the car to a gentle standstill. As the car stopped he pointed, and Roger, looking past him, saw two lights, red and green, stealing over the sea.

4

"There's the bleary old *bateau* . . ."

A ghost of merriment wraithed through the Saint's voice. Thus the approach of tangible peril always seized him with a stirring of stupendous laughter, and a surge of pride in all gay, glamorous things. And he slipped out of the car, and stood with his hands on his hips, looking down at the lights and the reflection of the lights in the smooth sea, and then away to his right, where the shreds of other lights were tattered between the trees. "Battle and sudden death," went a song in his heart," and he smiled in the starlight, remembering another adventure and an old bravado.

Then Roger was standing beside him.

"How long would you give it, Saint?"

"All the time in the world. Don't forget we're fifty feet above sea level, by your reckoning, and that alters the horizon. She's a good two miles out."

Simon's head went back; he seemed to be listening.

"What is it?" queried Roger.

"Nothing. That's the problem. We didn't pass Marius on the road here, and he didn't pass us. Question: did he get here first or is he still coming? Or isn't the Prince likely to find my bathroom decoration till next Saturday? What would you say, Roger?"

"I should say they were here. You had to wait for a slow train, and then we wasted an hour in Saxmundham."

"Not 'wasted,' sweetheart," protested the Saint absently. "We assimilated some ale."

He heard an unmistakable metallic snap at his side, and glanced down at the blue- black sheen of an automatic in Roger's hand.

"We'll soon find out what's happened," said Roger grimly.

"Gat all refuelled and straining at the clutch, old lad?"

"It is."

Simon laughed, softly, thoughtfully, and his hand fell on Conway's wrist.

"Roger, I want you to go back to London." There was an instant's utter silence.

Then—"You want—"

"I want you to go back to London. And find Lessing. Get at him somehow—if you have to shoot up the whole West End. And fetch him along here—even at the end of that gun!"

"Saint, what's the big idea?"

"I want him here—our one and only Ike—"

"But Sonia—"

"I'm staying, and that's what I'm staying for. You don't have to worry about her. And it's safer for you in London than it is for me. You've got to make record time on this trip."

"You can get ten miles an hour more out of that car than I can."

"And I can fight twice as many men as you can, and move about twice as quietly, and shoot twice as fast. No, Roger, this end of the game is mine, and you must know it. And Sir Isaac Lessing we must have. Don't you see?"

"Damn it, Saint—"

There were depths of bitterness in Roger's voice that the Saint had never heard there before, but Simon could understand.

"Listen, sonny boy," he said gently. "Don't we know that the whole of this part of the performance has been staged for Lessing's benefit? And mightn't there be one thing just a shade cleverer than keeping Lessing neutral? That's all we'd be doing if you had your way. But suppose we fetched Ikey himself along here—and showed him the whole frame-up from the wings? Lessing isn't a sack of peanuts. If Marius thinks enough of him to go to all this trouble to josh him into the show of an active partner, mightn't it be the slickest thing we ever did to turn Marius's battle-axe against himself with a vengeance—and get Lessing not just neutral, but a fighting man on our side? If Lessing can say 'War!' to the Balkans, and have them all cutting each other's throats in a week, why shouldn't he just as well say 'Nix!'—and send them all toddling home to their carpet slippers. Roger, it's the chance of a lifetime!"

He took Conway by the shoulders.

"You must see it, old Roger!"

"I know, Saint. But—"

"I promise you shall be in at the death. I don't know exactly what I'm going to do now, but I'm putting off anything drastic until the last possible minute. I don't want to make a flat tyre of our own private peep-show if I can possibly help it—not till Ike's here to share the fun. And you'll be here with him, bringing up the beer—rear—in the triumphal procession. Roger, is the bet on?"

They stood eye to eye for ten ticked seconds of silence, and Roger's bleak eyes searched the Saint's face as they had never searched it before. In those ten seconds, all that the Saint signified in Roger's life, all that he incarnated and inspired, all that they had been through together, the whole cumulative force of a lifelong loyalty, rose up and gave desperate battle to the seed of ugly suspicion that had been sown in Roger's mind nearly two hours ago, and devilishly fecundated by this last inordinate demand. The stress of the fight showed in Roger's face, the rebellion of unthinkable things, but Simon waited without another word.

And then, slowly, Roger Conway nodded.

"Shake," he said. "Atta-boy . . ."

Their hands met in a long grip, and then Roger turned away abruptly, and swung into the driving seat of the Hirondel. The Saint leaned on the door.

"Touch the ground in spots," he directed rapidly. "I've got my shirt on you, and I know you won't fizzle, but every minute matters. And understand—if you do have to prod Isaac with the snout of that shooting-iron, prod him gently. He's got to arrive here in good running order—but he's got to arrive. What happens after that is your shout. I'd have liked to make a definite date, and I'm sure you would, too, Roger, but that's more than any of us can do on a night like this, and we'd be boobs to try. If I can manage it, I'll be here myself. If I can't I'll try to leave a note—let's see—I'll slip something under a rock by that tree there. If I can't even do that—"

"Then what?"

"Then I'm afraid, Roger, it'll mean that you're the last wicket up, and you may give my love to all kind friends, and shoot Rayt Marius through the stomach for me, and raise what you can on my Ulysses and the photographs Dicky Tremayne sent me from Paris."

The self-starter whirred under Roger's foot, and he listened for a moment to the smooth purr of the great engine, and then he turned again to the Saint.

"I'll be carrying on," he said quietly.

"I know," said the Saint, in the same tone. "And if you don't find that note, it mayn't really be so bad as all that—it may only mean that I've had an attack of writer's cramp, or something. But it'll still be your call. So don't think you're being elbowed out—because you're not. Whatever else happens, you're more than likely to have to stand up to the worst of the bowling before we draw stumps, and the fate of the side may very well be in your hands. And that does not mean maybe." He clapped Roger on the shoulder. "So here's luck to you, sonny boy!"

"Good luck, Saint!"

"And give 'em hell!"

And Simon stepped back, with a light laugh and a flourish, and the Hirondel leaped away like an unleashed fiend.

CHAPTER SIX:
HOW SIMON TEMPLAR THREW
A STONE AND THE ITALIAN
DELEGATE WAS UNLUCKY

1

For a moment the Saint stood there, watching the tail light of the Hirondel skimming away into the darkness. He knew so well—he could not have helped knowing—the hideous doubts that must have tortured Roger's brain, the duel between jealousy and friendship, the agony that the struggle must have cost. For Roger could only have been thinking of the ultimate destiny of the girl who had been pitchforked into their lives less than twelve hours ago, who was now a prisoner in the house beyond the trees, from whom the Saint had already plundered such a fantastic allegiance. And Simon thought of other girls that Roger had known, and of other things that had been in their lives since they first came together, and of his own lady, and he wondered, with a queer wistfulness in the eyes that followed that tiny red star down the road.

And then the red star swept out of sight round a bend, and the Saint turned away with a shrug, and glanced down again at the sea, where lay another red star, with a green one beside it.

In that, at least, he had deliberately lied . . . The ship, he was sure, had been within a mile of the shore when he spoke, and now it had ceased to move. The rattle of a chain came faintly to his ears, and then he heard the splash of the anchor.

They had run their timetable close enough! And Roger Conway, with about a hundred and eighty miles to drive, to London and back, and a job of work to do on the way, had no mean gag to put over— even in the Hirondel. The Saint, who was a connoisseur of speed, swore by that car, and he knew that Roger Conway, for all his modesty, could spin a nifty wheel when he was put to it, but, even so, he reckoned that Roger hadn't a heap to beef about. Any verbiage about Roger having nothing to do that night would be so much apple sauce . . .

"And pray Heaven he doesn't pile that bus up on its front bumpers on the way," murmured Simon, piously.

As he slipped into the shadows of a clump of trees, his fingers strayed instinctively to his left sleeve, feeling for the hilt of Belle, the little throwing-knife that was his favourite weapon, which he could use with such a bewildering speed and skill. Once upon a time, Belle had been merely the twin sister of Anna, who was his darling, but he had lost Anna three months ago, in the course of his first fight with Marius. And, touching Belle, in her little leather sheath strapped to his forearm, the Saintly smile flickered over his lips, without reaching his eyes . . .

Then, beyond the clump of trees, he stood beside the wooden fence that walled off the estate. It was as tall as himself; he stretched up cautious fingers, and felt a thick entanglement of rusty barbed wire along the top. But a couple of feet over his head one of the trees in the clump through which he had just passed extended a long bare branch far over the fence. Simon limbered his muscles swiftly, judged his distance, and jumped for it. His hands found their hold as smoothly and accurately as if he had been performing on a horizontal bar in a gymnasium, and he swung himself back to the fence hand over hand, pulled up with his arms, carried his legs over, and dropped lightly to the ground on the other side.

Fastidiously settling his tie, which had worked a fraction of an inch out of place during the performance, he stepped through the narrow skirting of forestry in which he had landed, and inspected the view.

In front of him, and away round to his right, spread an expanse of park land, broken by occasional trees, and surrounding the house on the two sides that he could see. Also surrounding the house, and farther in, lay the gardens, trellises and terraces, shrubberies and outbuildings, dimly visible in the gloom. On his left, crowning a steady rise in the ground, a kind of balustraded walk cut a clean black line against the sky, and he guessed that this marked the edge of the cliffs.

In this direction he moved, keeping in the sheltering obscurity of the border of trees for as long as he could, and then breaking off at right angles, parallel with the balustrade, before he had mounted enough of the gentle slope for his silhouette to be marked against the skyline. He felt certain that his entrance upon the estate was not yet public knowledge, and he was inclined to stay cagey about it: the number and personal habits of the household staff were very much of an unknown quantity so far, and the Saint was not tempted to run any risk of provoking them prematurely. Swiftly as he shifted through the faint starlight, his sensitive ears were alert for the slightest sound, his restless eyes scanned every shadow, and the fingers of his right hand were never far from the chased ivory hilt of Belle. He himself made no more sound than a prowling leopard, and that same leopard could not have constituted a more deadly menace to any member of the opposition gang who might have chanced to be roaming about the grounds on Simon Templar's route.

Presently the house was again on his right, and much nearer to him, for he had travelled round two sides of a rough square. He began to move with an even greater caution. Then, in a moment, gravel grated under his feet He glanced sharply to his left, to see where the path led, and observed a wide gap in the balustrade at the cliff edge. That would be the top of a flight of steps running down the cliff face to the shore, he figured, and beside the gap he saw a tree that would provide friendly cover for another peep at the developments in the water below.

He turned off the path, and melted into the blackness beneath the tree. This grew on the very edge of the scarp, and the break in the balustrade meant what he had thought it meant—a rough stairway that vanished downwards into the darkness.

Looking out, Simon saw a thin paring of new moon slithering out of the rim of the sea. It wouldn't be the hell of a moon even when it was fully risen, he reflected, with a voiceless thanksgiving to the little gods that had made the adventure this much easier. For all felonious purposes, the light was perfect—nothing but the soft luminance of a sky spangled with a thousand stars—light enough for a cat-eyed *shikari* like Simon Templar to work by, without being bright enough to be embarrassing.

He switched his eyes downwards again, and saw, midway between the anchored ship and the thin white ribbon of sand at the foot of the cliff, a tiny black shape stealing over the waters. Motionless, instinctively holding his breath and parting his lips—the Saint's faculties worked involuntarily, whether they were needed or not—he could catch shreds of the sound of grating rowlocks.

And then he heard another sound, behind him, that was much easier to hear—the gritting of heavy boots on the gravel he had just quitted.

2

He merged a little deeper into the blackness of his cover, and looked round. A lantern was bobbing down the path from the house, and three men tramped along by its light. In a moment their voices came to him quite plainly.

"Himmel! I shall vant to go to bet. Last night—tonight—it iss never no sleep for der mans."

"Aw—ya big skeezicks! What sorta tony outfit d'ya think ya've horned in on?"

"Ah, 'e will-a always be sleeping, da Gerraman. He would-a make-a all his time sleeping and-a drinking—but I t'ink 'e like-a best-a da drinking."

"Maybe he's gotta toist like I got. Ya cain't do nuth'n about dat kinda toist . . ."

The Saint leaned elegantly against a tree, watching the advancing group, and there was a hint of genuine admiration in his eyes.

"A Boche, a Wop, and a Bowery Boy," he murmured. "Gee—that man Marius ought to be running the League of Nations!"

The three men marched a few more yards in silence, and they were almost opposite the Saint when the Bowery Boy spoke again.

"Who's bringin' down de goil?"

"Hermann," the Boche answered with guttural brevity.

"She is-a da nice-a girl, no?" The Wop took up the running sentimentally. "She remind-a me of-a a girl in Sorrento, 'oo I knew—"

"She sure is a classy skoit. But us poor fish ain't gotta break—it's de big cheese fer hers, sure . . ."

They passed so close by the Saint that he could have reached out and knifed the nearest of them without an effort—and he did actually meditate that manoeuvre for a second, for he had a forthright mind. But he knew that one minor assassination more or less would not make much difference, and he stood to lose more than he could hope to gain. Besides, any disturbance at that juncture would wreck beyond redemption the plan which he had just formed.

The League of Nations was descending the cliff stairway, the mutter of their voices growing fainter as they went. Simon took another look at the sea, and saw that the ship's boat had halved its distance from the shore. And then, after one quick glance round to see if anyone was following on immediately behind the three who had passed on, he slipped out of his shelter and flitted down the steps in the wake of the voices.

He could have caught them up easily, but he hung well behind. That cliff path was trickier country to negotiate than the smooth turf above, and a single loose stone, at close range, might tell good night to the story in a most inconvenient and disastrous fashion. Also, one of the three might for some reason take it into his head to return, and the Saint thought he would like warning of that tergiversation. So he saw to it that they kept their lead and walked with a delicacy that would have made Agag look like a rheumatic rhinoceros.

Then he found himself on the turn of the last zigzag while the party below were debouching on to the sands. At the same moment, the ship's boat ran alongside a little jetty, which had been screened from his view when he looked down from the top of the cliff.

He paused there, thinking rapidly, and surveying the scenery.

The shore itself was destitute of cover for the twenty yards of sand that lay between the end of the path and the jetty, but the miscellaneous grasses and shrubs which grew thickly over the sloping cliff extended right down to the beginning of the sands, without any bare patches that he could see, and appeared to become even thicker before they stopped altogether. This was certainly helpful, but . . . He looked out towards the ship, and stroked his chin thoughtfully. Then he gazed again at the jetty, where a man from the ship's boat was being helped up into the light of the lantern. Near that boat, alongside the wharf, but more in-shore, something else rode gently on the water . . . The Saint stiffened slowly, straining his eyes, with a kind of delirious ecstasy stealing through him. He was not quite sure—not quite—and it seemed too good to be true . . . But, while he stared, the man who had got out of the boat, and the man with the lantern, and one other of the three who had come down from the house, began to walk slowly towards the cliff path, and the man with the lantern walked on the outside by the edge of the jetty, and the light of the lantern turned speculation into certainty in the matter of the second craft which was moored by the wharf. It was, by the beard of the Prophet, an indisputable and incontrovertible outboard motor-boat . . .

The Saint drew a long lung-easing breath . . . Too good to be true, but—"Oh, baby!" sighed the Saint.

He was even able to ignore, for a short space, the disconcerting fact that this heaven- sent windfall coincided in the moment of its manifestation with a remarkably compensating disadvantage. For the third member of the reception committee was squatting on the wharf, talking to the boat's crew, and the other two were escorting the boat's passenger to the cliff stairway, and, at the same time as he perceived the movement of these events, Simon heard the sounds of a small party descending that same cliff stairway towards him.

Then he looked round, and saw the lantern of the descending party bobbing down the second flight above him; he could distinguish two figures, one of them tall and the other one much shorter.

Slightly annoying. But not desperate . . .

Reviewing the ground, he stepped lightly off the path, rounded a shrub, caught the stem of a young sapling, and drew himself silently up into the shadows. And it so happened that the two parties met directly beneath him, and he saw, as he had guessed, that the two who had descended after him were the man Hermann and Sonia Delmar.

The five checked their progress and gathered naturally into a little group, talking in an undertone. Sonia Delmar was actually outside the group, temporarily ignored. There was no need for her custodian to fear that she might duck out; Simon could see the cords that bound her wrists together behind her back, and the eighteen-inch hobble of rope between her ankles.

He was crouching where he was, with one arm locked about the slender trunk of the sapling that supported him precariously on the steep slope. The fingers of his free hand stroked tenderly over the ground, and picked up a tiny pebble; aiming carefully, he lobbed the stone down.

It struck the girl's hands, but she did not move at once. Then the toe of one shoe kicked restlessly at the gravel under her feet—and if any of the men below had heard the stone fall he would have thought the sound was due to her own movements. The Saint raised his eyes momentarily to the stars above. It was classic. That girl, playing his own game for the first time in her life, so far as he knew, after she'd already walked in under the shadow of the axe as coolly as any qualified adventurer—even with the axe in the act of falling she could watch the subtlest refinements of that game. When any other girl would have been shaking at the knees, thinking hysterically of escape and rescue, she was calmly and methodically chalking her cue . . .

And then, quite naturally and deliberately, she glanced round, and the Saint stood up out of the shadows so that he could be plainly seen.

She saw him. Even in that dim light he could make out the eager question in her face, and he knew that she must have seen his smile. He nodded, waved his hand, and pointed out to the waiting ship. Then he smiled again, and he crowded into that smile all that he could bring to it of reckless confidence. And when she smiled back, and nodded in semi-comprehension and utter trust, he could have thrown everything to the winds and leapt down to take her in his arms. But he did not. His right hand and arm went out and upwards in a gay cavalier gesture that matched his smile, and then he sank down again into the darkness as Hermann curtly urged her on down the slope and the other three resumed their climb.

3

But she had seen him; she knew that he was there, that there had been no mistake yet, that he had not betrayed her faith, that he was waiting, ready . . . And that was something to have shown her . . . And, as he dropped on his toes to the empty path, Simon remembered her fine courage, and Roger Conway, and many things. "Oh, glory," thought the Saint, sinking on to a convenient boulder, his hands on his knees . . .

He saw her marched along the jetty and lifted down into the boat. Hermann squatted down on his haunches, beside the other man who was chatting with the crew; the flare of the match which he struck to light his pipe brought up in sharp relief the lean predatory face that the Saint could recall so easily. And Simon waited.

Clearly the boat's crew were delaying for the return of the man they had brought ashore—one of the ship's officers, probably, if not the captain himself. And much seemed now to depend on what had happened to Marius, which in its turn depended upon the Crown Prince's ablutionary programme. And to the answers to these dependent questions the Saint had still no clue. When Marius came slavering into Saltham with the tale of the desecrated royal toothpaste, no small excitement might have been expected. Therefore the Saint was sure that this had not happened before his own arrival on the scene, for, if it had, there would have been a seething cordon of the ungodly around the grounds of the house, and his own modest entrance would have been a much livelier affair—unless Marius had banked on what he knew of the Saint's former ignorance of the Prince's language. And that was—well, a thin chance . . . Of course, Marius might have arrived while the Saint was doing his midnight mountaineering act, but even so, Simon would have expected to hear at least the echoes of some commotion. He estimated that, taken by and large, he and his record combined were an ingredient that might without conceit expect to commotate any brew of blowed-in-the-glass ungodliness, and he would have been very distressed to find that the ungodly had failed to commote as per schedule. Therefore he was blushingly inclined to rule out the possibility . . . But sooner or later the nocturnal tranquility of that part of the country was bound to be rudely shattered, and there were more votes for sooner than later, and the quintessential part of the plot, so far as Simon Templar was concerned, was how soon—with a very wiggly mark after it to indicate importunate interrogation.

But presently, after an age of grim anxiety, he heard voices above him, and slipped discreetly off the path. Two men came down—one of them, apparently, the Boche whose dulcet tones had a little earlier been complaining about his enforced insomnia, for they spoke in German. The Saint listened interestedly for any reference to himself as they came nearer, but there was none. The Boche complained about the steepness of the path, about the darkness, about the food on which he was fed, and about his lack of sleep, and the ship's officer expressed perfunctory sympathy at intervals; they passed on. They, at all events, were unperturbed by anything they had heard up at the house.

Simon watched them saunter down the jetty and shake hands. The officer re-entered the boat. A man in the bows pushed it off with a boathook. The crew bent to their oars.

In the light of the lanterns held by the men on the jetty Simon could see the girl looking back towards the cliff, but she could not have seen him even if he had stood out in the open. And then two of the men on the quay began to trudge back towards the cliff path.

Two of them . . . Simon saw them pass beneath him, and frowned. Then he looked down to the shore again, seeking the third man, and could not find him. The footsteps and voices of the two who climbed grew fainter and fainter, and presently were lost altogether. They had passed over the top of the scarp, and still the third man had not followed.

Simon hesitated, shrugged, and descended again to the path. Whatever the third man was doing, he would have to take his chance. Time was getting short. The ship must have been ready to weigh anchor as soon as its compulsory passenger was on board, and, besides—well, how soon . . . ?

And then, as he paused there, a very Saintly smile bared Simon's teeth in the darkness. For, if the third man was still lurking about on the shore—so much the better. His companions were gone, and the boat was some distance away . . . and the Saint was an efficient worker. The sounds of a slight scuffle need not be fatal. And the third man, whoever he was, could be used—very profitably and entertainingly used—in conjunction with that providential motor-boat . . .

Simon sped down the path like a flying shadow. As he rounded the last corner a stone dislodged by his foot went clinking over the side of the path and flurried into a bush. He heard a sharp movement at another point beneath him, and went on carelessly. Then a stocky figure loomed out of the dark directly in front of him.

"*Chi va là?*" rapped the startled challenge, in the man's own language, and Simon felt that the occasion warranted a demonstration of his own linguistic prowess.

"*L'uomo che ha la penna délia tua zia,*" he answered solemnly.

His feet grounded on the sand, a yard from the challenger, and, as the man opened his mouth to make some remark which was destined never to be given to the world, the Saint slashed a terrific uppercut into a jaw that was positively asking for it.

"Exit Signor Boloru, the Italian delegate," murmured the Saint complacently, and, stooping swiftly, he hoisted the unconscious man on to his shoulder and proceeded on his way thus laden.

4

In a few moments he stood on the jetty beside the motor-boat, and there he dumped his burden. Then, like lightning, he stripped himself to the skin.

The Saint possessed a very elegant and extensive wardrobe when he was at home, but, on this occasion, its extensiveness was not at his disposal, and the elegance of the excerpt that he was wearing therefore became an important consideration. He was certainly going to get wet, but he saw no good reason why his clothes should get wet with him. Besides, he felt that it would be an advantage to preserve immaculate the outward adornments of his natural beauty: there was no knowing how much more that Gent's Very Natty was going to have to amble through before the dawn, and to have been forced to exchange any breezy badinage with Rayt Marius and/or Prince Rudolf while looking like a deep-sea diver whose umbrella has come ungummed at twenty fathoms would have cramped the Saintly style more grievously than any other conceivable circumstance.

Therefore the Saint stripped. His clothes were of the lightest, and he was able to make them all into one compact bundle, which he wrapped in his shirt.

Then he returned his attention to the motor-boat. It was moored by two painters, and these he detached. A loose narrow floorboard taken from the bottom of the boat he lashed at right angles across the tiller, using strips of the Italian delegate's trousers, carved out with Belle, for the purpose; then, to the ends of this board, he fixed the ropes he had obtained, leaving them trailing in the water behind the boat. Finally, he deposited the Italian delegate himself in the stern sheets, propping him up as best he could with another couple of duck-boards.

The Saint had worked with incredible speed. The boat which carried Sonia Delmar had not reached the side of the ship when Simon took hold of the motor-boat's starting handle. With that he was lucky. The engine spluttered into life after a couple of pulls. And so, stark naked, with his bundle of clothes on his head and the sleeves of his shirt knotted under his chin to hold the bundle in place, the Saint slid into the water, holding one of his tiller ropes in each hand, and the motor-boat swerved out from the jetty and began to pick up speed as Sonia Delmar was lifted on to the gangway of the waiting ship.

That crazy surf-ride remained ever afterwards as one of Simon Templar's brightest memories. The motor-boat had a turn of speed that he had not anticipated; its creaming wake stung his eyes, half blinding him, and strangled his nostrils when he breathed; if he had not had fingers of steel his hold on the ropes by which it towed him would have been broken in the first two minutes. And with those very ropes he had to steer a course at the same time, an accurate course—with the hull of the boat in front of him blacking out most of his field of vision, and so much play on his crude steering apparatus that it was a work of art to do no more than prevent the tiller locking over on one side or the other and hereafter ceasing to function at all. Whereupon he would, presumably, have travelled round in a small circle till the petrol tank dried up . . .

He found that the only way he could keep control of his direction was by travelling on a series of progressive diagonal tacks; otherwise it was impossible to keep his objective in view. Even then, the final rush would have to be a straight one . . . The blinding stammer of the motor was a hellish affair. Long ago the men out on the water must have been asking questions. Probably the din could have been heard up at the house on the cliffs as well, and he wondered what that section of the unrighteous would make of it . . . As he swung over on another tack— he had to do this very gently, for any vertical banking business would have been liable to upset the Italian delegate, and Simon wanted the Italian delegate to stay put—he glimpsed the ship's boat hanging from the falls, clear of the water, and little knots of black figures clustered along the starboard rail. Surely they must be asking questions . . .

He realized, suddenly, that it was time to attempt the last straight dash.

He sighted for it as best he could, rolled all his weight on to one rope for a moment, and then flattened out again. Now, if he hit the side of the ship the fishes would do themselves proud on what was left of him . . . But he didn't hit. Far from it. Through a lashing lather of spray, he saw the anchor-chain flash past him, half a dozen yards away.

Not good enough . . .

As he went by, he heard the faint shred of a shout from the deck, above, and the Saintly smile twitched a trifle grimly at the corners of his mouth. Then the motor-boat was speeding out to sea, and again he rolled his weight carefully on to one rope.

The roughness of the ropes was scorching the inside of his hands. The cords were too thin to be gripped comfortably, and his fingers were numbed and aching with the strain. In spite of his strength, he felt as if his arms were being torn from their sockets, and it seemed centuries since he had drawn a full free breath . . .

The Saint set his teeth. It had got to be done this next time—he doubted whether he could hang on for a third attempt. Ordinary surf-riding was another matter, when you had a good board beneath you to skim the surface of the water, but when you were immersed yourself . . . Again he sighted, turned the boat, and prayed . . . And, as he did so, he heard, high and clear above the clamour of the engine, the sharp sound of a shot.

Well, that was inevitable—and that was what the Italian delegate was sitting in the boat for, anyway.

"But what about us?" thought the Saint, and, at that moment, he felt the boat quiver against the ropes he held. "Here goes," thought the Saint, and relaxed his tortured hands. The cords whipped out of his grip like live things. Then the anchor-chain seemed to materialize out of space. It leapt murderously at his head; he grabbed desperately, caught, held it . . .

As he hauled himself wearily out of the water, drawing great gulps of air into his bursting lungs, he saw the Italian delegate flop sideways over the tiller. The boat heeled over dizzily; then the Italian tumbled forwards into the bilge, and the boat straightened up somehow, gathered itself, and headed roaring out to sea. A second shot cracked out from the deck.

Simon felt as if he had been stretched on the rack, but he dared not rest for more than a few seconds. This was his chance, while the attention of everyone on deck was focused on the flying motor-boat. Somehow he clambered upwards. If it had been a rope that he had to climb he could never have done it, for there seemed to be no strength left in his arms, but he was able to get his toes into the links of the chain, and only in that way could he manage the ascent. As he went higher, the bows of the ship cut off the motor-boat from his view, but he heard a third shot, and a fourth . . .

Then he was able to reach up and grip a stanchion. With a supreme effort, he drew himself up until he could get one knee over the side.

No one was looking his way, and, for all his weariness, he made no sound.

As he came over the rail, he saw the motor-boat again, scudding towards the rising moon. A figure stood up in the boat, swaying perilously, waving frantic arms. Then it gripped the tiller, and the boat reeled over on its beam-ends and headed once more towards the ship.

The man must have been shouting, but whatever he shouted was lost in the snarl of the motor. And then, for the fifth time, a gun barked somewhere on the deck, and the Italian delegate clutched at his chest and went limply into the dark sea.

CHAPTER SEVEN:

HOW SONIA DELMAR HEARD A
STORY AND ALEXIS VASSILOFF WAS
INTERRUPTED

1

Sonia Delmar heard the shooting as she was hustled across the deck and up an outside companion. Before that, she had seen the speeding motor-boat and the shape of the man crouched in the stern. The drone of its engine had rattled deafeningly across the waters as she was hurried up the gangway, she had heard the perplexed mutterings of her captors, without being able to understand what they said, and she herself, in a different way, had been as puzzled as they were. She had seen the Saint on the cliff path, and had understood from the signs he made that he was not yet proposing to interfere; after a fashion, she had been relieved, for so far she had gained no useful information. But she appreciated that, if he had meant to interfere, his chance had been then and there, on the cliff path, when he could have taken by surprise a mere handful of men who would have been additionally hampered by the difficulty of distinguishing friend from foe, and she wondered what could have made him elect instead to come so noisily against a whole boatload.

But these questions had no hope of a leisured survey at that moment; they rocketed hazily across the back of her consciousness as she stumbled on to the upper deck. The two men in charge of her, at least, placed the mysterious motor-boat second in their considerations, whatever their fellows might be doing. There was a quietly efficient discipline about everything that she had seen done that was unlike anything she had expected to find in such a criminal organization as Simon Templar had pictured for her. Nor had anything that she had read of the ways of crime prepared her for such an efficiency: the gangs on her native side of the Atlantic, by all reports, were not to be compared with this. Again came that vicious snap of the rifle on the lower deck, but the men who led her took no notice. She tripped over a cleat in the darkness, and one of the men caught her and pulled her roughly back to her balance; then a door was opened, and she barely had a glimpse of the lighted cabin within before she herself was inside it, and she heard the key turned in the lock behind her.

The howl of the motor-boat grew steadily louder, and then died down again to a fading moan.

Crack . . . ! Crack . . . !

The clatter of two more shots came to her ears as she reached an open porthole, and then she could see the boat itself and the swaying figure in the stern. She saw the boat turn and make for the ship again, and then came the last shot . . .

Slowly she sank on to a couch and closed her eyes. She felt no deep emotion—neither grief, nor terror, nor despair. Those would come afterwards. But at the time the sense of unreality was too powerful for feeling. It seemed incredible that she should be there, on that ship, alone, alive, destined for an unknown fate, with her one hope of salvation lost in the smooth waters outside. Quite quietly she sat there. She heard the empty motor-boat whine past, close by, for the last time, and hum away towards the shore. Her mind was cold and numb. When she heard a new sound in the night—a noise not unlike that of the motor-boat, but more deep-throated and reverberating—she did not move. And when upon that sound was superimposed the thrum and clatter of a steam winch forward, she opened her eyes slowly, and felt dully surprised that she could see . . .

Mechanically she took in her prosaic surroundings.

The cabin in which she sat was large and comfortably furnished. There were chairs, a table, a desk littered with papers, and one bulkhead completely covered with well-filled bookcases. One end of the cabin was curtained off, and she guessed that there would be a tiny bedroom beyond the curtain, but she did not move to investigate.

Presently she knelt up on the couch and looked up again. The ship was turning, and the dark coast swung lazily into view. Somewhere on the black line of land, a tiny light winked intermittently for a while, and vanished. After a pause, the light flickered again, more briefly. She knew that it must have been a signal from the house on the cliffs, but she could not read the code. It would not have profited her to know that a question had been asked and answered, and felicitations returned, for the answer said that the Saint was dead . . .

She lay down again, and stared at the ceiling with blind eyes. She did not think. Her brain had ceased to function. She would have liked to weep, to fling herself about in a panic of fear, but though there was the impulse to do both, she knew that neither outlet would have been genuine. That kind of thing was not in her. She could only lie still, in a paralysing daze of apathy. She lost track of time. It might have been five minutes or fifty before the cabin door opened, and she turned her head to see who had come.

"Good evening, Miss Delmar."

It was a tall man, weather-beaten of face and trimly bearded, in a smart blue uniform picked out with gold braid. His greeting was perfectly courteous.

"Are you the captain?" she asked, and he nodded.

"But I am not responsible for your present position," he said. "That is the responsibility of my employer."

"And who's he?"

"I am not at liberty to tell you."

He spoke excellent English; she could only guess at his nationality.

"I suppose," she said, "you know that you're also responsible to the American Government?"

"For you, Miss Delmar? I do not think I shall be charged."

"Also to the British Government—for murder."

He shrugged.

"There is no great risk, even of that accusation."

She was silent for a moment. Then she asked, casually, "And what's your racket—ransom?"

"You have not been informed?"

"I have not."

"Good. That was a question I came to ask."

He sat down at the desk and selected a thin cigar from a box which he produced from a drawer. "You have been brought here, frankly, in order that you may be married to a gentleman who is on board—a Mr Vassiloff. The ceremony will be performed whether you consent or not, and if there should ever be a need to bring forward witnesses, we have those who will swear that you consented. I am told that it is necessary for you to marry Mr Vassiloff—I do not know why."

2

The news did not startle her. It came as a perfect vindication of the Saint's deductions, but, now, it had a grim significance that had been lacking before. Yet the sense of unreality that lay at the root of her inertia became by that much greater instead of less. She could not imagine that she was dreaming—not in that bright light, that commonplace atmosphere—but still she could not adjust herself to the facts. She found herself speaking mechanically, as calmly as if she had been sitting in the drawing-room of the American Embassy in London, carrying on the game exactly as she had set out to play it, as if nothing had gone amiss. Her conscious mind was stunned and insentient, but some blind indomitable instinct had emerged from the recesses of her subconscious to take command, so that she amazed whatever logic was left sensible enough within her to be amazed.

"Who is this man Vassiloff?"

"I am not informed. I have hardly spoken to him. He has kept to his cabin ever since he came on board, and he only came out when we were—shooting. He is on the bridge now, waiting to be presented."

"Don't you even know what he looks like?"

"I have scarcely seen him. I can tell you that he is tall, that he wears glasses, that he has a moustache. He may be young or old—perhaps he has a beard—I do not know. When I have seen him he has always had the collar of his coat buttoned over his chin. I assume that he does not wish to be known."

"Do you even know where we're going?"

"We go to Leningrad."

"And then?"

"As far as you are concerned, that is a matter for Mr Vassiloff. My own employment will be finished."

His manner was impeccably restrained and impeccably distant. It made her realize the futility of her next question before she asked it.

"Aren't you at all interested in the meaning of what you're doing?"

"I am well paid not to be interested."

"People have been punished for what you're doing. You're very sure that you're going to escape."

"My employer is powerful as well as rich. I am well protected."

She nodded . . . "But do you know who I am?"

"I have not been told."

"My father is one of the richest men in America. It's possible that he might be able to do even more for you than your present employer."

"I am not fond of your country, Miss Delmar." He rose, deferential and yet definite, dismissing her suggestion without further speech, as if he found the discussion entirely pointless. "May I tell Mr Vassiloff that he may present himself?"

She did not answer, and, with a faintly cynical bow, he passed to the door and went out.

She sat without moving, as he had left her. In those last few moments of conversation her consciousness had begun to creep back to life, but not at all in the way she would have expected. She was still unaware of any real emotion; only she became aware of the frantic pounding of her heart as the sole sign of a nervous reaction which she felt in no other way. But a queer fascination had gripped her, born, perhaps, of the utter hopelessness of her plight, a fantastic spell that subordinated every rational reflexion to its own grotesque seduction. She was a helpless prisoner on that ship, weaponless, bound hand and foot, without a single human soul to stand by her, and every pulse of the rhythmic vibrations that she could feel beneath her was speeding her farther and farther from all hope of rescue; she was to be married with or without her consent to a man she had never seen, and whose very name she had only just heard for the first time, and yet she could feel nothing but an eerie, nightmare curiosity. The hideous bizarreness of the experience had taken her in a paralysing hold; the stark certainty that everything that the captain had announced would inexorably follow in fact seemed to sharpen and vivify all her senses, while it stupefied all initiative, so that a part of her seemed to be detached and infinitely aloof, watching with impotent eyes the drama that was being enacted over herself. There was nothing else that she could do, and so, with that strange fatalism wrapping her in an inhuman impassivity she had only that one superbly insane idea—to see the forlorn game through to the bitter end, for what it was worth . . . facing the inevitable finale with frozen eyes . . .

And, if she thought of anything else, she thought with a whimsical homesickness of a sunny room on a quiet Sunday morning, and the aromatic hiss and crackle of grilling bacon, and she thought she would like a cigarette . . .

And then the door opened again.

It was not the captain. This man came alone—a man such as the captain had described, with the wide brim of a black velour overshadowing his eyes, and the fur collar of a voluminous coat turned up about his face.

"Good evening—Sonia."

She answered quietly, with soft contempt: "You're Vassiloff, I suppose?"

"Alexis."

"Once," she said, "I had a dog called Alexis. It's a nice name—for a dog."

He laughed, sharply.

"And in a few moments," he said, "you will have a husband of the same name. So are you answered."

He pushed a chair across to the couch where she sat, and settled himself, facing her, his hands clasped over his knees. Through his thick spectacles a pair of pale blue eyes regarded her fixedly.

"You are beautiful," he remarked presently. "I am glad. It was promised me that you would be beautiful."

When he spoke it was like some weird Oriental chant; his voice rose and fell monotonously without reference to context, and remained horribly dispassionate. For the first time the girl felt a qualm of panic, that still was not strong enough to shake her bleak inertia. She cleared her throat.

"And who made this promise?" she inquired calmly.

"Ah, you would like to know!"

"I'm just naturally interested."

"It was an old friend of me." He nodded ruminatively, still staring, like a bearded mandarin. "Yess—I think Sir Isaac Lessing will be sorry to have lost you . . ."

Then the nodding slowed up and stopped abruptly, and the stare went on.

"You love him—Sir Isaac?"

"Does that matter? I don't see what difference it makes—now."

"It makes a difference."

"The only difference I can see is that Sir Isaac Leasing has a few gentlemanly instincts. For instance, he did take the trouble to ask my permission before he arranged to marry me."

"Ah!" Vassiloff bent forward. "You think Sir Isaac is a gentleman? Yet he is an enemy of me. This"—he spread out one hand and returned it to his knee—"has been done because he is an enemy."

Sonia shrugged, returning the man's stare coldly. Her composed indifference seemed to infuriate Vassiloff. He leaned farther forwards, so that his face was close to hers, and a pale flame glinted over his eyes.

"You are ice, yess? But listen. I will melt you. And first I tell you why I do it."

He put his hand on her shoulder, and she recoiled from the touch, but he took no notice.

"Once," he said, in that crooning voice, "there was a very poor young man in London. He went to ask for work of a rich man. He was starving. He could not see the rich man at his office, so he went to the rich man's house, and there he see him. The rich man strike in his face, like he was dirt. And then, for fear the young man should strike him back, he call his servants, and say, 'Throw him out in the street.' I was that young man. The rich man is Sir Isaac Lessing."

"I should call that one of the most commendable things Lessing ever did," said the girl gently.

He ignored her interruption.

"Years go by. I go back to Russia, and there are revolutions. I am with them. I see many rich men die—men like Lessing. Some of them I kill myself. But always I remember Lessing, who strike in my face. I promote myself—I have power—but always I remember."

Overhead, on the bridge, could be heard the regular pacing of the officer of the watch, but in that brightly lighted cabin Sonia felt as if there was no one but Alexis Vassiloff on the ship. His presence filled her eyes; his sing-song accents filled her ears.

"Lessing makes money with oil. I, also, make control of the oil. He does not remember me, but still he try to strike in my face—but this time it is in the oil. I, too, try to fight him, but I cannot. There are great ones with him. And then I meet a great one, and he becomes a friend of me, and I tell him my story. And he make the plan. First, he will take you away from Lessing and give you to me. He show me your picture, and I say—yess. That will make Lessing hurt. It is for the strike in the face he once give me. But that is not enough. I must make to ruin Lessing. And my friend make another plan. He say that when he tell Lessing you are with me, Lessing will try to make war. 'Now,' he say, 'I will make Lessing think that when he make war against you he will have all Europe with him, but when the war come he will find all the big countries fight among themselves, and they cannot take notice of the little country Lessing will use to make his war against you.' All this my friend can do, because he is a great one. He is greater than Lessing. He is Rayt Marius. You know him?"

"I've heard of him."

"You have heard of him? Then you know he can do it. Behind him there are other great ones, greater than there are behind Lessing. He show me his plans. He will send out spies, and make the big countries hate each other. Then, when we have take you, he send men to kill someone—the French President, perhaps—and there is the war. It is easy. It is just another Sarajevo. But it is enough. And I have my revenge—I, Vassiloff—for the strike in the face. I will have Sir Isaac Lessing crawl to my feet, but I will not be merciful. And our Russia will be great also. The big countries will fight each other, and they will be tired, and when we have finished one little country we will conquer another, and we shall be victorious over all Europe, we of the Revolution . . ."

The Russian's voice had risen to a higher pitch as he spoke, and the light of madness burned in his eyes.

Sonia watched him, listening, hypnotized. At no time before, even when she had heard and incredulously accepted the Saint's inspired deductions, had she fully grasped the immensity of the plot in which she had been made a pawn. And now she saw it in a blinding flash, and the vision appalled her.

As Vassiloff went on, the hideously solid facts on which his insanity was balanced showed up with greater and greater definition through his raving. It was there—all the machinery of which the Saint had spoken was there, and strains and stresses and counter-actions measured and calculated and balanced, every cog in the whole ghastly engine cut and ground and trued up ready for Marius to play with as he chose. How the mechanism would be put together did not matter—whether Marius had lied to Vassiloff, or meant to lie to Lessing. The rocks had been drilled in their most vital parts, the charges loaded and tamped in, the fuses laid; the tremendous fact was that the Saint had been right right in every prophecy, vague only in the merest details. The axe had been laid to the root of the tree . . .

She saw the conspiracy then as the Saint himself had seen it, months before: intrigue and counterplot, deception and deception again, and the fiendish forces that had been disentombed for this devil's sleight-of-hand. And she saw in imagination the unleashing of those forces—the tapping drums and the blast of bugles, the steady tramp of marching feet, the sonorous drone of the war birds snarling through the sky. Almost she could hear the earth-shaking reverberations of the guns, the crisp clatter of rifle fire, and she saw the swirling mists of gas, and men reeling and stumbling through hell; she had seen and heard these things for a dollar's worth of evening entertainment, in a comfortably upholstered chair. But the men there had been only actors, fighting again the battles of a generation that was already left behind; the men she saw in her vision were of her own age, men she knew . . .

She hardly heard Vassiloff anymore. She was thinking, instead, of that morning. "Have we the right?" Simon Templar had asked . . . And she saw once again the sickening sway and plunge of the figure in the motor-boat . . . Roger Conway—where had he been? What had happened to him? He should have been somewhere around, but she had not seen him. And if he were not to be counted in it meant that no power on earth could prevent her vision coming true . . .

"That'd mean we'd given Marius the game . . ."

Slowly, grotesquely, the presence of Alexis Vassiloff drifted in again upon her tempestuous thought. His voice had sunk back to that eerie crooning note to which it had been tuned before. "But you—you will not be like the others. You will stand beside me, and we will make a new empire together, you and I. You will like that?"

She started up.

"I'll see you damned first!"

"So you are still cold . . ."

His arms went round her, drawing her to him. With her hands still securely bound behind her back she was at his mercy—and she knew what that mercy would be. She kicked at his legs, but he bore her down upon the couch; she felt his hot breath on her face . . .

"Let me go—you swine—"

"You are cold, but I will melt you. I will teach you how to be warm—soft—loving. So—"

Savagely she butted her head into his face, but he only laughed. His lips stung her neck, and an uncontrollable shudder went through her. His hands clawed at her dress.

"Are you ready, Mr Vassiloff?"

The captain spoke suavely from the doorway, and Vassiloff rose unsteadily to his feet.

"Yess," he said thickly. "I am ready."

Then he leered down again at the girl.

"I go to prepare myself," he said. "It is perhaps better that we should be married first. Then we shall not be disturbed . . ."

3

The door closed behind him.

Without a flicker of expression, the captain crossed the cabin and sat down at his desk. He drew towards him a large book like a ledger, found a place in it, and left it open in front of him; then, from the box in his drawer, he selected another of his thin cigars, lighted it, and leaned back at his ease. He scarcely spared the girl a glance.

Sonia Delmar waited without speaking. She remembered, then, how often she had seen such situations enacted on the stage and on the screen, how often she had read of them . . .

She found herself trembling, but the physical reaction had no counterpart in her mind. She could not help recalling all the stereotyped jargon that had been splurged upon the subject by a hundred energetic parrots. "A fate too horrible to contemplate"—"a thing worse than death." . . . All the heroines she had encountered faced the horror as if they had never heard of it before. She felt that she ought to have experienced the same emotions as they did, but she could not. She could only think of the game that had been thrown away—the splendid gamble that had failed.

At the desk, the captain uncrossed his legs, and inhaled again from his cigar.

It seemed to Sonia Delmar that that little cabin was the centre of the world—and the world did not know it. It was hard to believe that in other rooms, all over the world, men and women were gathered together in careless comradeship, talking perhaps, reading perhaps, confident of a thousand tomorrows as tranquil as their yesterdays. She had felt the same when she had read that a criminal was to be executed the next day—that same shattering realization that the world was going on unmoved, while one lonely individual waited for dawn and the grim end of the world . . .

And yet she sat upright and still, staring ahead with unfaltering eyes, buoyed with a bleak and bitter courage that was above reason. In that hour she found within herself a strength that she had not dreamed of, something in her breed that forbade any sign of fear—that would face death, or worse than death, with scornful lips.

And then the door opened and Vassiloff came in.

Anything that he had done to "prepare" himself was not readily visible. He still wore his hat, and his fur collar was muffled even closer about his chin; only his step seemed to have become more alert.

He gave the girl one cold-blooded glance, and then he turned to the captain.

"Let us waste no more time," he said harshly.

The captain stood up.

"I have the witnesses waiting, Mr Vassiloff. Permit me . . ."

He went to the door and called two names curtly. There was a murmured answer, and the owners of the names came in—two men in coarse trousers and blue seamen's jerseys, who stood gazing uncomfortably about the cabin while the captain wrote rapidly in the book in front of him. Then he addressed them in a language that the girl could not understand, and, hesitantly, one of the men came forward and took the pen. The other followed suit. Then the captain turned to Vassiloff.

"If you will sign—"

As the Russian scrawled his name the captain spoke a brusque word of dismissal, and the witnesses filed out.

"Your wife should also sign," added the captain, turning back to the desk. "Perhaps you will arrange that?"

"I will." Vassiloff put down the pen. "I want to be left alone now—for a little while—with my wife. But I shall require to see you again. Where shall I find you?"

"I shall finish my cigar on the bridge—"

"Good. I will call you."

Vassiloff waved his hand in a conclusive gesture, and, with a slightly sardonic bow, the captain accepted his discharge.

The door closed, but Vassiloff did not turn round. He still stood by the desk, with his back to the girl. She heard the snap of a cigarette case, the sizzle of a match, and a cloud of blue smoke wreathed up towards the ceiling. He was playing with her—cat and mouse . . .

"So," he said softly, "we are married—Sonia."

The girl drew a deep breath. She was shivering, in spite of the warmth of the evening, and she did not want to shiver. She did not want to add that relish to his gloating triumph—to see the sneer of sadistic satisfaction that would flame across his face. She wanted to be what he had called her—ice . . . To save her soul aloof and undefiled, infinitely aloof and terribly cold . . .

She said swiftly, breathlessly, "Yes—we're married—if that means anything to you . . . But it means nothing to me. Whatever you do to me, you'll never be able to call me yours—never—"

He had unbuttoned his coat and flung it back; it billowed away from his wide shoulders, making him loom gigantically under the light.

"Perhaps," he said, "you think you love someone else."

"I'm sure of it," she said in a low voice.

"Ah! Is it, after all, that you were not being sold to Sir Isaac Lessing for the help he could give your father?"

"Lessing means nothing to me—"

"So there is another?"

"Does that matter?"

Another cloud of smoke went up towards the ceiling. "His name?"

She did not answer.

"Is it Roger Conway?" he asked, and a new fear chilled her heart.

"What do you know about him?" she whispered.

"Nearly everything, old dear," drawled the Saint, and he turned round, without beard, without glasses, smiling at her across the cabin, a mirthful miracle with the inevitable cigarette slanted rakishly between laughing lips.

CHAPTER EIGHT:
HOW SIMON TEMPLAR
BORROWED A GUN AND THOUGHT
KINDLY OF LOBSTERS

1

"Saint!"

Sonia Delmar spoke the name incredulously, storming the silence and the dream with that swift husky breath. And the silence was broken, but the dream did not break . . .

"Well—how's life, honey?" murmured the dream, but no dream could have miraged that gay, inspiring voice, or the fantastic flourish that went with it.

"Oh, Saint!"

He laughed softly, a sudden lilt of a laugh, and in three strides he was across the cabin, his hands on her shoulders.

"Weren't you expecting me, Sonia?"

"But I saw them shoot you—"

"Me? I'm bullet-proof, lass, and you ought to have known it. Besides, I wasn't the man in the comic canoe. That was an Italian, exhibit—a sentimental skeezicks with tender memories of the girl he left behind him in Sorrento. And I'm afraid his donna is completely mobile now."

She, too, was half laughing, trembling unashamedly now that the tense cord of suspense was snapped.

"Set me loose, Saint!"

"Half a sec. Has Vassiloff sung his song yet?"

"Yes—everything—"

"And all done by kindness . . . Sonia, you wonderful kid!"

"Oh, but I'm glad to see you, boy!"

"Are you?" The Saint's smile must have been the gayest thing in Europe. "But my show was easy! I came aboard off the motor-boat several minutes before Antonio stopped the bit of lead that was meant for me. I'd got all my clothes with me, as good as new, but when I say that my own personal corpse was damp I don't mean peradventure, and just naturally wandered into the nearest cabin in search of towels. I'd just got dried and dressed, and I was busy putting this beautiful shoe-shine on my chevelure with a pair of gold-mounted hair-brushes that were lying around, when who should beetle in but old Popoffski himself. There followed some small argument about the tenancy of the cabin, but I got half a pillow into our friend's mouth before he could raise real hell. Then I trussed him up with the sash of his own dressing-gown, and after that there was nothing for it but to take his place."

Simon's deft fingers were working on the ropes that bound the girl's hands, and she felt the circulation prickling back through her numbed wrists.

"But how did you get here?"

"I breezed in pretty much on the off-chance. I'd still got the beard I used this morning, and that was good enough for the moment, with Vassiloff's own coat buttoned round my chin and his glasses on my nose, but I couldn't trust to it indefinitely. The performance had to be speeded up—particularly, I had to find you. If Vassiloff hadn't laid his egg I should have had to go back to the cabin and perform a Caesarean operation with a hot iron, or something—otherwise the accident that

I'd chosen his cabin for my dressing-room might have mucked things badly. When I came in here and saw you and the skipper, I just said the first thing that came into my head, and after that I had to take my cue from him." Simon twitched the last turn of Manila from her ankles and grinned. "And there's the bitter blow, old dear: behold us landed in the matrimonial casserole. What sort of a husband d'you think I'll make?"

"Terrible."

"So do I. Now, if it had been Roger—"

"Simon—"

"My name," said the Saint cheerfully. "I know—I owe you an apology for that last bit of cross-examination before the unveiling of the monument, but the chance was too good to miss. The prisoner pleaded guilty under great provocation, and threw himself upon the mercy of the court. Now tell me about Marmaduke."

He sank on to the couch beside her, flicking open his cigarette-case. She accepted gratefully, and then, as quietly and composedly as she could, she told him all she had heard.

He was a surprisingly sober listener. She found that the flippant travesty of his real character with which he elected to entertain the world at large was a flimsy thing, and, when he was listening, it fell away altogether. He sat perfectly still, temporarily relaxed but still vivid in repose, alert eyes intent upon her face; the boyish effervescence that was his lighter charm bubbled down into the background, and the tempered metal of the man stood out alone and unmistakable. He only interrupted her at rare intervals—to ask a question that went to the heart of the story like aimed lightning, or to help her to make plain a point that she had worded clumsily. And, as he listened, the flesh and blood of the plot built itself up with a frightful solidity upon the skeleton that was already in his mind . . .

It must have taken her a quarter of an hour to give him all the information she had gained, and at the end of that time the clear vision in the Saint's brain was as stark and monstrous as the thing he had imagined so few months ago—only a little while before he had thought that the ghost was laid forever. All that she told him fitted faultlessly upon the bones of previous knowledge and speculation that were already his, and he saw the thing whole and real, the incarnate nightmare of a megalomaniac's delirium, gigantic, bloated, hideous, crawling over the map of Europe in a foul suppuration of greed and jealousy, writhing slimy tentacles into serene and precious places. The ghost was not laid. It was creeping again out of the poisoned shadows where it had grown up, made stronger and more savage yet by its first frustration, preparing now to fashion for itself a foetid physical habitation in the bodies of a holocaust of men . . .

And the Saint was still silent, absorbed in his vision, for a while after Sonia Delmar had finished speaking, and even she could not see all that was in his mind.

Presently she said, "Didn't I find out enough, Simon? You see, I believed you'd been killed—I thought it was all over—"

"Enough?" repeated the Saint softly, and there was a queer light in the steady sea-blue eyes. "Enough . . . ? You've done more than enough—more than I ever dreamed you'd do. And as for thinking it was all over—well, lass, I heard you. I've never heard anything like it in my life. It was plain hell keeping up the act. But—I was just fascinated. And I've apologized . . . But the game goes on, Sonia!"

2

The Saint stared at the carpet, and for a time there was no movement at all in the cabin; even the cigarette that lay forgotten between his fingers was held so still that the trail of smoke from it went up as straight as a pencilled line. The low-pitched thrum of the ship's engines, and the chatter of stirred waters about the hull, formed no more than an undercurrent of sound that scarcely disturbed the silence.

Much later, it seemed, Sonia Delmar said, "What happened to Roger?"

"I sent him back to London to find Lessing," answered the Saint. "It came to me when I was on my way out here—I didn't see why Marius should just break even after we'd got you back, and bringing Ike on the scene seemed a first-class way of stirring up the stew. And the more I think of that scheme, after what you've told me, old girl, the sounder it looks to me . . . Only, it doesn't seem big enough now—not for the kettle of hash we've dipped our ladles into."

"How long ago was that?"

"Shortly before I heaved that rock at you." Simon glanced at his watch. "By my reckoning, if we turned this ship round about now, we should all fetch up at Saltham around the same time. I guess that's the next move . . ."

"To hold up the ship?"

The Saint grinned, and in an instant the old mocking mischief was back in his eyes. She knew at once that if the business of holding up the ship single-handed had been thrust upon him, he would have duly set out to hold up the ship single-handed—and enjoyed it. But he shook his head.

"I don't think it'll be necessary. I shall just wander up on the bridge and make a few suggestions. There'll only be the captain and the helmsman and one officer to deal with, and the watch has just been changed, so no one will be butting in for hours. There's no reason why the rest of the crew should wake up to what's happening until we're home."

"And when they do wake up?"

"There will probably be a certain amount of bother," said the Saint happily. "Nevertheless, we shall endeavour to retire with dignity."

"And go ashore?"

"Exactly."

"And then?"

"And then—let us pray. I've no more idea than you have what other cards Rayt Marius is wearing up his sleeve, but from what I know of him I'd say he was certain to be carrying a spare deck. We've got to check up on that. Afterwards—"

The girl nodded quietly.

"I remember what you said last night"

"RIP." The Saint laughed softly. "I guess that's all there is to it . . . And then the last chapter, with you marrying Ike, and Roger and I starting a stamp collection. But who says nothing ever happens?"

And the lazy voice, the cool and flippant turning of the words, scarcely masked the sterner challenge of those reckless eyes.

And then the Saint rose to his feet, and the butt of his cigarette went soaring through the open port-hole, and, as he turned, she found that the set of the fine fighting lips had changed again completely. But that was just pure Saint. His normal temperament held every mood at once; he could leap from grave to gay without pause or parley, as the fancy moved him, and do it in such a way that neither seemed inconsequent. And now Sonia Delmar looked at him and found in his changed face an answer to the question that she had no need to ask, and he saw that she understood.

"But all that's a long way off yet, isn't it?" he murmured. "So I think we'll go right ahead and stick up this hoary hooker for a start. Shall we?"

"We?"

"I don't see why you shouldn't come along, old dear. It isn't every day of your life that you have the chance to shove your oar into a spot of twenty five carat piracy. Burn It!—what's the use of being raised respectable if you never go out for the frantic fun of bucking plumb off the rails and stepping off the high spring-board into the dizzy depths of turpitude?"

"But what can I do?"

"Sit in a ring seat and root for me, sweetheart. Cheer on the gory brigand." Swiftly the Saint was replacing beard and glasses and settling Vassiloff's hat to a less rakish angle, and two blue devils of desperate delight danced in his eyes. "It seems to me," said the Saint, "that there's a heap more mirth and horseplay on the menu before we settle down to the speechifying. You ain't heard nothin' yet." And the Saint was buttoning the great fur collar about his chin with sinewy fingers that had an air of playing their own independent part in the surge of joyous anticipation that had suddenly swept up through every inch of his splendid frame. "And it seems to me," said the Saint, "that the best and brightest moments of the frolic are still ahead—so why worry about anything?"

He smiled down at her—at least, there was a Saintly glitter behind the thick glasses that he had perched upon his nose, though his mouth was hidden. And as Sonia Delmar stood up she was shaken by a great wave of unreasoning gratefulness—to the circumstances that made it necessary to switch off thus abruptly from the line of thought that he had opened up so lightly, and to the Saint himself, for making it so easy for her to turn away from the perilous path on which she might have stumbled. And she knew quite definitely that it was as deliberate and calculated a move as ever he made in his life, and he let her know it, yet that took none of the inherent gentleness from the gesture. And she accepted the gesture at its worth.

"You're right," she said. "There's a long way to go yet. First the crew and then Marius . . . Haven't you any idea of what you're going to do?"

"None. But the Lord will provide. The great thing is that we know we shall find Marius at Saltham, and that's bound to make the entertainment go with a bang!"

"But how do you know that?"

"My dear, you must have heard the aeroplane—"

"Just after they shot the man in the motor-boat?"

"Sure."

"I didn't realize—"

"And I thought you knew! But I didn't only hear it—I saw its lights and the flares they lit for it to land by. I haven't had time to tell you, but my trip to the Ritz this morning produced some real news—after I was supposed to have lit out for the tall timber. I left my card in Rudy's bathroom, and right up to the time that kite came down I was wondering how long it'd be before the Heavenly Twins found the memento and got busy. Oh yes—Rayt Marius is at Saltham all right, and the best part of it is that he thinks I'm at the bottom of the deep blue sea with the shrimps nibbling my nose. There was a great orgy of signalling to that effect shortly after we upped anchor.

"So now you know why this is going to be no ordinary evening . . . And with Roger and Ike rolling in on their cue, if all goes well—I ask you, is that or is that not entitled to be called a real family reunion?"

"If you think Roger will be able to bring Sir Isaac—"

"Roger has a wonderful knack of getting things done."

She nodded, very slowly.

"It will be—a reunion—"

"Yes." Simon took her hands. "But it's also a story—and so few people have stories. Why not live your story, Sonia? I'm living mine . . ."

And for a moment, through all his fantastic disguise, she saw that his eyes were bright and level again, with a sober intentness in their gaze that she had yet to read aright.

3

But the Saint was away before she could speak, the Saint was the most elusive man on earth when he chose to be, and he chose it then, with a breath of careless laughter that took him to the door and left the spell half-woven and adrift behind him. He was away with a will-o'-the-wisp of sudden mischievous mirth that he had conjured out of that moment's precipitous silence, waking the moment to surer hazards and less strange adventure.

"Strange adventure! Maiden wedded . . ."

And the words of the song that he had sung so lightly twenty-four hours ago murmured mockingly in the Saint's ears as he paused for a second outside the cabin, under the stars, glancing round for his bearings and giving his eyes a chance to take the measure of the darkness.

"And it's still a great life," thought the Saint, with a tingle of unabated zest in his veins, and then he found Sonia Delmar at his shoulder. Their hands met. "This way," said the Saint softly, serenely, and steered her to the front of the starboard companion. She went up after him. Looking upwards, she saw him in the foreground of a queer perspective, like an insurgent giant escalading the last toppling pinnacle of a preposterous tower; the pinnacle of the tower swayed crazily against the spangled pageant of the sky; the slithering rush of invisible waters filtered up out of an infinite abyss . . . And then she saw another figure, already bestriding the battlements of the last tower; then the Saint was also there, speaking with a quiet and precise insistence . . . Then she also stood on the battlements of the swaying tower beside Simon Templar and the captain, and, as her feet found level boards, and the sea breeze sighed clearly to her face, the illusion of the tower fell away, and she saw the whole black bulk of the ship, sheering through dark waters that were no longer infinitely far below, and over the dark waters was laid a golden carpet leading to the moon. And the captain's shoulders shrugged against the stars.

"If you insist—"

"It is necessary."

The moonlight glinted on the dull sheen of an automatic changing hands; then she saw the glimmer of a brighter metal, and the captain's start of surprise.

"Quietly!" urged the Saint.

But the captain was foolish. For an instant he stood motionless, then he snatched . . . The Saint's steely fingers took him by the throat . . .

Involuntarily the girl closed her eyes. She heard a swift rustle of cloth, a quiver of fierce muscular effort, and then, away from the ship and down towards the sea, a kind of choking sob . . . a splash . . . silence . . . And she opened her eyes again, and saw the Saint alone. She saw the white flash of his teeth.

"Now his wives are all widows," said the Saint gently, and she shuddered without reason.

Other feet grated on the boards farther along the bridge; a man stood in the strip of light that came from the open door of the wheel-house, pausing irresolute and half-interrogative. But the Saint was leaning over the side, looking down to the sea.

"Look !"

The Saint beckoned, but he never turned round. And the officer came forwards. He also leaned over the side and looked down, but Simon stepped back. The Saint's right hand rose and fell, with a blue-black gleam in it. The sound of the dull impact was vaguely sickening . . .

"Two," said the Saint calmly. The officer was a silent heap huddled against the rail. "And that only leaves the quartermaster. Who says piracy isn't easy? Hold on while I show you . . . !"

He slipped away like a ghost, but the girl stayed where she was. She saw him enter the wheel-house, and then his shadow bulked across one lighted window. She held her breath, tensing herself against the inevitable outcry—surely such luck could not hold for third encounter . . . ! But there was no sound. He appeared again, calling her name, and she went to the wheel-house in a trance. There was a man sprawled on the floor—she tried to keep her eyes from the sight.

"Shelling peas is hard labour compared to this," Simon was murmuring cheerfully, and then he saw how pale she was. "Sonia!" drawled the Saint reproachfully, "don't say it gives you the wiggles in your little tum-tum to see the skids going under the ungodly!"

"But it doesn't, really. Look." She held up her hand—it was as steady as his own. "Only I'm not so used to it as you are . . ."

He chuckled.

"You'll learn," he said. "It's surprising how the game grows on you. You get so's you can't do without it. Why, if I didn't have plenty of this sort of exercise, I should come out all over pimples and take to writing poetry . . . See here, sweetheart—what you want is something to do. Now, d'you think you could wangle this wheel effect, while I get active on something else?"

He was stripping off beard and glasses; hat and coat followed them into a corner. She was irresistibly reminded of a similar transformation that very morning in Upper Berkeley Mews, and with the memory of the action returned also a vivid memory of the atmosphere in which it had first been performed. And the Saint was smiling in the same way, as gay and debonair as ever, and his careless confidence was like a draught of wine to her doubts.

She smiled, too.

"If it's the same as it is on daddy's yacht—"

"The identical article . . . So I'll leave you to it, lass. Make a wide circle round, and hold her a fraction south of south-south-east— I took a peek at that bouncing binnacle before I strafed the nautical gent over there by the cuspidor, and I reckon that course ought to take us back to somewhere pretty near where we came from. Got it?"

"But where are you going?"

"Well, there's the third officer very busy being unconscious outside—at the moment—and Barnacle Bill under the spittoon isn't dead yet, either, and I'd be happier to feel that they wouldn't be dangerous when they woke up. I won't heave them overboard, because I'm rather partial to lobsters, and you know what lobsters are, but I guess I'll fossick around for some rope and do the next best thing."

"And suppose anyone comes—could you spare a gun?"

"I could." And he did. "That belonged to the late lamented. So long as you don't get rattled and shoot me by mistake everything will be quite all right . . . All set, lass?"

"All set, Saint?"

"Good enough. And I'll be right back." He had hitched the sleeping quartermaster on to his shoulder, and he paused on the return journey to touch one of the cool, small hands that had taken over the helm. "Yo-ho-ho," said the Saint, smiling, and was gone like a wraith.

4

He dumped the quartermaster beside the third officer, and went quickly down the companion to the upper deck. There he found a plentiful supply of rope, and cut off as much as he required. On his way back he re-entered the cabin in which he had found the girl, and borrowed a couple of towels from the bedchamber section beyond the curtains. That much was easy. He flitted silently back to the bridge, and rapidly bound and gagged the two unconscious men with an efficient hand; the task called for hardly any attention, and while he worked his mind was busy with the details of the job that would have to be done next— which was not quite so easy. But when his victims lay at his feet giving two creditable imitations of Abednego before entering the hot room, the Saint went back to the upper deck without seeing the girl again.

On his first trip he had located one of the most important items in the catalogue—the boat in which Sonia Delmar had been taken to the ship. It still hung over the side, obviously left to be properly stowed away the next morning, and, which was even more important, the gangway still trailed low down by the water, as a glance over the side had revealed.

"And a lazy lot of undisciplined sea-cooks that makes them out," murmured the Saint when he had digested all this good news. "But I'm making no complaints tonight!"

But for that providential slackness, the job he had to do would have been trebly difficult. Even so, it was none too easy, but it had come to him, during part of the buccaneering business on the bridge, that there was no real need to look forward to any superfluous unpleasantness on the return to Saltham, and that a resourceful and athletic man might very well be able to rule that ship's crew out of the list of probable runners for the Death-or-Glory Stakes. That was what the Saint was out to do, being well satisfied with the prospect of the mainline mirth and horseplay that lay ahead, without inviting the intrusion of any imported talent en route, and he proceeded to put the first part of this project into execution forthwith, by lowering the boat gingerly, foot by foot, from alternate davits, until it hung within a yard of the water. Then, with a rope from another boat coiled over his shoulder, he slid down the falls. One end of the rope he made fast in the bows of the boat, and then he spent some time adjusting the fenders. The other end of the rope he carried back with him on his return climb, stepping off on the main deck, and then, going down the gangway, he made that end fast to a convenient stanchion near the water level. Then he went back to the upper deck and paid out some more rope, even more gingerly at first, and then with a rush. The tackle creaked and groaned horrifically, and the boat finally hit the water with a smack that seemed loud enough to wake the dead, but the Saint had neither seen nor heard any sign of life on any of the expeditions connected with the job, and the odds were that the crew were all sleeping soundly in their bunks . . . unless an oiler or someone had taken it into his head to come up on deck for a breather about then . . . But it was neck or nothing at that point, anyhow, and the Saint gave way on the falls recklessly until the ropes went slack. Then he leaned out over the side and looked down, and saw the boat floating free at the length of the rope by which he had moored it to the gangway, and he breathed a sigh of relief.

"Praise the Lord!" breathed the Saint, and meant it.

He belayed again, and made a second trip down the falls to cast off the blocks. The cockleshell bucked and plunged perilously in the ship's wash, but he noted with renewed satisfaction that it had sustained no damage in the launching, and was shipping no water in spite of its present maltreatment. Again he took a rest on the main deck on his way up, and listened in silence for several seconds, but he heard no suspicious sound.

Back on the upper deck, it was the work of a moment to haul the falls well up and clear, and then he made his last trip down the gangway and bent his back to the hardest physical labour of the whole performance—the task of taking in the tow-rope until the boat was near enough to be easily reached from the grating at the bottom of the gangway. He got it done after a struggle that left every muscle aching, and left the boat less than half a fathom away, with all the slack of the tow-rope secured in a seaman-like sheepshank. And then he went back to the bridge.

"Strange adventure that we're trolling. Modest maid and gallant groom—"

The song came again to his lips as he turned into the wheel-house and looked down the barrel of the girl's automatic.

"Put it away, honey," he laughed. "I have a tender regard for my thorax, and I've seen fingers less wobbly on the trigger!"

"But what have you been doing?"

"Preparing our getaway. Did I make a lot of noise?"

"I don't know—it seemed a frightful din to me—"

Simon grinned, and took out his cigarette-case.

"It seemed the same to me, old dear," he remarked. "But I don't think anyone else noticed it."

With a lighted cigarette between his lips, he relieved her of the wheel, and told her briefly what he had done.

"In its way, it should be a little gem of an escape," he said. "We bring the old tub in as near to the shore as we dare, and then we turn her round again and step off. When the next watch comes on duty they find out what's happened, but the old tub is blinding through the North Sea at its own sweet will, and they won't know whether they're coming or going. Gosh, wouldn't you give a couple of years of your life to be able to listen in on the excitement?"

She moved away, and brought up a chair to sit beside him. Now she definitely felt that she was dreaming. Looking back, it seemed incredible that so much could have happened in such a short time— that even the present position should have come to pass.

"When do you think we should get back?" she asked.

"We ought to sight land in about an hour, the way I figure it out," he answered. "And then—more fun!"

The smiling eyes rested on her face, reading there the helpless incredulity that she could not hide from her expression any more than she could dispel it from her mind, and the Saint laughed again, the soft lilting laughter of sheer boyish delight that carried him through all the adventures that his gods were good enough to send.

"I meant to tell you it was a great life," said the Saint, with that lazy laughter dancing like sunshine through his voice. "Here you are, Sonia—have another of these cigarettes, and tell me your story. We've got all the time in the world!"

CHAPTER NINE:

HOW SIMON TEMPLAR LOOKED
FOR LAND AND PROVED HIMSELF
A TRUE PROPHET

1

But it was the Saint who talked the most on that strange return voyage, standing up to the wheel, with the breeze through the open door fluttering his tie, and his shoulders sweeping wide and square against the light, and his tanned face seeming more handsome and devil-may-care and swaggeringly swift of line than ever.

She came to know him then as otherwise she might never have come to know him. It was not that he talked pointedly of himself—he had too catholic a range of interests to aim any long speech so monotonously—and yet it would be idle to deny that his own personality impregnated every subject on which he touched, were the touch never so fleeting. It was inevitable that it should be so for he spoke of things that he had known and understood, and nothing that he said came at second-hand. He told her of outlandish places that he had seen, of bad men that he had met, of forlorn ventures in which he had played his part, and yet it was nothing like a detailed autobiography that he gave her—it was a kaleidoscope, an irresponsibly shredded panorama of a weird and wonderful life, strewn extravagantly under her eyes as only the Saint himself could have strewn it, seasoned with his own unique spice of racy allusion and flippant phrase, and it was out of this squandered prodigality of inconsequent reminiscence, and the gallant manner of its telling, that she put together her picture of the man.

And, truly, he told her much of his amazing career, and even more of the ideals that had shaped it to the thing it was. And because she was no fool she gleaned from the tale a clear vision of the fantastic essence of the facts—of D'Artagnan born again without his right to a sword . . .

"You see," he said, "I'm mad enough to believe in romance. And I was sick of this age—tired of the miserable little mildewed things that people racked their brains about, and wrote books about, and called Life. I'm not interested to read about maundering epileptics, and silly nymphomaniacs, and anaemic artists with a Message, and I'm not interested to meet them. If I notice them at all, they make me want to vomit. There's no message in life but the message of splendid living—which doesn't mean crawling about on a dunghill yapping about your putrid little repressions. Nor does it mean putting your feet on the mantelpiece and a soapily beatific expression on your face, and concentrating on God in the image of a musical-comedy curate or Aimée Semple McPherson. It means the things that our forefathers were quite contented with, though their children have got so damned refined that they really believe the said forefathers would have been much 'naicer' if they'd spent their days picking over the scabs on their souls instead of going in for the noisy vulgar things they did go in for—I mean battle, murder, and sudden death, with plenty of good beer and a complete callousness about blipping the ungodly over the beezer. The low-down shocker is a decent and clean and honest-to-God form of literature, because it does deal with things that have a right to occupy a man's mind—a primitive chivalry, and damsel in distress, and virtue triumphant, and a wholesale slaughter of villains at the end, and a real fight running through it all. It mayn't be true to life as we know it, but it ought to be true, and that's why it's the best stuff for people to read—if they must read about things instead of doing them. Only I preferred to do them . . ."

And he told her other things, so that the vision grew even clearer in her mind—that vision of a heroic revolt against circumstance, of a huge and heroic impatience against the tawdry pusillanimity that had tried and failed to choke his spirit, of a strange creed and a challenge . . . And with it all there was a lack of bitterness, a joyous fatalism, that lent the recital half its glamour; the champion of lost causes fought with a smile . . .

"Of course," he said, "it makes you an outlaw—in spirit as well as in fact. But that again seems worthwhile to me. Isn't the outlaw one of the most popular figures in fiction? Isn't Robin Hood every schoolboy's idol? There's a reason for everything that people love, and there must be a reason for that—it must be the response of one of the most fundamental impulses of humanity. And why? For the same reason that Adam fell for the apple—because it's in the nature of man to break laws—because there's no real difference between the thrill of overthrowing a legitimate obstacle and the thrill of overthrowing a legitimate thou-shalt-not. Man was given legs to walk the earth, and therefore, out of the divine cussedness of his inheritance, he chooses his heroes, not from the men who walk superlatively well, but from the men who trespass into the element for which they were never intended, and fly superlatively well. In the same way, man was also given moral limitations by his ancestors after God Almighty, and therefore he reserves his deepest and most secret admiration for those who defy those limitations. He would like to do it himself, but he hasn't the courage, and so he enjoys the defiance even more when it's done for him by someone else. But compare that pleasure with the pleasure of the outlaw himself, when he chooses his outlawry because he loves it, and goes forth into the wide world to rob bigger and better orchards than he ever dreamed of when he was a grubby little urchin with a feather in his cap!"

"Yes, but the end of it!"

"The end?" said the Saint, with far-away eyes and a reckless smile. "Well—

> *'What gifts hath Fate for all his chivalry?*
> *Even such as hearts heroic oftenest win:*
> *Honour, a friend, anguish, untimely death.'*

"And yet—I don't know that that's a bad reward . . . Do you remember me telling you about Norman Kent? I found his grave when I came back to England, and I had those lines carved over it. And, do you know, I've often thought I should be proud to have earned them on my own."

He could talk like that with fresh blood upon his hands and his heart set upon another killing! For a moment the girl felt that it could not be true—she could not be sitting there listening to him with no feeling of revulsion for such a smug hypocrisy. But it was so. And she knew, at the same time, that that charge would not have been true— his simple sincerity was as natural as the half-smile that went with the words.

So they talked . . . And the Saint opened up for her a world of whose existence she had never known, a world of flamboyant colours and magnificently medieval delights. His magic made her see it as he saw it—a rich romance that depended on no cloaks or ruffles or other laboriously picturesque trapping for its enchantment, a play of fierce passions and grim dangers and quixotic loyalties, a tale that a man had dreamed and gone out to live. It was Gawain before the Grail, it was Bayard on the bridge of Garigliano, it was Roland at the gates of Spain; a faith that she had thought was dead went through it all, a thread of fairy gold with power to transmute all baser metals that it touched. Thus and thus he showed her glimpses of the dream, and he would have shown her more, but all at once she faltered, she who from the first matched his stride so easily, she saw a step that he had deliberately missed, and she could not be silent. She said, "Oh yes, but there are other things—in your own life! Even Robin Hood had to admit it!"

"You mean Maid Marian?"

"Roger told me. I asked him."

"About Patricia?"

"Yes."

The Saint gazed across the tiny cabin, but he could not see beyond the windows.

"Patricia—happened. She came in an adventure, and she stayed. She's been more to me than anyone can ever know."

"Do you love her?"

The Saint turned.

"Love?" said the Saint softly. "What is love?"

"You should know," she said.

"I've wondered."

Now they had been talking for a long time. "Have you never been in love?" she asked.

The Saint drew back his sleeve and looked thoughtfully at his watch.

"We ought to be getting near land," he said. "Would you mind taking over the wheel again, old dear, while I go and snoop round the horizon?"

2

He was gone for several minutes, and when he came back it was like the return of a different man. And yet, in truth, he had not changed at all; if anything, he was an even more lifelike picture of himself. It was the Saint as she had first met him who came back, with a Saintly smile, and a Saintly story, and a spontaneous Saintly mischief rekindling in his eyes, but that very quintessential Saintliness somehow set him infinitely apart. Suddenly, in a heart-stopping flash of understanding, she knew why . . .

"Do they keep a look-out on any of your father's yachts?" he drawled. "Or don't you do any night work?"

"A look-out? I don't know—"

"Well, they certainly stock one on this blistered *buque*, as they do on any properly conducted ship, but blow me if I hadn't forgotten the swine!"

"Then he must have heard you lowering that boat!"

The Saint shook his head. His smile was ridiculously happy.

"Not he! That's just one more point we can chalk up to ourselves for the slovenliness of this bunch of Port Mahon sodgers. He must have been fast asleep—if he hadn't, we'd have known all about him before now. But he woke up later, by the same token—I saw him lighting a cigarette up in the bows when I went out on the bridge. And it was just as well for us that he did take the idea of smoking a cigarette at that moment, for there was land, on the starboard bow as plain as the hump on a camel, and in another few minutes he couldn't have helped noticing it."

"But what shall we do?"

Simon laughed.

"It's done, old darling," he answered cheerfully, and she did not have to ask another question.

He lounged against the binnacle, a fresh white cylinder between his lips, his lighter flaring in his hand. The adventure had swept him up again: she could mark all the signs. The incident of which he had returned to speak so airily was a slight thing in itself, as he would have seen it, but it had turned a subtle scale. Though he lounged there so lazily relaxed, so easy and debonair, it was a dynamic and turbulent repose. There was nothing about it of permanence or even pause: it was the calm of a crouched panther. And she saw the mocking curve of the eager fighting lips, the set of the finely chiselled jaw, the glimmer of laughter in the clear eyes half-sheathed by languid lids, and she read his destiny again in that moment's silence.

Then he straightened up, and it was like the uncoiling of tempered steel. His hand fell on her shoulder.

"Come and have a look," he said.

She followed him outside.

The wind touched her hair, cool and sweet as a sea-nymph's breath; it whispered in the rigging, a muted chant to the rustle and throb of the ship's passage. Somewhere astern, between the bridge and the frayed white feather of their wake, the rattle and swish of a donkey-engine shifting clinker jarred into the softness of the night. The sky was a translucent veil of purple, spangled with silver dust, a gossamer canopy flung high above the star-spearing topmasts, with a sliver of moon riding between yard-arm and water. And away ahead and to her right, as the Saint had prophesied, a dark line of land was rousing half a hand's-breadth from the sea.

She heard the Saint speaking, with a faint tremor of reckless rapture in his voice.

"Only a little while now and then the balloon . . . I wonder if they're all gone to bed, to dream about my obituary notice in the morning papers . . . You know, that'd make the reunion too perishingly perfect for words—to have Angel Face trying to do his stuff in a suit of violently striped pyjamas and pink moccasins. I'm sure Angel Face is the sort of man who would wear striped pyjamas," said the Saint judicially . . .

It did not occur to her to ask why the Saint should take the striping of pyjamas as such an axiomatic index of villainy, but she remembered, absurdly, that Sir Isaac Lessing had a delirious taste in stripes. They had been members of the same house-party at Ascot that summer, and she had met him on his way back from his bath . . . And Sonia said abruptly: "Aren't you worried about Roger?"

"In a way . . . But he's a great lad. I trained him myself."

"Did he—think the same as you?"

"About the life?"

"Yes."

Simon leaned on the rail, gazing out to the slowly rising land.

"I don't know," he said. "I'm damned if I know . . . I led him on, of course, but he wasn't hard to lead. It gave him something to do. Then he got tied up with a girl one time, and that ought to have been the end of him, but she let him down rather badly. After that—maybe you'll understand—he was as keen as knives. And I can't honestly say I was sorry to have him back."

"Do you think he'll stay?"

"I've never asked him, old dear. There's no contract—if that's what you mean. But I do know that nothing short of dynamite would shift him out of this particular party, and that's another reason why I'm not fretting myself too much about him tonight. You see, he and I and Norman were the original Musketeers, and—well, I guess Roger wants to meet Rayt Marius again as much as I do . . ."

"And you mean to kill Marius?" said the girl quietly.

The Saint's cigarette-end glowed brighter to a long, steady inhalation, and she met the wide, bland stare of Saintly eyes.

"But of course," he said simply. "Why not?"

And Sonia Delmar made no answer, turning her face again towards the shore. Words blazed through her brain; they should have come pelting—but her tongue was tied. He had shown her the warning, made it so plain that only a swivel-eyed half-wit could have missed it: "No Entry—One Way Street," it said. And not once, but twice, he had edged her gently off the forbidden road, before her own unmannered obstinacy had pricked him to the snub direct. Yet he had broken the strain as easily and forthrightly as he had broken the spell; by now the entire circumstance had probably slipped away to the spacious background of his mind. He was as innocent of resentment as he was innocent of restraint; he pointed her retreat for the third time with no whit less of gentle grace, and she could not find the hardihood to breach the peace again.

3

The ship ploughed on through a slow swell of dark shining steel, and the Saint's lighter gritted and flared again in the gloom. His soft chuckle scarcely rose above the sigh of the breeze.

"If you want to powder your nose, or anything, Sonia," he murmured, "this is your chance. I guess we'll be decanting ourselves in a few minutes now. We don't want to drive this gondola right up to the front door—I've no idea what the coast is like around here, and it might be infernally awkward to run aground at the critical moment."

"And even then we don't know where we are," she said.

"Well, I'm not expecting we'll find ourselves a hundred miles away, and the nearest signpost will give us our bearings . . . Glory be! Do you know, old dear?—I believe I shall be more interested in Marius's pantry than in his pyjamas when we do arrive!"

He had had so many other things to think about that he was only just becoming aware that he had gone through a not uneventful day on nothing but breakfast and a railway-station sandwich, and when the Saint developed an idea like that he never needed roller-skates to help him catch up with it. After another wary glance at the land he wandered off the bridge in search of the galley, and in a few minutes he was back, with bulging pockets and a large sandwich in each hand. Even so, he had run it rather fine—the shore was looming up more quickly than he had thought.

"Here we are, che-ild—and off you go," he said briskly. "The orchestra's tuned up again, and we're surely going to start our symphony right now." He grinned, thrusting the sandwiches into her hands. "Paddle along down the gangway, beautiful, and begin gnawing bits out of these, and I'll be with you as soon as I've ported the plurry helm."

"OK, Simon . . ."

Yet she did not go at once. She stood there facing him in the starlight. He heard her swift breath, and a puzzled question shaped itself in his mind, on the brink of utterance, but then, before he could speak, her lips brushed his mouth, very lightly . . .

Then he was alone.

"Thank you, Sonia," whispered the Saint.

He knew there was no one to hear.

Then he went quickly into the wheel-house, and his hands flashed over the spokes as he put the wheel hard over. And once again he remembered his song.

> "Modest maiden will not tarry:
> Though but sixteen year she carry,
> She must marry, she must marry,
> Though the altar be a tomb—"

The Saint smiled crookedly.

For a space he held the wheel locked over, judging his time, and then he went out again on to the bridge. The line of land was slipping round to the starboard quarter, dangerously near. He went back and held the wheel for a few moments longer; when he emerged for a second survey the coast was safely astern, and he permitted himself a brief prayer of contented thanksgiving.

The quartermaster and the third officer, at the starboard end of the bridge, had both returned to life. Simon observed them squirming in helpless fury as he made for the companion, and paused to sweep them a mocking bow.

"*Bon soir, mes enfants,*" he murmured. "Remember me to Monsieur Vassiloff."

He sped down the upper deck to the cabin below. His business there detained him only for a matter of seconds, and then he raced down another companion to the main deck. Every second lost, now that the ship was headed away from the shore, meant so much more tedious rowing after the location, and the Saint, when pruning down an affliction of that kind of toil, was in the habit of moving so fast that a pursuing jack-rabbit would have suffocated in his dust.

The girl was waiting at the foot of the gangway.

"Filled the aching void, baby . . . ? Well, stand by to make the jump when I give the word. It's a walk-over really—but don't lose your nerve, because I shan't be able to hold the boat for ever."

He dropped on one knee, locking one arm round the lowest handrail stanchion and gripping the tow-rope with his other hand. Inch by inch he edged the boat up to the grating on which they stood, until it was plunging dizzily through the wash only a foot away.

"Go!" said the Saint through his teeth, and she went.

He saw her stumble as the boat heaved up on a vicious flurry of water, and held his breath, but she fell inside the boat—though only just—with one hand on the gunwale and the other in the sea. He watched her scramble away towards the stern, and then he let go the slack of the rope, buttoned his coat, and leapt lightly after her.

A loose oar caught him across the knees, almost bringing him down, but he found his balance, and pivoted round with Belle flashing in his hand. Once, twice, he hacked at the straining rope, and it parted with a dull twang. The side of the ship seemed to gather speed, slipping by like a huge moving wall.

"Hallelujah!" said the Saint piously.

The transshipment had been a merry moment, in its modest way, as he had known all along it would be, though he had characteristically refused to grow any grey hairs over it in anticipation. And in this case his philosophy was justified of the result . . .

He waved a cheery hand to the girl, and clambered aft. It was like travelling over a rabid cake-walk. As he flopped on to a thwart and started to unship a pair of oars the black bulge of the steamer's haunches went past him, so close that he could have put out a hand and touched it, and the flimsy cockleshell, slithering into the unabated maelstrom of the ship's wake, lurched up on its tiller and smashed down into a seething trough with a report like a gunshot. An undercarry of fine spray whipped into his eyes. "Matchless for the complexion," drawled the Saint, and dipped the first powerful oar.

The lifeboat yawed round, reeling back into easier water. A few strong pulls, and the merry moment was over altogether.

"Attaboy! . . ."

He rested on his oars, with the frail craft settling down under him to comparative equilibrium, and carefully mopped the salt spume from his face. Over the girl's shoulder he could watch the shadowy hull of the departing ship sliding monstrously away into the darkness. The steady pulse-beats of its engines came more and more faintly to his ears—fainter, very soon, than the booming and boiling of its wash against the coast . . .

The Saint reached forwards, lifted a battered sandwich from the girl's lap, and took a large contented bite.

"Feelin' good again, lass?"

"All right now, Big Chief."

"That's the spirit." All the Saint's buoyant optimism reached her through his voice. "And now you'd better get gay with those vitamins, old dear, while I do my Charon act. You can't keep your end up on an empty stomach—and this wild party is just getting into its stride!"

And, with his mouth full, Simon bent again to the oars.

4

It was a stiff twenty minutes' pull to the shore, but the Saint took it in his night's work cheerfully. It gave him a deep and enduring satisfaction to feel his muscles limbering up to the smooth rhythm of the heavy sweeps, and the fact that the boat had never been designed for one-man sculling practice robbed him of none of his pleasure. The complete night's party wasn't everyone's idea of a solo piece, anyway, if it came to that, but the Saint wasn't kicking. He was essentially a solo performer, and, if the circumstances required him to turn himself into a complete brass band—well, he was quite ready to warm himself up for the concert. So he rowed with a real physical enjoyment of the effort, and when the boat grounded at last, with a grating bump, there was a tingle of new strength rollicking joyously through every inch of his body.

"This way, sweetheart!"

He stood up in the bows. Fortunately the beach shelved steeply; watching his chance with the ebb of a wave he was able to jump easily to dry land. The girl followed. As her feet touched the shingle he caught her up and swung her bodily out of reach of the returning water, and stood beside her, his hands on his hips.

"Home is the sailor, home from the spree . . . And now what price Everest?"

With a hand on her arm he steered her over the stones. Something like a low wall rose in front of them. He lifted her to the top of it like a feather, and joined her there himself a moment later, and then he laughed.

"Holy Haggai—this is indubitably our evening!"

"Why—do you know where we are?"

"That's more than I could tell you. But I do know that there's going to be no alpine work. Pass down the car, Sonia!"

The land reared up from where they stood—not the scarp that he had expected, but a whale's back, overgrown with stunted bushes. They moved on in a steady climb, the Saint's uncanny instinct picking a way through the straggling obstacles without a fault. For about fifty yards the slope was steep and the foothold precarious; then, gradually, it began to flatten out gently for the summit. Their feet stumbled off the rubble on to grass . . .

He stopped by a broken-down fence at the top of the climb to give the girl a breather.

Eighty feet below the sea was like a dark cloth laid over the floor of the world, and over the cloth moved two steady points of luminance— the masthead lights of the ship that they had left. To right and left of them the coast was shrouded in unbroken obscurity. Behind them, the land fell smoothly away in an easy incline, rising again in the distance to the line of another hill, a long slow undulation with one lonely spangle of light on its farthest curve.

"Where there's a house there's a road," opined the Saint. "We may even find a road before that, but we might as well head that way. Ready?"

"Sure."

He picked her up lightly in his arms and set her down on the other side of the fence. In a moment they were pushing on again together.

His zest was infectious. She found that the spirit of the adventure was gathering her up again, even as it had gathered up the Saint. Reason went by the board; the Saint's own fantastic delight took its place. She managed a glance at the luminous dial of her wrist watch, and could have gasped when she saw the time. A truly comprehensive realization of all that she had lived through in a day and two half-nights was only just beginning to percolate into her brain, and the understanding of it dazed her. In four circuits of the clock she had lived through an age, and yet with no sense of incongruity until that moment; her whole life had been speeded up in one galvanic acceleration, mentally and emotionally as well as in event, and somewhere in that fabulous rush she had found something that would have amazed herself of yesterday.

Long ragged grasses rustled about their ankles. They dropped into a hollow, rose again momentarily, faced a hedge, but the Saint found a gap for them as if he could see as clearly in the dark as he could have seen by daylight. Then they plodded over a ploughed field. Once she stumbled, but he caught her in a moment. He himself had an almost supernatural sense of country; in the next field he checked her abruptly and guided her round a fallen tree that she would have sworn he could not have been told of by his eyes. Came another hedge, a ditch, and a field of corn; he found a straight path through it, and she heard him husking a handful of ears as he walked.

"It's not even Sunday any longer," he remarked, "so we shan't be bawled out."

And once again she was bewildered by a mind that could remember such pleasant far-off things at such a time—Scribes and Pharisees, old family Bibles, fields of Palestine!

Presently they came to a gate; the Saint ran his fingers lightly along the top, feeling for wire; then he stood still.

"What is it?" she asked.

"The road!"

He might have been Cortes at gaze before the Pacific; his ravishment could not have been greater.

He vaulted over; she followed more cautiously, and he lifted her down, with a breath of laughter. They went on. Road he might have called it, but it was really no more than a lane, yet it was something—a less nerve-racking surface for her feet, at least. For about half a mile they took its winding course, until she had lost her bearings altogether. With that loss she lost also an iota of the fickle enthusiasm that had helped her over the fields; about a road, or even a lane, there was a brusque reminder of more prosaic atmospheres and more ordinary nights. And it was definitely the threshold of a destination . . .

But Simon Templar was happy; as he walked he hummed a little tune; she could feel, as by a sixth sense, the quickened spring in his step, though he never set a pace that would have spent her endurance. His presence was even more vital for this restraint. For the destination and the destiny were his own, and she knew that there was a song in his heart as well as on his lips, an exultation that no one could share.

So they were following the lane. And then, of a sudden, he stopped, his song stopping with him, and she saw that the lane had at last brought them out upon an unquestionable road. She saw the telegraph poles reaching away on either side—not very far, for they stood between two bends. But it was a road . . .

"I don't see a signpost," she remarked dubiously. "Which way shall we—"

"Listen!"

She strained her ears, and presently she was able to pick up the sound he had heard—the purr of a powerful car.

"Who cares about signposts?" drawled the Saint. "Why, this bird might even give us a lift—it might even be Roger!"

They stood by the side of the road, waiting. Slowly the purr grew louder. Simon pointed, and she saw the reflection of the headlights as a pale nimbus in the sky; then, suddenly, a clump of trees stood out black and stark against a direct glare.

"Stand by to glom the Saltham Limited!"

The Saint had slipped out into the middle of the road. Beyond him, at the next bend in the road, a hedge and a tree were picked out in a strengthening shaft of light. The voice of the car was rising to a querulous drone. Then, all at once, the light began to sweep along the hedge; then, in another instant, it blazed clear down the road itself, corrugating the tarmac with shadows, and the Saint stood full in the centre of the blinding beam, waving his arms.

She heard the squeal of the brakes as he stepped aside, and the car slid past with an expiring swish of wind, and came to rest a dozen yards beyond.

The Saint sprinted after it, and Sonia Delmar was only just behind him. "Could you tell me—"

The monosyllable cracked out with a guttural swiftness that sent the Saint's hand flying to his hip, but the man in the car already had him covered. Simon grasped the fact—in time.

But the girl was not a yard away, and she also had a gun. Simon tensed himself for the shot . . .

"Put up your hands, Herr Saint."

There was a note of leering triumph in the harsh voice, and the Saint, blinking the last of the glare of the headlights out of his eyes, recognized the man. Slowly he raised his hands, and his breath came in a long sigh.

"Bless my soul!" said the Saint, who was never profane on really distressing occasions. "It's dear old Hermann. And he's going to give us our lift!"

CHAPTER TEN:

HOW SIR ISAAC LESSING TOOK EXERCISE AND RAYT MARIUS LIGHTED A CIGAR

1

Roger Conway's foot shifted off the accelerator and trod urgently upon the brake, and the Hirondel skidded to a protesting standstill.

"We've arrived," said Roger grimly.

The man beside him glanced at the big iron gates a few yards down the road and gained one momentary glimpse of them before the headlights went out under Roger's hand on the switch.

"This is the place?" he asked.

"It is."

"And where is your friend?"

"If I were a clairvoyant, Sir Isaac, I might be able to tell you. But you saw me get out and look for the message where he arranged to leave one if he could—and there was no message. That's all I know, except— have you ever seen a man shot through the stomach, Sir Isaac?"

"No."

"You probably will," said Roger, and Lessing was silent.

He had no idea why he should have been silent. He knew that he ought to have said things—angry and outraged and ordinary things. He ought to have been saying things like that all the way from London.

But, somehow, he hadn't said them. He'd certainly started to say them, once, two hours ago, when he had been preparing his second after-dinner Corona, and this curt and crazy young man had forced his way past butler and footman and penetrated in one savage rush to the sanctum sanctorum of the Oil Trade; he had nobly gone on trying to say them for a while after that, while the butler and the footman, torn between duty and discretion, had wavered apoplectically before the discouragement of the automatic in the curt and crazy young man's hand, and yet—somehow that had been as far as he'd got. The young man had had facts. The young man, compelling audience at the business end of his Webley, had punched those facts home one on top of the other with the shattering effect of a procession of mule-kicks, and the separate pieces of that preposterous jig-saw had fitted together without one single hiatus that Sir Isaac Lessing could discover—and he was a man cynically practised at discovering the flaws in ingenious stories. And the whole completed edifice, fantastic as were its foundations, and delirious as were the lines on which it reared itself, stood firm and unshakable against the cyclone of reasonable incredulity that he loosed upon it when he got his turn. For the young man spoke freely of the Saint, and that name ran through the astounding structure like a webwork of steel girders, poising its most extravagant members, bearing it up steadfast and indefeasible against the storm. And the climax had come when, at the end of narrative and cross-examination, the crazy young man had laid his gun on the table and invited the millionaire to take his choice—Saltham or Scotland Yard . . .

"Come on," snapped Roger.

He was already out of the car, and Lessing followed blindly. Roger had his finger on the bell beside the gate when Lessing caught up with him—Lessing was not built for speed. He stood beside his guide, breathing heavily, and they watched a window light up in the cottage that served for a lodge. A grumbling figure came through the gloom to the other side of the gates.

"Who is that?"

"A message for the Prince."

"He is not here."

"I said from the Prince. Open quickly, fool!"

A key grated in the massive lock, and, as the gate swung open on creaking hinges, Roger slipped through in a flash. The muzzle of his gun jabbed into the man's ribs.

"Quiet," said Roger persuasively. 'The man was very quiet.

"Turn round."

The gatekeeper obeyed. Roger reversed his gun swiftly, and struck accurately with the butt and intent to do enduring damage . . .

"Hurry along, please," murmured Roger briskly.

He went padding up the drive, and Sir Isaac Lessing plodded after him short-windedly. It was a long time since the millionaire had taken any exercise of this sort, and his palmiest athletic days were over, anyway, but Roger Conway hustled him along mercilessly. Having hooked his fish, according to the Saint's instructions, he meant to keep it on the line, but he was in no mood to play it with a delicate hand. He had never seen Isaac Lessing in his life before, and his first glimpse of the man had upset all his expectations, but he had a fundamental prejudice against the Petroleum Panjandrum which could not be uprooted merely by discovering that he neither lisped nor oleaginated.

The drive cut straight to the front door of the house, and Roger travelled as straight as the drive, his automatic swinging in his hand. He did not pause until he had reached the top of the steps, and there he waited an impatient moment to give Lessing a chance. Then, as the millionaire set the first toiling foot on the wide stone stair, Roger pressed the bell.

He braced himself, listening to the approach of heavy footsteps down the hall, as Lessing came panting up beside him. There was the sound of two bolts socketing back, then the rattle of the latch, then, as the door opened the first cautious inch, Roger hurled his weight forwards . . .

The man who had opened the door looked down the snout of the gun, and his hands voyaged slowly upwards.

"Turn round," said Roger monotonously . . .

As he brought the gun-butt back into his hand he found the millionaire at his elbow, and surprised a certain dazed admiration in Lessing's crag-like face.

"I wish I had you in my office," Lessing was saying helplessly. "You're such a very efficient young man, Mr—er—Conway—"

"I'm all of that," agreed an unsmiling Roger.

And then he heard a sound in the far corner of the hall, and whipped round to see an open door and a giant blocking the doorway. And Roger laughed.

"Angel Face!" he breathed blissfully. "The very man . . . We've just dropped in to see you, Angel Face!"

2

Marius stood perfectly still—the automatic that was focused on him saw to that. And Roger Conway walked slowly across the hall, Lessing behind him.

"Back into that room, Angel Face!"

The giant turned with a faint shrug, and led the way into a richly furnished library. In the centre of the room he turned again, and it was then that he first saw Lessing in the full light. Yet the wide, hideous face remained utterly impassive—only the giant's hands expressed a puzzled and faintly cynical surprise.

"You, too, Sir Isaac? What have you done to incur our friend's displeasure?"

"Nothing," said Roger sweetly. "He's just come along for a chat with you, like I have. Keep your hands away from that desk, Angel Face—I'll let you know when we want to be shown the door."

Lessing took a step forwards. For all his bulk, he was a square-shouldered man, and his clean-shaven jaw was as square as his shoulders.

"I'm told," he said, "that you have, or have had, my fiancée—Miss Delmar—here." Marius's eyebrows went up.

"And who told you that, Sir Isaac?"

"I did," said Roger, comfortably. "And I know it's true, because I saw her brought here—in the ambulance you sent to take her from Upper Berkeley Mews, as we arranged you should."

Marius still looked straight across at Lessing.

"And you believed this story, Sir Isaac?" he inquired suavely, and the thin, soft voice carried the merest shadow of pained reproach.

"I came to investigate it. There were other circumstances—"

"Naturally there are. Sir Isaac. Our friend is a highly competent young man. But surely—even if his present attitude and behaviour are not sufficient to demonstrate his eccentric character—surely you know who he is?"

"He was good enough to tell me."

The giant's slitted gaze did not waver by one millimetre. "And you still believed him. Sir Isaac?"

"His gang has a certain reputation."

"Yes, yes, yes!" Marius fluttered one vast hand. "The sensational newspapers and their romantic nonsense! I have read them myself. But our friend is still wanted by the police. The charge is—murder."

"I know that."

"And yet you came here with him—voluntarily?"

"I did."

"You did not even inform the police?"

"Mr Conway himself offered to do that. But he also pointed out that that would mean prison for himself and his friend. Since they'd been good enough to find my fiancée for me, I could hardly offer them that reward for their services."

"So you came here absolutely unprotected?"

"Well, not exactly. I told my butler that unless I telephoned him within three hours he was to go to the police."

Marius nodded tolerantly.

"And may I ask what were the circumstances in which our friend was so ready to go to prison if you refused to comply with his wishes?"

"A war—which I was to be tricked into financing."

"My dear Sir Isaac!"

The giant's remonstrance was the most perfect thing of its kind that Roger had ever seen or heard; the gesture that accompanied it would have been expressive enough in itself. And it shook Lessing's confidence. His next words were a shade less assertive, and the answer to them was a foregone conclusion.

"You still haven't denied anything, Marius."

"But I leave it to your own judgement!"

"And still you haven't denied anything, Angel Face," said Roger gently. Marius spread out eloquent hands.

"If Sir Isaac is still unconvinced," he answered smoothly, "I beg that he will search my house. I will summon a servant—"

"You'll keep your hands away from that bell!"

"But if you will not allow me to assist you—"

"I'll let you know when I want any help."

The giant's huge shoulders lifted in deprecating acquiescence. He turned again to Lessing.

"In that case, Sir Isaac," he remarked, "I am unfortunately deprived of my proof that Miss Delmar is not in this house."

"So you got her away on that ship, did you?" said Roger very quietly.

"What ship?"

"I see . . . And did you meet the Saint?"

"I have seen none of your gang."

Slowly Roger sank down to the arm of a chair, and the hand that held the gun was as cold and steady as an Arctic rock. The knuckle of the trigger finger was white and tense, and for a moment Rayt Marius looked at death with expressionless eyes . . .

And then the giant addressed Lessing again without a change of tone.

"You will observe, Sir Isaac, that our impetuous young friend is preparing to shoot me. After that, he will probably shoot you. So neither of us will ever know his motive. It is a pity—I should have been interested to know it. Why, after his gang have abducted your fiancée for some mysterious reason, they should have elected to make such a crude and desperate attempt to make you believe that I was responsible—unless it was nothing but an elaborate subterfuge to trap us both simultaneously in this house, in which case I cannot understand why he should continue with the accusation now that he has achieved his end . . . Well, we are never likely to know, my dear Sir Isaac. Let us endeavour to extract some consolation from the reflection that your butler will shortly be informing the police of our fate."

3

Roger's face was a mask of stone, but behind that frozen calm two thoughts in concentric circles were spinning down through his brain, and nothing but those thoughts sapped from his trigger finger the last essential milligram of pressure that would have sent Rayt Marius to his death.

He had to know definitely what had happened to the Saint, and perhaps Marius was the only man who could tell him.

Nothing else was in doubt. Marius's brilliantly urbane cross-examination of Lessing had been turned to its double purpose with consummate skill. In a few minutes, a few lines of dialogue, innocently and unobtrusively, Marius had gained all the information that he needed—about their numbers, about the police, about everything . . . And at the same time, in the turning of those same questions, he had attacked the charge against him with the most cunning weapon in his armoury—derision. Inch by inch he had gone over it with a distorting lens, throwing all its enormities into high relief, flooding its garish colours with the cold, merciless light of common, conventional sense, and then, scorning even to deny, he had simply stepped back and sardonically invited Lessing to form his own conclusions . . .

It was superb—worthy in every way of the strategic genius that Roger remembered so well. And it had had its inevitable effect. The points that Marius had scored with those subtly mocking rhetorical question-marks in their tails had struck home one after another with deadly aim. And Lessing was wavering. He was looking at Roger steadily, not yet in downright suspicion, but with a kind of grim challenge.

And there was the impasse. Roger faced it. For Lessing, there was a charge to be proven: and if Marius was not bluffing, and Sonia Delmar had really left the house, how could there be any proof? For Roger himself, there was an unconscious man down by the gates who would not remain permanently unconscious, and another in the hall who might be discovered even sooner, and before either of them revived Roger had got to learn things—even as Marius had had to learn things. Only Roger was not Rayt Marius . . .

But the tables were turned—precisely. In that last speech with, murder staring him in the face, the giant had made a counter-attack of dazzling audacity. And Sir Isaac Lessing waited . . .

It was Roger's cue.

A queer feeling of impotence slithered into the pit of his stomach. And he fought it down—fought and lashed his brains to match themselves against a man beside whom he was a newborn babe.

"Still the same old Angel Face!"

Roger found his voice somehow, and levelled it with all the dispassionate confidence at his command, striving to speak as the Saint would have spoken—to bluff out his weakness as the Saint would have bluffed. And he caught a sudden glitter in the giant's eyes at the sound of that very creditably Saintly drawl, and gathered a new surge of strength.

He turned to Lessing.

"Perhaps," he said, "I didn't make it quite plain enough that in the matter of slipperiness you could wrap Angel Face in sand-paper, and still have him giving points to an eel. But I'll put it to you in his very own words. If I only wanted to trap you both here, why should I keep up the deception?"

"I believe I discarded that theory as soon as I had propounded it," said Marius imperturbably.

Roger ignored him.

"On the other hand, Sir Isaac, if I wanted to bring any charge against Marius—well, he was generous enough to say that I was competent. Don't you think I might have invented something a little more plausible? And when I had invented something, wouldn't you have thought I'd have taken steps to see that I had some evidence—faked, if necessary? But I haven't any, except my own word. D'you think a really intelligent crook would try to put over anything like that?"

"I said our young friend was competent," murmured the giant, and Lessing looked at him.

"What do you mean?"

"Merely that he is even more competent than I thought. Consider it, Sir Isaac. To—er—fake evidence is not so easy as it sounds. But boldly to admit that there is no evidence, and then brazenly to adduce that confession as evidence in itself—that is a masterpiece of competence which can rarely have been equalled."

Roger laughed shortly.

"Very neat, Angel Face," he remarked. "But that line is wearing a little thin. Now, I've just had a brain-wave. You know a lot of things which I certainly don't know, and which I very much want to know—where Sonia Delmar has gone, and what's happened to the Saint, for instance. And you won't tell me—yet. But there are ways of making people talk, Angel Face. You may remember that the Saint nearly had to demonstrate one of those ways on you a few months ago. I've always been sorry that something turned up to stop him, but it mayn't be too late to put that right now."

"My dear young friend—"

"I'm talking," said Roger curtly. "As I said—there are ways of making people talk. In the general circumstances I'm not in a position to apply any of those methods single-handed, and Sir Isaac won't help me unless he's convinced. But you're going to talk, Angel Face—in your proper turn—you've got to be made to. And therefore Sir Isaac has got to be convinced, and that's where my brain-wave comes in."

Marius shrugged.

"So far," he said, "you have not been conspicuously successful, but I suppose we cannot prevent you making further efforts."

Roger nodded.

"You don't mind, do you?" he said. "You're quite ready to let me go on until somebody comes in to rescue you. But this will be over very quickly. I'm going to give you a chance to prove that innocence— smashingly. Sir Isaac will remember that in my very competent story I mentioned other names besides yours—among them, one Heinrich Dussel and a certain Prince Rudolf—"

"Well?"

"Do you deny that you know them?"

"That would be absurd."

"But you say they know absolutely nothing of this affair?"

"The suggestion is ridiculous. They would be as astonished as I am myself."

"Right." Roger drew a deep breath. "Then here's your chance. Over in that corner there's a telephone—with a spare receiver. We'll ring up Heinrich or the Prince—whichever you like—and as soon as they answer you'll give your name and you'll say "the girl has got away again"—and let Sir Isaac hear them ask you what you're talking about!"

4

There had been silence before but now for an instant there was a silence that seemed to Roger's over-wrought nerves like the utter dreadful stillness before the unleashing of a hurricane, that left his throat parched and his head singing. He could hear the beating of his own heart, and the creak of the chair as he moved shrieked in his ears. Once before he had known the same feeling—had waited in the same electric hush, his nerves raw and strained with the premonition of peril, quiveringly alert and yet helpless to guess how the blow would fall . . .

And yet the tension existed only in himself. The silence was for a mere five seconds—just such a silence as might reasonably greet the proposition he had put forward. And not a flicker of expression passed across the face he watched—that rough-hewn nightmare face of some abominable heathen idol. Only, for one sheer scintilla of time, a ferine, fiendish malignance seared into the gaze of those inhuman eyes.

And Lessing was speaking quite naturally.

"That seems a sensible way of settling the matter, Marius." Marius turned slowly.

"It is an admirable idea," he said. "If that will satisfy you—although it is a grotesque hour at which to disturb my friends—"

"I shall be perfectly satisfied—if the answer is satisfactory," returned Lessing bluntly. "If I've been misled I'm ready to apologize. But Mr Conway persists with the charge, and I'd be glad to have it answered."

"Then I should be delighted to oblige you."

In another silence, deeper even than the last, Roger watched Marius cross to the telephone.

He knew—he was certain—that the giant was cornered. Exactly as Marius had swung the scale over in his own favour during the first innings, so Roger had swung it back again, with the inspired challenge that had blazed into his brain at the moment of his need. And Lessing had swung back with the scale. The millionaire was looking at Roger, curiously studying the young profile, and the grimness was gone again from the set of the jaw.

"A trunk call to London, please . . . Hanover eight five six five . . . Yes . . . Thank you." Marius's voice was perfectly self-possessed.

He put down the instrument and turned again blandly.

"The call will be through in a few minutes," he said. "Meanwhile, since I am not yet convicted, perhaps you will accept a cigar, Sir Isaac?"

"He might if you kept well away from that desk," said Roger relentlessly. "Let him help himself, and he can pass you one if you want it."

Lessing shook his head.

"I won't smoke," he said briefly. Marius glanced at Roger.

"Then, with your permission, perhaps Mr—er—Conway—"

Roger stepped forward, took a cigar from the box on the desk, and tossed it over. Marius caught it, and bowed his thanks.

Roger had to admire the man's self-control. The giant was frankly playing for time, gambling the whole game on the hope of an interruption before the call came through that would inevitably damn him beyond all redemption; his brain, behind that graven mask, must have been a seething ball-race of whirling schemes, yet not by the most infinitesimal twitch of a muscle did he betray one scantling of concern. And before that supernatural impassivity, Roger's glacial vigilance keyed up to aching pitch . . .

Deliberately Marius bit off the tip of the cigar and removed the band; his right hand moved to his pocket in the most natural way in the world, and Roger's voice rang out like the crack of a whip.

"Stop that!"

Marius's eyebrows went up.

"But surely, my dear young friend," he protested mildly, "you will permit me to light my cigar!"

"I'll give you a light."

Roger fished a match out of his pocket, struck it on the sole of his shoe, and crossed the room.

As he held it out, at arm's length, and Marius carefully put his cigar to the flame, their eyes met . . .

In the stillness, the shout from the hall outside came plainly to their ears . . . "Lessing—we'll see this through!" Roger Conway stood taut and still; only his lips moved. "Come over here . . . ! Marius, get back—"

And then, even as he spoke, the door behind him burst open, and instinctively he looked round. And the explosion of his own gun came to him through a bitter numbness of despair, for the hand that held it was crushed and twisted in such a grip as he had never dreamed of, and he heard the giant's low chuckle of triumph too late.

He was flung reeling back, disarmed—Marius hurled him away as if he had been a wisp of thistledown. And as he lurched against the wall he saw, through a daze of agony, the Saint himself standing within the room, cool and debonair, and behind the Saint was Sonia Delmar, with her right arm twisted up behind her back, and behind Sonia was Hermann, with an automatic in his hand.

"Good evening, everybody," said the Saint.

CHAPTER ELEVEN:

HOW SIMON TEMPLAR
ENTERTAINED THE
CONGREGATION AND HERMANN
ALSO HAD HIS FUN

1

"Love, your magic spell is everywhere . . ."

Gay, mocking, cavalier, the old original Saintly voice! And there was nothing but a mischievous laughter in the clear blue eyes that gazed so delightedly at Marius across the room—nothing but the old hell-for-leather Saintly mirth. Yet the Saint stood there unarmed and at bay, and Roger knew then that the loss of his own gun made little difference, for Hermann was safely sheltered behind the girl and his Browning covered the Saint without a tremor.

And Simon Templar cared for none of these things . . . Lot's wife after the transformation scene would have looked like an agitated eel on a hot plate beside him. By some trick of his own inimitable art, he contrived to make the clothes that had been through so many vicissitudes that night look as if he had just taken them off his tailor's delivery van; his smiling freshness would have made a rosebud in the morning dew appear to wear a positively debauched and scrofulous aspect, and that blithe, buccaneering gaze travelled round the room as if he were reviewing a rally of his dearest friends. For the Saint in a tight corner had ever been the most entrancing and delightful sight in all the world . . .

"And there's Roger. How's life, sonny boy? Well up on its hind legs—what . . . ? Oh, and our one and only Ike! Sonia—your boyfriend—"

But Lessing's face was grey and drawn. "So it was true, Marius!" he said huskily.

"Sure it was," drawled the Saint. "D'you mean to say you didn't believe old Roger? Or did Uncle Ugly tell you a naughty story?" And again the Saint beamed radiantly across at the motionless giant. "Your speech, Angel Face: 'Father, I cannot tell a lie. I am the Big Cheese . . .' Sobs from pit and gallery. But you seem upset, dear heart—and I was looking to you to be the life and soul of the party. 'Hail, smiling morn,' and all that sort of thing."

Then Marius came to life.

For a moment his studied impassivity was gone altogether. His face was the contorted face of a beast, and the words he spat out came with the snarl of a beast, and the gloating leer on the lips of the man Hermann froze where it grimaced, and faded blankly. And then the Saint intervened.

"Hermann meant well, Angel Face," he murmured peaceably, and Marius swung slowly round.

"So you have escaped again, Templar," he said.

"In a manner of speaking," agreed the Saint modestly. "Do you mind if I smoke?" He took out his cigarette-case, and the giant's mouth writhed into a ghastly grin.

"I have heard about your cigarettes," he said. "Give those to me"

"Anything to oblige," sighed the Saint.

He wandered over, with the case in his hand, and Marius snatched it from him. The Saint sighed again, and settled himself on the edge of the big desk, with a scrupulous regard for the crease in his trousers. His eye fell on the box of cigars, and he helped himself absent-mindedly.

Then Lessing was facing Marius.

"What have you to say now?" he demanded, and the last atom of emotion drained out of Marius's features as he looked down at the millionaire.

"Nothing at all, Sir Isaac." Once again that thin, soft voice was barren of all expression, the accents cold and precise and unimpassioned. "You were, after all, correctly informed—in every particular."

"But—my God, Marius! That war—everything—do you realize what this means?"

"I am perfectly well aware of all the implications, my dear Sir Isaac."

"You were going to make me your tool in that—"

"It was an idea of mine. Perhaps even now—"

"You devil!"

The words bit the air like hot acid, and Marius waved protesting and impatient hands. "My dear Sir Isaac, this is not a Sunday School. Please sit down and be quiet for a moment, while I attend to this interruption—"

"Sit down?" Lessing laughed mirthlessly. The stunned incredulity in his eyes had vanished, to be replaced by something utterly different. "I'll see you damned first! What's more, I'm going to put you in an English gaol for a start—and when you come out of that I'll have you hounded out of every capital in Europe. That's my answer!"

He turned on his heel.

Between him and the door Hermann still held the girl. And Roger Conway stood beside her.

"One moment."

Marius's voice—or something else—brought Lessing up with a snap, and the millionaire faced slowly round again. And, as he turned, he met a stare of such pitiless malevolence that the flush of fury petrified in his face, leaving him paler than before.

"I am afraid you cannot be allowed to leave immediately, my dear Sir Isaac," said the giant silkily, and there was no mistaking the meaning of the slight movement of the automatic in his hand. "A series of accidents has placed you in possession of certain information which it would not suit my purpose to permit you to employ in the way which you have just outlined. In fact, I have not yet decided whether you will ever be allowed to leave."

2

The Saint cleared his throat.

"The time has come," he remarked diffidently, "for me to tell you all the story of my life." He smiled across at Lessing, and that smile, and the voice with it, slashed like a blast of sunshine through the tenuous miasma of evil that had spawned into the room as Marius spoke.

"Just do what Angel Face told you, Sir Isaac," said the Saint winningly. "Park yourself in a pew and concentrate on Big Business. Just think what a half-nelson you'll have on the Banana Oil market when Angel Face has unloaded his stock, And he won't hurt you, really. He's a plain, blunt man, and I grant you his face is against him, but he's a simple soul at heart. Why, many's the time we've sat down to a quiet game of dominoes—haven't we, Angel Face?—and all at once, after playing his third double-six, he's said, in just the same dreamy way, 'Templar, my friend, have you ever thought that there is something embolismal about Life?' And I've said, brokenly, 'It's all so—so umbilical,' Just like that. 'It's all so umbilical . . .' Doesn't it all come back to you, Angel Face?"

Marius turned to him.

"I have never been amused by your humour, Templar," he said. "But I should be genuinely interested to know how you have spent the evening."

All the giant's composure had come back, save for the vindictive hatred that burned on in his eyes like a lambent fire. He had been secure in the thought that the Saint was dead, and then for a space the shock of seeing the Saint alive had battered and reeled and ravaged his security into a racketing chaos of raging unbelief, and at the uttermost nadir of that havoc had come the cataclysmic apparition of Sonia Delmar herself, entering that very room, to overwhelm his last tattered hope of bluff and smash down the ripening harvest of weeks of brilliant scheming and intrigue into one catastrophic devastation, and he had certainly been annoyed . . . Yet not for an instant could his mind have contained the shred of an idea of defeat. He stood there by the desk where the Saint stood, a poised and terrible colossus, and behind that unnatural calm the brain of a warped genius was fighting back with brute ferocity to retrieve the irretrievable disaster. And Simon looked at him, and laughed gently.

"Tonight's jaunt," said the Saint, "is definitely part of the story of my life."

"And of how many more of your friends?"

Simon shook his head.

"You never seem to be able to get away from the distressing delusion that I am some sort of gang," he murmured. "I believe we've had words about that before. Saint Roger Conway you've met. That in the middle distance is a new recruit—Saint Isaac Lessing, Regius Professor of Phlebology at the University of Medicine Hat and Consulting Scolecophagist to the Gotherington Gasworks, recently canonized for his article in *The Suffragette*, advocating more clubs for women. 'Clubs, tomahawks, flat-irons, anything you like,' he said . . . And here we all are. I'm sorry to disappoint you, but that's all there is—as the bishop said to the actress."

"And how many more?" repeated Marius.

"Isn't that quite clear?" sighed the Saint. "I said there are no more. Let me put it in words of one syllable. The unadulterated quintessence of nihility—"

Savagely Marius caught his arm in one gigantic hand, and the Saint involuntarily tensed his muscles.

"Not that way, Angel Face," he said softly. "Or there might be a vulgar brawl . . ."

Yet perhaps it was that involuntary tensing of an arm of leather and iron, rather than the change in the Saint's voice, that made Marius loose his grip. With a tremendous effort the giant controlled himself again, and his lips relaxed from the animal snarl that had distorted them; only the embers of his fury still glittered in his eyes.

"Very good. There are no more of you. And what happened on the ship?"

"Well, we went for a short booze—cruise."

"And the man who was shot in the motor-boat—was he another of your friends?" Simon surveyed the ash of his cigar approvingly.

"One hates to cast aspersions on the dead," he answered, "but I can't say that we ever became what you might call bosom pals. Not," said the Saint conscientiously, "that I had anything against the man. We just didn't have the chance to get properly acquainted. In fact, I'd hardly given him the first friendly punch on the jaw, and dumped him in that motor-boat to draw the fire, when some of the sharp-shooting talent pulled the *voix céleste* stop on him for ever. I don't even know his name, but he addressed me in Grand Opera, so if your ice-cream plant is a bit diminuendo—"

Hermann spoke sharply.

"It was Antonio, *mein Herr*! He stayed on the beach after we took the girl down—"

"So!" Marius turned again. "It was one of my own men!"

"Er—apparently," said the Saint with sorrow.

"And you were already on the ship?"

"Indeed to goodness. But only just." The Saint grinned thoughtfully. "And then I met Comrade Vassiloff—a charming lad, with a beautiful set of hair-brushes. We exchanged a little backchat, and then I tied him up and passed on. Then came the amusing error."

"What was that?"

"You see, it was a warm evening, so I'd borrowed Comrade Vassiloff's coat to keep the heat out. The next cabin I got into was the captain's and he promptly jumped to the conclusion that Comrade Vassiloff was still inhabiting the coat—"

Marius stiffened.

"Moeller! The man always was a fool! When I meet him again—"

The Saint shook his head.

"What a touching scene it would have been!" he murmured. "I almost wish it could come true . . . But it cannot be. I'm afraid, Angel Face, that Captain Moeller has also been translated."

"You killed him?"

"That's a crude way of putting it. Let me explain. Overcome with the shock of discovering his mistake, he went slightly bughouse, and seemed to imagine that he was a seagull. Launching himself into the empyrean—oh, very hot, very hot!—he disappeared from view, and I have every reason to believe that he made a forced landing a few yards further on. As I didn't know how to stop the ship—"

"When was this?"

"Shortly after the ceremony. That was the amusing error. When I rolled into his cabin Sonia was there as well and there was a generally festive air about the gathering. The next thing I knew was that I was married." He saw Marius start, and laughed softly. "Deuced awkward, wasn't it, Angel Face?"

He gazed at Marius benevolently, but, after that first un-purposed recoil, the giant stood quite still. The only one in the room who moved was Lessing, who came slowly to his feet, his eyes on the girl.

"Sonia—is that true?"

She nodded, without speaking, and the millionaire sank back again, white-faced. The Saint slewed round on his perch, and it was at Roger that he looked.

"It was quite an unofficial affair," said the Saint deliberately. "I doubt if the Archbishop of Canterbury would have approved. But the net result—"

"Saint!"

Roger Conway took a pace forwards, and the name was cried so fiercely that Simon's muscles tensed again. And then the Saint's laugh broke the hush a second time, with a queer blend of sadness and mockery.

"That's all I wanted," said the Saint, and Roger fell back, staring at him.

But the Saint said no more. He deposited an inch and a half of ash in an ashtray, flicked a minute flake of the same from his knee, adjusted the crease in his trousers, and returned his gaze again to Marius.

Marius had taken no notice of the interruption. For a while longer he continued to stare fixedly at the Saint, and then, with an abrupt movement, he turned away and began to pace the room with huge, smooth strides. And once again there was silence.

The Saint inhaled meditatively.

An interval of bright and breezy badinage, he realized distinctly, had just been neatly and unobtrusively bedded down in its appointed niche in the ancient history of the world, and the action of the piece was preparing to resume. And the coming action, by all the portents, was likely to be even brighter and breezier than the badinage—in its own way.

Thus far, Simon Templar had to admit that he had had all the breaks, but now Rayt Marius was definitely in play. And the Saint understood, quite quietly and dispassionately, as he had always understood these things, that a succulent guinea-pig in the jaws of a lion made more than ordinary carnivorous by a coincidence of toothache and the loss of a consignment of grape-nuts would have been just as much a lead-pipe cinch for an enterprising vendor of annuities as he was. For the milk of human kindness had never entered the reckoning—on either side—and now that Marius had the edge . . . As the Saint watched the ruthless, deliberate movements of that massive Neolithic figure, there came back to him a vivid recollection of the house by the Thames where they had faced each other at the close of the last round, and of the passing of Norman Kent . . . and the Saint's jaw tightened a little grimly. For between them now there was infinitely more than there had been then. Once again the Saint had wrecked a cast-iron hand at the very moment when failure must have seemed impossible, and he had never thought of the giant as a pious martyr to persecution. He knew, in that quiet and dispassionate way, that Marius would kill him—would kill all of them—without a moment's compunction, once it was certain that they could not be more useful to him alive.

Yet the Saint pursued the pleasures of his cigar as if he had nothing else to think about. In his life he had never walked very far from sudden death, and it had been a good life . . .

It was Lessing who broke first under the strain of that silence. The millionaire started up with a kind of gasp.

"I'm damned if I'll stay here like this!" he babbled. "It's an outrage! You can't do things like this in England—"

Simon looked at him coldly.

"You're being obvious, Ike," he remarked, "and also futile. Sit down."

"I refuse—"

Lessing swung violently towards the door, and even the Saint could not repress a smile of entirely unalloyed amusement as the millionaire fetched up dead for the second time of asking before the discourteous ugliness of Hermann's automatic.

"You'll pick up the rules of this game as we go along, Ike," murmured the Saint consolingly, and then Marius, whose measured pacing had not swerved by a hair's breadth for Lessing's protests, stopped by the desk with his finger on the bell.

"I have decided," he said, and the Saint turned with a seraphic smile.

"Loud and prolonged applause," drawled the Saint.

He stood up, and Roger Conway, watching the two men as they stood there eye to eye, felt a queer cold shiver trickle down his spine like a drizzle of ghostly icicles.

3

Just for a couple of seconds it lasted, that clash of eyes—as crisp and cold as a clash of steel. Just long enough for Roger Conway to feel, as he had never felt before, the full primitive savagery of the volcanic hatreds that seethed beneath the stillness. He felt that he was a mere spectator at the climax of a duel to the death between two reincarnate paladins of legend, and for once he could not resent this sense of his own unimportance. There was something prodigious and terrifying about the culmination of that epic feud—something that made Roger pray blasphemously to awake and find it all a dream . . . And then the Saint laughed; the Saint didn't give a damn, and the Saint said, "You're a wonderful asset to the gaiety of nations, Angel Face . . ."

With a faint shrug Marius turned away, and he was placidly lighting a fresh cigar when the door opened to admit three men in various stages of undress.

Simon inspected them interestedly. Evidently the household staff was not very large, for he recognized two of the three at once. The bullet-headed specimen in its shirtsleeves, unashamedly rubbing the sleep out of its eyes with two flabby fists, was obviously the torpescent and bibulous Bavarian, who had spoken so yearningly of his bed. Next to him, the blue-chinned exhibit without a tie, propping itself languidly against a bookcase, could he identified without hesitation as the Bowery Boy who was a suffering authority on thirsts. The third argument for a wider application of capital punishment was a broken-nosed and shifty-eyed individual whom the Saint did not know—nor, having surveyed it comprehensively, did Simon feel that his life had been a howling wilderness until the moment of that meeting.

It was to Broken Nose that Marius spoke.

"Fetch some rope, Prosser," he ordered curtly, "and tie up these puppies."

"Spoken like a man, Angel Face," murmured the Saint approvingly as Broken Nose departed. "You think of everything, don't you . . . ? And may one ask what you've decided?"

Marius looked at him. "You shall hear," he said.

The Saint bowed politely and returned to the serene enjoyment of his cigar. Outwardly he remained as unperturbed as he had been throughout the interview, but all his faculties were tightening up again into cool co-ordination and razor-edged alertness. Quietly and inconspicuously he flexed the muscles of his forearm—just to feel the reassuring pressure of the straps that secured the little leather sheath of Belle. When Hermann had taken his gun he had not thought of Belle, nor, since then, had the thought seemed to occur to Marius, and with Belle literally up his sleeve the Saint felt confident of being able to escape from any system of roping that might be employed—providing he was left unobserved for a few minutes. But there were others to think of—particularly the girl. Simon stole a glance at her. Hermann still held her with her right arm twisted up behind her back—holding her like that, in the back seat, he had forced the Saint to drive the car back. "And if you do not behave, English swine," he had said, "I will break the arm." It had been the same on the walk up the long drive. "If you escape, and I do not shoot you, English swine, she will scream until you return." Hermann had the most sweet and endearing inspirations, thought the Saint, with his heart beating a little faster, and then his train of thought was interrupted by the return of Mr Prosser in charge of a coil of rope.

As he placed his hands helpfully behind his back the Saint's thoughts switched off along another line. And that line ranged out in the shape of a series of question marks towards the decision of Marius which he had yet to hear. From the first he had intended to make certain that the giant's machinations should this time be ended for ever, not merely checked, and with this object he had been prepared to take almost any risk in order to discover what other cards Marius might have to play, and now he was surely going to get his wish . . . Though what the revelation could possibly be was more than Simon Templar could divine. That there could be any revelation at all, other than the obvious one of revenge, Simon would not have believed of anyone but Marius. The game was smashed—smithereened—blown to ten different kinds of Tophet. There couldn't be any way of evading the fact—unless Marius, with Lessing in his power, had conceived some crazy idea of achieving by torture what cunning had failed to achieve. But Marius couldn't be such a fool . . .

The rope expert finished his task, tested the knots, and passed on to Roger Conway, and the Saint shifted over to the nearest wall and lounged there elegantly. Marius had seated himself at the desk, and nothing about him encouraged the theory that he was merely plotting an empty vengeance. After a brief search through a newspaper which he took from the waste-basket beside him, he had spread out a large-scale map on the desk in front of him and taken some careful measurements, and now, referring at intervals to an open timetable, he was making some rapid calculations on the blotter at his elbow. The Saint watched him thoughtfully, and then Marius looked up, and the sudden sneering glitter in his eyes showed that he had misconstrued the long silence and the furrows of concentration that had corrugated the Saint's forehead.

"So you are beginning to realize your foolishness. Templar?" said the giant sardonically. "Perhaps you are beginning to understand that there are times when your most amusing bluff is wasted? Perhaps you are even beginning to feel a little—shall we say—uneasy?"

The Saint beamed.

"To tell you the truth," he murmured, "I was composing one of my celebrated songs. This was in the form of an ode on the snags of life which Angel Face could overcome with ease and grace. The limpness of asparagus meant nothing to our Marius: not once did he, with hand austere, drip melted butter in his ear. And with what *maestria* did Rayt inhale spaghetti from the plate! Pursuing the elusive pea—"

For a moment the giant's eyes blazed, and he half rose from his chair, and then, with a short laugh, he relaxed again, and picked up the pencil that had slipped from his fingers.

"I will deal with you in a moment," he said. "And then we shall see how long your sense of humour will last."

"Just as you like, old dear," murmured the Saint affably. "But you must admit that Ella Wheeler Wilcox has nothing on me."

He leaned back once more against the wall and watched Broken Nose getting busy with the girl. Roger and Lessing had already been attended to. They stood side by side—Lessing with glazed eyes and an unsteady mouth, and Roger Conway pale and expressionless. Just once Roger looked at the girl, and then turned his stony gaze upon the Saint, and the bitter accusation in that glance cut Simon like a knife. But Sonia Delmar had said nothing at all since she entered the room, and even now she showed no fear. She winced once, momentarily, when the rope expert hurt her, and once, when Roger was not looking at her, she looked at Roger for a long time; she gave no other sign of emotion. She was as calm and queenly in defeat as she had been in hope, and once again the Saint felt a strange stirring of wonder and admiration . . .

But—that could wait . . . Or perhaps there would be nothing to wait for . . . The Saint became quietly aware that the others were waiting for him—that there was more than one reason for their silence. Even as two of them had followed him blindly into the picnic, so they were now looking to him to take them home . . . The fingers of the Saint's right hand curled tentatively up towards his left sleeve. He could just reach the hilt of his little knife, but he released it again at once. The only chance there was lay in those six inches of slim steel, and if that were lost he might as well ask permission to sit down and make his will: he had to be sure of his time . . .

At length the rope expert had finished, and at the same moment Marius came to the end of his calculations and leaned back in his chair. He looked across the room.

"Hermann!"

"*Ja, mein Herr?*"

"Give your gun to Lingrove and come here."

Without moving off the bookcase the Bowery Boy reached out a long arm and appropriated the automatic lethargically, and Hermann marched over to the desk and clicked his heels.

And Marius spoke.

He spoke in German, and, apart from Hermann and the somnolent Bavarian, Simon Templar was probably the only one in the room who could follow the scheme that Marius was setting forth in cold staccato detail. And that scheme was one of such a stupendous enormity, such a monstrous inhumanity, that even the Saint felt an icy thrill of horror as he listened.

4

He stared, fascinated, at the face of Hermann, taking in the shape of the long narrow jaw, the hollow cheeks, the peculiar slant of the small ears, the brightness of the sunken eyes. The man was a fanatic, of course—the Saint hadn't realized that before. But Marius knew it. The giant's first curt sentences had touched the chords of that fanaticism with an easy mastery, and now Hermann was watching the speaker raptly, with one high spot of colour burning over each cheekbone, and the fanned flames of his madness flickering in his gaze. And the Saint could only stand there, spellbound, while Marius's gentle, unimpassioned voice repeated his simple instructions so that there could be no mistake . . .

It could only have taken five minutes altogether, yet in those five minutes had been outlined the bare and sufficient essentials of an abomination that would set a torch to the powder-magazine of Europe and kindle such a blaze as could only be quenched in smoking seas of blood . . . And then Marius had finished, and had risen to unlock a safe that stood in one corner of the room, and the Saint woke up.

Yet there was nothing that he could do—not then . . . Casually his eyes wandered round the room, weighing up the grouping and the odds, and he knew that he was jammed—jammed all to hell. He might have worked his knife out of its sheath and cut himself loose, and that knife would then have kissed somebody good night with unerring accuracy, but it wouldn't have helped. There were two guns against him, besides the three other hoodlums who were unarmed, and Belle could only be thrown once. If he had been alone, he might have tried it—might have tried to edge round until he could stick Marius in the back and take a lightning second shot at the Bowery Boy from behind the shelter of that huge body—but he was not alone . . . And for a moment, with a deathly soberness, the Saint actually considered that idea in spite of the fact that he was not alone. He could have killed Marius, anyway—and that fiendish plot might have died with Marius . . . even if Lessing and Roger and Sonia Delmar and the Saint himself also died . . .

And then Simon realized, grimly, that the plot would not have died. To Hermann alone, even without Marius, the plot would always have been a live thing. And again the Saint's fingers fell away from his little knife . . .

Marius was returning from the safe. He carried two flat metal boxes, each about eight inches long, and Hermann took them from him eagerly.

"You had better leave at once." Marius spoke again in English, after a glance at the clock. "You will have plenty of time . . . if you do not have an accident."

"There will be no accident, *mein Herr*."

"And you will return here immediately."

"*Jawohl!*"

Hermann turned away, slipping the boxes into the side pockets of his coat. And, as he turned, a new light was added to the glimmering madness in his eyes, for his turn brought him face to face with the Saint.

"Once, English swine, you hit me."

"Yeah." Simon regarded the man steadily. "I'm only sorry, now, that it wasn't more than once."

"I have not forgotten, pig," said Hermann purringly, and then, suddenly, with a bestial snarl, he was lashing a rain of vicious blows at the Saint's face. "You also will remember," he screamed, "that I hit you—pig—like that—and that—and that—"

It was Marius who caught and held the man's arms at last.

"*Das ist genug*, Hermann. I will attend to him myself. And he will not hit you again."

"*Das ist gut*." Panting, Hermann drew back. He turned slowly, and his eyes rested on the girl with a gloating leer. And then he marched to the door. "I shall return, *werter Herr*," he said thickly, and then he was gone.

Marius strolled back to the desk and picked up his cigar. He gazed impassively at the Saint.

"And now, Templar," he said, "we can dispose of you." He glanced at Roger and Lessing. "And your friends," he added.

There was the faintest tremor of triumph in his voice, and for an instant the Saint felt a qualm of desperate fear. It was not for himself, nor for Roger. But Hermann had been promised a reward . . .

And then Simon pulled himself together. His head was clear—Hermann's savage attack had been too unscientific to do more than superficial damage—and his brain had never seemed to function with more ruthless crystalline efficiency in all his life. Over the giant's shoulder he could see the clock, and that clock face, with the precise position of the hands, printed itself upon the forefront of the Saint's mind as if it had been branded there with red-hot irons. It was exactly twenty-eight minutes past two. Four hours clear, and a hundred and fifteen miles to go. Easy enough on a quiet night with a powerful car—easy enough for Hermann. But for the Saint . . . for the Saint, every lost minute sped the world nearer to a horror that he dared not contemplate.

He saw every facet of the situation at once, with a blinding clarity, as he might have seen every facet of a pellucid jewel suspended in the focus of battery upon battery of thousand-kilowatt sun-arcs—saw everything that the slightest psychological nuke might mean—heard, in imagination, the dry, sarcastic welcome of his fantastic story . . . Figures blazed through his brain in an ordered spate—figures on the speedometer of the Hirondel, trembling past the hairline in the little window where they showed—seventy-five—eighty—eighty-five . . . Driving as only he could drive, with the devil at his shoulder and a guardian angel's blessing on the road and on the tyres, he might average a shade over fifty. Give it two hours and a quarter, then—at the forlorn minimum . . .

And once again the Saint looked Marius in the eyes, while all these things were indelibly graven upon a brain that seemed to have turned to ice, so clear and smooth and cold it was. And the Saint's smile was very Saintly.

"I hope," he drawled, "that you've invented a really picturesque way for me to die."

CHAPTER TWELVE:

HOW MARIUS ORGANIZED AN ACCIDENT AND MR PROSSER PASSED ON

1

"It is certainly necessary for you to die, Templar," said Marius dispassionately. "There is a score between us which cannot be settled in any other way."

The Saint nodded, and for a moment his eyes were two flakes of blue steel.

"You're right, Angel Face," he said softly. "You're dead right . . . This planet isn't big enough to hold us both. And you know as surely as you're standing there that if you don't kill me I'm going to kill you, Rayt Marius!"

"I appreciate that," said the giant calmly.

And then the Saint laughed.

"But still we have to face the question of method, old dear," he murmured, with an easy return of all his old mocking banter. "You can't wander round England bumping people off quite so airily. I know you've done it before—on one particular occasion—but I haven't yet discovered how you got away with it. There are bodies to be got rid of, and things like that, you know—it isn't quite such a soft snap as it reads in story-books. It's an awful bore, but there you are. Or were you just thinking of running us through the mincing-machine and sluicing the pieces down the kitchen sink?"

Marius shook his head.

"I have noticed," he remarked, "that in the stories to which you refer, the method employed for the elimination of an undesirable busybody is usually so elaborate and complicated that the hero's escape is as inevitable as the reader expects it to be. But I have not that melodramatic mind. If you are expecting an underground cellar full of poisonous snakes, or a trap door leading to a subterranean river, or a man-eating tiger imported for your benefit, or anything else so conventional—pray disillusion yourself. The end I have designed for you is very simple. You will simply meet with an unfortunate accident—that is all."

He was carefully trimming the end of his cigar as he spoke, and his tremendous hands moved to the operation with a ruthless deliberation that was more terrible than any violence.

The Saint had to twist his bound hands together until the cords bit into his wrists—to make sure that he was awake. Vengeful men he had faced often, angry men a thousand times; more than once he had listened to savage, triumphant men luxuriously describing, with a wealth of sadistic detail, the arrangements that they had made for his demise: but never had he heard his death discussed so quietly, with such an utterly pitiless cold-bloodedness. Marius might have been engaged in nothing but an abstract philosophical debate on the subject—the ripple of vindictive satisfaction in his voice might have passed unnoticed by an inattentive ear . . .

And as Marius paused, intent upon his cigar, the measured tick of the clock and Lessing's stertorous breathing seemed to assault the silence deafeningly, mauling and mangling the nerves like the tortured screech of a knife blade dragged across a plate . . .

And then the sudden scream of the telephone bell jangled into the tenseness and the torture, a sound so abruptly prosaic as to seem weird and unnatural in that atmosphere, and Marius looked round.

"Ah—that will be Herr Dussel."

The Saint turned his head in puzzled surprise, and saw that Roger Conway's face was set and strained.

And then Marius was talking.

Again he spoke in German, and Simon listened, and understood. He understood everything—understood the grim helplessness of Roger's stillness . . . understood the quick compression of Roger's lips as Marius broke off to glance at the clock. For Roger Conway's German was restricted to such primitive necessities as *Bahnof, Speisewagen*, and *Bier*, but Roger could have needed no German at all to interpret that renewed interest in the time.

The Saint's fingers stole up his sleeve, and Belle slid gently down from her sheath.

And Simon understood another reason why Roger had been so silent, and had played such an unusually statuesque part in the general exchange of genial persiflage. Roger must have been waiting, hoping, praying, with a paralysing intentness of concentration, for Marius to overlook just the one desperate detail that Marius had not overlooked . . .

The Saint leaned very lazily against the wall. He tilted his head back against it, and gazed at the ceiling with dreamy eyes and a look of profound boredom on his face. And very carefully he turned the blade of Belle towards the ropes on his wrists.

"An unfortunate accident," Marius had said. And the Saint believed it. Thinking it over now, he didn't know why he should ever have imagined that a man like Marius would indulge in any of the theatrical trappings of murder. The Saint knew as well as anyone that the blood-curdling inventions of the sensational novelist had a real foundation in the mentality of a certain type of crook, that there were men constitutionally incapable of putting the straightforward skates under an enemy whom they had in their power—men whose tortuous minds ran to electrically fired revolvers, or tame alligators in a private swimming bath, as inevitably as water runs downhill. The Saint had met that type of man. But to Rayt Marius such devices would not exist. Whatever was to be done would be done quickly . . .

And the same applied to the Saint—consequently. Whatever he was going to do, by way of prophylaxis, he would have to do instantly. Whatever sort of a gamble it might be, odds or no odds, handicaps or no handicaps, Bowery Boys and miscellaneous artillery notwithstanding, hell-fire and pink damnation inasmuch and hereinafter—be b-blowed . . . Simon wondered why he hadn't grasped that elementary fact before.

"*Gute Nacht, mein Freund. Schlafen Sie wohl . . .*"

Marius had finished. He hung up the receiver, and the Saint smiled at him.

"I trust," said Simon quietly, "that Heinrich will obey that last instruction—for his own sake. But I'm afraid he won't."

The giant smiled satirically.

"Herr Dussel is perfectly at liberty to go to sleep—after he has followed my other instructions." He turned to Roger. "And you, my dear young friend—did you also understand?"

Roger stood up straight.

"I guessed," he said, and again Marius smiled.

"So you realize—do you not—that there is no chance of a mistake? There is still, I should think, half an hour to go before Sir Isaac's servants will be communicating with the police—plenty of time for them also to meet with an unfortunate accident. And there will be no one to repeat your story."

"Quate," said the Saint, with his eyes still on the ceiling. "Oh, quate."

Marius turned again at the sound of his voice.

"And this is the last of you—you scum!" The sentence began as calmly as anything else that the giant had said, but the end of it was shrill and strident. "You have heard. You thought you had beaten me, and now you know that you have failed. Take that with you to your death! You fool! You have dared to make your puny efforts against me—me—Rayt Marius!"

The giant stood at his full height, his gargantuan chest thrown out, his colossal fists raised and quivering.

"You! You have dared to do that—you dog—!"

"Quate," said the Saint affably.

And even as he spoke he braced himself for the blow that he could not possibly escape this time, and yet the impossible thing happened. With a frightful effort Marius mastered his fury for the last time; his fists unclenched, and his hands fell slowly to his sides.

"Pah! But I should flatter you by losing my temper with you." Again the hideous face was a mask, and the thin, high-pitched voice was as smooth and suave as ever. "I should not like you to think that I was so interested in you, my dear Templar. Once you kicked me; once, when I was in your hands, you threatened me with torture, but I am not annoyed. I do not lose my temper with the mosquito who bites me. I simply kill the mosquito."

2

A severed strand of rope slipped down the Saint's wrist, and he gathered it in cautiously. Already the cords were loosening. And the Saint smiled.

"Really," he murmured, "that's awfully ruthless of you. But then, you strong, silent men are like that . . . And are we all classified as mosquitoes for this event?"

Marius spread out his hands.

"Your friend Conway, personally, is entirely unimportant," he said. "If only he had been wise enough to confine his adventurous instincts to activities which were within the limits of his intelligence—" He broke off with a shrug. "However, he has elected to follow you into meddling with my affairs—"

"And Lessing?"

"He also has interfered. Only at your instigation, it is true, but the result is the same."

The Saint continued to smile gently.

"I get you, Tiny Tim. And he also will have an unfortunate accident?"

"It will be most unfortunate." Marius drew leisurely at his cigar before proceeding. "Let me tell you the story as far as it is known. You and your gang kidnapped Sir Isaac—for some reason unknown—and killed his servants when they attempted to resist you. You brought him out to Saltham—again for some reason unknown. You drove past this house on to the cliff road, and there—still for some reason unknown—your car plunged over the precipice. And if you were not killed by the fall, you were certainly burnt to death in the fire which followed . . . Those are the bare facts—but the theories which will be put forward to account for them should make most interesting reading."

"I see," said the Saint very gently. "And now will you give us the low-down on the tragedy, honeybunch? I mean, I'm the main squeeze in this blinkin' teal—"

"I do not understand all your expressions. If you mean that you would like to know how the accident will be arranged, I shall be delighted to explain the processes as they take place. We are just about to begin,"

He put down his cigar regretfully, and turned to the rope expert.

"Prosser, you will find a car at the lodge gates. You will drive it out to the cliff road, and then drive it over the edge of the cliff. Endeavour not to drive yourself over with it. After this, you will return to the garage, take three or four tins of petrol, and carry them down the cliff path. You will go along the shore until you come to the wreckage of the car, and wait for me there."

The Saint leaned even more lazily against the wall. And the cords had fallen away from his wrists. He had just managed to turn his hand and catch them as they fell.

"I may be wrong," he remarked earnestly, as the door closed behind Mr Prosser, "but I think you're marvellous. How do you do it, Angel Face? Is it Pelmanism?"

"We will now have you gagged," said Marius unemotionally. "Ludwig, fetch some cloths."

Stifling a cavernous yawn, the Boche roused himself from the corner and went out. And the Saint's smile could never have been more angelic.

The miracle . . . ! He could scarcely believe it. And it was a copper-bottomed wow. It was too utterly superfluously superlative for words . . . But the blowed-in-the-glass, brass-bound, seventy-five-point-three-five-over-proof fact was that the odds had been cut down by half.

Quite casually, the Saint made sure of his angles.

The Bowery Boy was exactly on his right; Marius, by the desk, was half-left. And Marius was still speaking.

"We will take you to the top of the cliffs—bound, so that you cannot struggle, and gagged, so that you cannot cry out—and we throw you over. At the bottom we are ready to remove the ropes and the gags. We place you beside the car; the petrol is poured over you; a match . . . And there is a most unfortunate accident . . ."

The Saint looked round.

Instinctively Roger Conway had drawn closer to the girl. Ever afterwards the Saint treasured that glimpse of Roger Conway, erect and defiant, with fearless eyes.

"And if the fall doesn't quite kill us?" said Roger distinctly.

"It will be even more unfortunate," said Marius. "But for any one of you to be found with a bullet wound would spoil the effect of the accident. Naturally, you will see my point . . ."

There were other memories of that moment that the Saint would never forget. The silence of the girl, for instance, and the way Lessing's breath suddenly came with a choking sob. And the stolid disinterestedness of the Bowery Boy. And Lessing's sudden throaty babble of words. "Good God—Marius—you can't do a thing like that! You can't—you can't—"

And Roger's quiet voice again, cutting through the babble like the slash of a sabre. "Are we really stuck this time, Saint?"

"We are not," said the Saint.

He said it so gently that for a few seconds no one could have realized that there was a significant stone-cold deliberateness, infinitely too significant and stone-cold for bluff, about that very gentleness. And for those few seconds Lessing's hysterical incoherent babble went on, and the clock whirred to strike the hour . . .

And then Marius took a step forwards. "Explain!"

There was something akin to fear in the venomous crack of that one word, so that even Lessing's impotent blubbering died in his throat, and the Saint laughed.

"The reason is in my pocket," he said softly. "I'm sorry to disappoint you, Angel Face, my beautiful, but it's too late now— "

In a flash the giant was beside him, fumbling with his coat.

"So! You will still be humorous. But perhaps, after all, you will not be thrown down the cliff before your car is set on fire—"

"The inside breast pocket, darlingest," murmured the Saint very softly. And he turned a little. He could see the bulge in the giant's pocket, where Roger's captured automatic dragged the coat out of shape. And for a moment the giant's body cut off most of the Saint from the Bowery Boy's field of vision. And Marius was intent upon the Saint's breast pocket . . .

Simon's left hand leapt to its mark as swiftly and lightly as the hand of any professional pickpocket could have done . . .

"Don't move an inch, Angel Face!"

The Saint's voice rang out suddenly like the crack of a whip—a voice of murderous menace, with a tang of tempered steel. And the automatic that backed it up was rammed into the giant's ribs with a savagery that made even Rayt Marius wince.

"Not one inch—not half an inch, Angel Face," repeated that voice of tensile tungsten. "That's the idea . . . And now talk quickly to Lingrove—quickly! He can't get a bead on me, and he's wondering what to do. Tell him! Tell him to drop his gun!"

Marius's lips parted in a dreadful grin.

And the Saint's voice rapped again through the stillness.

"I'll count three. You die on the three. One!" The giant was looking into Simon's eyes, and they were eyes emptied of all laughter. Eyes of frozen ultramarine, drained of the last trace of human pity . . . And Marius answered in a whisper.

"Drop your gun, Lingrove."

The reply came in a muffled thud on the carpet, but not for an instant did those inexorable eyes cease to bore into the giant's brain.

"Is it down, Roger?" crisped the Saint, and Conway spoke the single necessary word.

"Yes."

"Right. Get over in that corner by the telephone, Lingrove." The Saint, with the tail of his eye, could see the Bowery Boy pass behind the giant's shoulder, and the way was clear. "Get over and join him, Angel Face . . ."

Marius stepped slowly back, and the Saint slid silently along the wall until he was beside the door. And the door opened.

As it opened it hid the Saint, and the Boche came right into the room. And then Simon closed the door gently, and had his back to it when the man whipped round and saw him.

"*Du bist wie eine Blume,*" murmured the Saint cordially, and a glimmer of the old lazy laughter was trickling back into his voice. "Incidentally, I'll bet you haven't jumped like that for years. Never mind. It's very good for the liver . . . And now would you mind joining your boss over in the corner, sweet Ludwig? And if you're a very good boy, perhaps I'll let you go to sleep . . ."

3

"Good old Saint!"

The commendation was wrung spontaneously from Roger Conway's lips, and Simon Templar grinned.

"Hustle this way, son," he remarked, "and we'll have you loose in two flaps of a cow's pendulum. Then you can be making merry with that spare coil of hawser while I carry on with the good work—Jump!"

The last word detonated in the end of the speech like the fulmination of a charge of high explosive at the tail of a length of fuse. And Roger jumped—no living man could have failed to obey that trumpet-tongued command.

A fraction of a second later he saw—or rather heard—the reason for it.

As he crossed the room he had carelessly come between the Saint and Marius. And, as he jumped, ducking instinctively, something flew past the back of his neck, so close that the wind of it stirred his hair, and crashed into the wall where the Saint had been standing. Where the Saint had been standing, but Simon was a yard away by then . . .

As Roger straightened up he saw the Saint's automatic swinging round to check the rush that followed. And then he saw the telephone lying at the Saint's feet.

"Naughty," said the Saint reproachfully.

"Why didn't you shoot the swine?" snapped Roger, with reasonable irritation, but Simon only laughed.

"Because I want him, sonny boy. Because it wouldn't amuse me to bounce him like that. It's too easy. I want our Angel Face for a fight . . . And how I want him!"

Roger's hands were free, but he stood staring at the Saint helplessly.

He said suddenly, foolishly, "Saint—what do you mean? You couldn't possibly—"

"I'm going to have a damned good try. Shooting is good—for some people. But there are others you want to get at with your bare hands . . ."

Very gently Simon spoke—very, very gently. And Roger gazed in silent wonder at the bleak steel in the blue eyes, and the supple poise of the wide limber shoulders, and the splendid lines of that reckless fighting face, and he could not find anything to say.

And the Saint laughed again.

"But there are other things to attend to first. Grab that rope and do your stuff, old dear—and mind you do it well. And leave that iron on the floor for a moment—we don't want anyone to infringe our patent in that pickpocket trick."

A moment later he was cutting the ropes away from Sonia Delmar's wrists. Lessing came next, and Lessing was as silent during the operation as the girl had been, but for an obviously different reason. He was shaking like a leaf, and, after one comprehensive glance at him, Simon turned again to the girl.

"How d'you feel, lass?" he asked, and she smiled.

"All right," she said.

"Just pick up that gun, would you . . . ? D'you think you could use it?"

She weighed the Bowery Boy's automatic thoughtfully in her hand. "I guess I could, Simon."

"That's great!" Belle was back in the Saint's sleeve, and he put out his free hand and drew her towards him. "Now, park yourself right over here, sweetheart, so that they can't rush you. Have you got them covered?"

"Sure!"

"Atta-baby. And don't you take your pretty eyes off the beggars till Roger's finished his job. Ike, you flop into that chair and faint in your own time. If you come blithering into the line of fire it'll be your funeral. Sonia, d'you feel really happy?"

"Why?"

"Could you be a real hold-up wizard for five or ten minutes, all on your ownsome?" She nodded slowly.

"I'd do my best, Big Boy."

"Then take this other gat as well." He pressed it into her hand. "I'm leaving you to it, old dear—I've got to see a man about a sort of dog, and it's blamed urgent. But I'll be right back. If you have the least sign of trouble let fly. The only thing I ask is that you don't kill Angel Face—not fatally, that is . . . S'long!"

He waved a cheery hand, and was gone—before Roger, who had been late in divining his intention, could ask him why he went.

But Roger had not understood Hermann's mission.

And even the Saint had taken fully a minute to realize the ultimate significance of the way that hurtling telephone had smashed into the wall, but there was nothing about it that he did not realize now, as he raced down the long, dark drive. That had been a two-edged effort— by all the gods! It was a blazing credit to the giant's lightning grasp on situations—a desperate bid for salvation, and simultaneously a vindictive defiance. And the thought of that last motive lent wings to the Saint's feet . . .

He reached the lodge gates, and looked up and down the road, but he could see no car. And then, as he paused there, he heard, quite distinctly, the unmistakable snarl of the Hirondel with an open throttle.

The Saint spun round.

An instant later he was flying up the road as if a thousand devils were baying at his heels.

He tore round a bend, and thought he could recognize a clump of trees in the gloom ahead. If he was right, he must be getting near the cliff. The snarl of the Hirondel was louder . . .

He must have covered the last hundred yards in a shade under evens. And then, as he rounded the last corner, he heard a splintering crash.

With a shout he flung himself forwards. And yet he knew that it was hopeless. For one second he had a glimpse of the great car rearing like a stricken beast on the brink of a precipice, with its wide flaming eyes hurling a long white spear of light into the empty sky, and then the light went out, and down the cliff side went the roar of the beast and a racking, tearing thunder of breaking shrubs and battered rocks and shattering metal . . . And then another crash. And a silence . . .

The Saint covered the rest of the distance quite calmly, and the man who stood in the road did not try to run. Perhaps he knew it would be useless.

"Mr Prosser, I believe?" said the Saint caressingly.

The man stood mute, with his back to the gap which the Hirondel had torn through the flimsy rails at the side of the road. And Simon Templar faced him.

"You've wrecked my beautiful car," said the Saint, in the same caressing tone.

And suddenly his fist smashed into the man's face, and Mr Prosser reeled back, and went down without a sound into the silence.

4

Which was certainly very nice and jolly, reflected the Saint, as he walked slowly back to the house. But not noticeably helpful . . .

He walked slowly because it was his habit to move slowly when he was thinking. And he had a lot to think about. The cold rage that had possessed him a few minutes before had gone altogether: the prime cause of it had been fully dealt with, and the next thing was to weigh up the consequences and face the facts.

For all the threads were now in his hands, all ready to be wormed and parcelled and served and put away—all except one. And that one was now more important than all the others. And it was utterly out of his reach—not even the worst that he could do to Marius could recall it or change its course . . .

"Did you get your dog, old boy?" Roger Conway's cheerful accents greeted him as he opened the door of the library, but the Saintly smile was unusually slow to respond.

"Yes and no," Simon answered after a short pause. "I got it, but not soon enough." The smile had gone again, and Roger frowned puzzledly.

"What was the dog?" he asked.

"The late Mr Prosser," said the Saint carefully, and Roger jumped to one-half the right conclusion.

"You mean he'd crashed the car?"

"He had crashed the car."

The affirmation came flatly, precisely, coldly—in a way that Roger could not understand.

And the Saint's eyes roved round the room without expression, taking in the three bound men in the corner, and Lessing in a chair, and Sonia Delmar beside Roger, and the telephone on the floor. The Saint's cigarette-case lay on the desk where Marius had thrown it, and the Saint walked over in silence and picked it up.

"Well?" prompted Roger, and was surprised by the sound of his own voice.

The Saint had lighted a cigarette. He crossed the room again with the cigarette between his lips, and picked up the telephone. He looked once at the frayed ends of the flex, and then he held the instrument close to his ear and shook it gently.

And then he looked at Roger.

"Have you forgotten Hermann?" he asked quietly.

"I had forgotten him for the moment, Saint. But—d"

"And those boxes he took with him—had you guessed what they were?"

"I hadn't."

Simon Templar nodded.

"Of course," he said. "You wouldn't know what it was all about. But I'm telling you now, just to break it gently to you, that the Hirondel's been crashed and the telephone's bust, and those two things together may very well mean the end of peace on earth for God knows how many years. But you were just thinking we'd won the game, weren't you?"

"What do you mean, Saint?"

The newspaper that Marius had consulted was in the waste-basket. Simon bent and took it out, and the paragraph that he knew he would find caught his eye almost at once.

"Come here, Roger," said the Saint, and Roger came beside him wonderingly.

Simon Templar did not explain. His thumb simply indicated the paragraph, and Conway read it through twice—three times—before he looked again at the Saint with a fearful comprehension dawning in his eyes.

CHAPTER THIRTEEN:
HOW SIMON TEMPLAR ENTERED
A POST OFFICE AND A BOOB WAS
BLISTERED

1

"But it couldn't be that!"

Roger's dry lips framed the sane denial mechanically, and yet he knew that sanity made him a fool even as he spoke. And the Saint's answer made him a fool again.

"But it is that!"

The Saint's terrible calm snapped suddenly, as a brittle blade snaps at a turn of the hand. Sonia Delmar came over and took the paper out of Roger's hands, but Roger scarcely noticed it—he was gazing, fascinated, at the blaze in the Saint's eyes.

"That's what Hermann's gone to do. I tell you, I heard every word. It's Angel Face's second string. I don't know why it wasn't his first—unless because he figured it was too desperate to rely on except in the last emergency. But he was ready to put it into action if the need arose, and it just happened that there was a chance this very night—by the grace of the devil—"

"But I don't see how it works," Roger said stupidly.

"Oh, for the love of Pete!" The Saint snatched his cigarette from his mouth, and his other hand crushed Roger's shoulder in a vice-like grip.

"Does that count? There are a dozen ways he could have worked it. Hermann's a Boche. Marius could easily have fixed for him to be caught later, with the necessary papers on him—and there the fat would have been in the fire. But what the hell does it matter now, anyway?"

And Roger could see that it didn't matter, but he couldn't see anything else. He could only say: "What time does it happen?"

"About six-thirty," said the Saint, and Roger looked at the clock. It was twenty-five minutes past three.

"There must be another telephone somewhere," said the girl. Simon pointed to the desk.

"Look at that one," he said. "The number's on it—and it's a Saxmundham number. Probably it's the only private phone in the village."

"But there'll be a post office—"

"I wonder."

The Saint was looking at Marius. There might have been a sneer somewhere behind the graven inscrutability of that evil face, but Simon could not be sure. Yet he had a premonition . . .

"We might try," Roger Conway was saying logically, and the Saint turned.

"We might. Coming?"

"But these guys—and Sonia—"

"Right. Maybe I'd better go alone. Give me one of those guns!"

Roger obeyed.

And once again the Saint went flying down the drive. The automatic was heavy in his hip pocket, and it gave him a certain comfort to have it there, though he had no love for firearms in the ordinary way. They made so much noise . . . But it was more than possible that the post office would look cross-eyed at him, and it might boil down to a hold-up. He realized that he wasn't quite such a paralysingly respectable sight as he had been earlier in the evening, and that might be a solid disadvantage when bursting into a village post office staffed by startled females at that hour of the morning. His clothes were undamaged, it was true, but Hermann's affectionate farewell had left certain traces on his face. Chiefly, there was a long scratch across his forehead, and a thin trickle of blood running down one side of his face, as a souvenir of the diamond ring that Hermann affected. Nothing much as wounds went, but it must have been enough to make him look a pretty sanguinary desperado—and if it did come to a hold-up, how the hell did telegraph offices work? The Saint had a working knowledge of Morse, but the manipulation of the diverse gadgets connected with the sordid mechanism of transmission of the same was a bit beyond his education . . .

How far was it to the village? Nearly a mile, Roger had said when they drove out. Well, it was one river of gore of a long mile . . . It was some time since he had passed the spot where Mr Prosser's memorial tablet might or might not be added to the scenic decorations. And, like a fool, he'd started off as if he were going for a hundred yards' sprint, and, fit as he was, the pace would kill his speed altogether if he didn't ease up. He did so, filling his bursting lungs with great gulps of the cool sea air. His heart was pounding like a demented trip-hammer . . . But at that moment the road started to dip a trifle, and that must mean that it was nearing the village. He put on a shade of acceleration—it was easier going downhill—and presently he passed the first cottage.

A few seconds later he was in some sort of village street, and then he had to slacken off almost to a walk.

What the hairy hippopotamus were the visible distinguishing marks or peculiarities of a village post office? The species didn't usually run to a private building of its own, he knew. Mostly, it seemed to house itself in an obscure corner of the grocery store. And what did a grocery store look like in the dark, anyway . . . ? His eyes were perfectly attuned to the darkness by this time, but the feebleness of the moon, which had dealt so kindly with him earlier in the evening, was now catching him on the return swing. If only he had a flashlight . . . As it was, he had to use his petrol lighter at every door. Butcher—baker—candle-stick maker—he seemed to strike every imaginable kind of shop but the right one . . .

An eternity passed before he came to his goal.

There should have been a bell somewhere around the door . . . but there wasn't. So there was only one thing to do. He stepped back, and picked up a large stone from the side of the road. Without hesitation he hurled it through an upper window . . .

Then he waited.

One—two—three minutes passed, and no indignant head was thrust out into the night to demand the reason for the outrage. Only, somewhere behind him in the blackness, the window of another house was thrown up.

The Saint found a second stone . . .

"'Oo's that?"

The quavering voice that mingled with the tinkle of broken glass was undoubtedly feminine, but it did not come from the post office. Another window was opened. Suddenly the woman screamed. A man's shout answered her . . .

"Hell," said the Saint through his teeth.

But through all the uproar the post office remained as silent as a tomb. "Deaf, doped, or dead," diagnosed the Saint, without a smile. "And I don't care which . . ."

He stepped into the doorway, jerking the gun from his pocket. The butt of it crashed through the glass door of the shop, and there was a hole the size of a man's head. Savagely the Saint smashed again at the jagged borders of the hole, until there was a gap big enough for him to pass through. The whole village must have been awake by that time, and he heard heavy footsteps running down the road.

As he went in his head struck against a hanging oil lamp, and he lifted it down from its hook and lighted it. He saw the post office counter at once, and had reached it when the first of the chase burst in behind him.

Simon put the lamp down and turned. "Keep back," he said quietly.

There were two men in the doorway; they saw the ugly steadiness of the weapon in the Saint's hand and pulled up, open-mouthed.

The Saint sidled along the counter, keeping the men covered. There was a telephone box in the corner—that would be easier than tinkering at a telegraph apparatus—

And then came another man, shouldering his way through the crowd that had gathered at the door. He wore a dark-blue uniform with silver buttons, and there was no mistaking his identity.

"'Ere, wot's this?" he demanded truculently.

Then he also saw the Saint's gun, and it checked him for a moment—but only for a moment.

"Put that down," he blustered, and took another step forwards.

2

Simon Templar's thoughts moved like lightning. The constable was coming on—there wasn't a doubt of that. Perhaps he was a brave man, in his blunt way, or perhaps Chicago was only a fairy-tale to him, but certainly he was coming on. And the Saint couldn't shoot him down in cold blood, without giving him a chance. Yet the Saint realized at the same time how thread-bare a hope he would have of putting his preposterous story over on a turnip-headed village cop. At Scotland Yard, where there was a different type of man, he might have done it, but here . . .

It would have to be a bluff. The truth would have meant murder— and the funeral procession would have been the cop's. Even now the Saint knew, with an icy intensity of decision, that he would shoot the policeman down without a second's hesitation, if it proved to be necessary. But the man should have his chance . . .

The Saint drew himself up.

"I'm glad you've come, officer," he remarked briskly. "I'm a Secret Service agent, and I shall probably want you."

A silence fell on the crowd. For the Saint's clothes were still undeniably glorious to behold, and he spoke as one having authority. Standing there at his full height, trim and lean and keen-faced, with a cool half-smile of greeting on his lips, he looked every inch a man to be obeyed. And the constable peered at him uncertainly.

"Woi did you break them windoos, then?"

"I had to wake the people here. I've got to get on the phone to London—at once. I don't know why the post office staff haven't shown up yet—everyone else seems to be here—"

A voice spoke up from the outskirts of the crowd.

"Missus Fraser an' 'er daughter doo 'ave goorn to London theirselves, sir, for to see 'er sister. They ain't a-comin' back till morning."

"I see. That explains it." The Saint put his gun down on the counter and took out his cigarette-case. "Officer, will you clear these good people out, please? I've no time to waste."

The request was an order—the constable would not have been human if he had not felt an automatic instinct to carry it out. But he still looked at the Saint.

"Oi doo feel Oi've seen your face befoor," he said, with less hostility, but Simon laughed.

"I don't expect you have," he murmured. "We don't advertise."

"But 'ave you got anything on you to show you're wot you says you are?"

The Saint's pause was only fractional, for the answer that had come to him was one of pure inspired genius. It was unlikely that a hayseed cop like this would know what evidence of identity a secret agent should properly carry; it was just as unlikely that he would recognize the document that Simon proposed to show him . . .

"Naturally," said the Saint, without the flicker of an eyelid. "The only difficulty is that I'm not allowed to disclose my name to you. But I think there should be enough to convince you without that."

And he took out his wallet, and from the wallet he took a little book rather like a driving licence, while the crowd gaped and craned to see. The constable came closer.

Simon gave him one glimpse of the photograph which adorned the inside, while he covered the opposite page with his fingers and then he turned quickly to the pages at the end.

For the booklet he had produced was the certificate of the Fédération Aéronautique Internationale, which every amateur aviator must obtain—and the Saint, in the spare time of less strenuous days, had been wont to amateurly aviate with great skill and dexterity. And the two back pages of the certificate were devoted to an impressive exhortation to all whom it might concern, translated into six different languages, and saying:

The Civil, Naval, and Military authorities, including the Police, are respectfully requested to aid and assist the holder of this certificate.

Just that, and nothing more . . .

But it ought to be enough. It ought to be . . . And the Saint, with his cigarette lighted, was quietly taking up his gun again while the constable read, but he might have saved himself the trouble, for the constable was regarding him with a kind of awe.

"Oi beg your pardon, sir . . ."

"That," murmured the Saint affably, "is OK by me."

He replaced the little book in his pocket with a silent prayer of thanksgiving, while the policeman squared his shoulders importantly and began to disperse the crowd, and the dispersal was still proceeding when the Saint went into the telephone booth.

He should have been feeling exultant, for everything should have been plain sailing now . . . And yet he wasn't. As he took up the receiver he remembered the veiled sneer that he had seen—or imagined—in the face of Marius. And it haunted him. He had had a queer intuition then that the giant had foreseen something that the Saint had not foreseen, and now that intuition was even stronger. Could it be that Marius was expecting the Prince, or some other ally, due to arrive about that time, who might take the other by surprise while the Saint was away? Or might the household staff be larger than the Saint had thought, and might there be the means of a rescue still within the building? Or what . . . ? "I'm growing nerves," thought the Saint, and cursed all intuitions categorically.

And he had been listening for some time before he realized that the receiver was absolutely silent—there was none of the gentle crackling undertone that ordinarily sounds in a telephone receiver . . .

"Gettin' on all roight, sir?"

The crowd had gone, and the policeman had returned. Simon thrust the receiver into his hand.

"Will you carry on?" he said. "The line seems to have gone dead. If you get a reply, ask for Victoria six eight two seven. And tell them to make it snappy. I'm going to try the telegraph."

"There's noo telegraph, sir."

"What's that?"

"There's noo telegraph, sir."

"Then how do they send and receive telegrams? Or don't they?"

"They doo coom through on the telephoon, sir, from Sexmundam." The constable jiggered the receiver hook. "And this loine doo seem to be dead, sir," he added helpfully.

Simon took the receiver from him again.

"What about the station?" he snapped. "There must be a telephone there."

The policeman scratched his head.

"Oi suppose there is, sir . . . But, now Oi coom to think of it, Oi did 'ear earlier in the day that the telephoon loine was down somewhere. One o' they charry-bangs run into a poost on Saturday noight—"

He stopped, appalled, seeing the blaze in the Saint's eyes.

Then, very carefully, Simon put down the receiver. He had gone white to the lips, and the twist of those lips was not pleasant to see.

"My God in Heaven!" said the Saint huskily. "Then there's all hell let loose tonight!"

3

"Is it as bad as that, sir?" inquired the constable weakly, and Simon swung round on him like a tiger.

"You blistered boob!" he snarled. "D'you think this is my idea of being comic?" And then he checked himself. That sort of thing wouldn't do any good.

But he saw it all now. The first dim inkling had come to him when Marius had hurled that telephone at him in the house, and now the proof and vindication was staring him in the face in all its hideous nakedness. The telegraph post had been knocked down on Saturday night; being an unimportant line, nothing would be done about it before Monday, and Marius had known all about it. Marius's own line must have followed a different route, perhaps joining the other at a point beyond the scene of the accident . . .

Grimly, gratingly, the Saint bedded down the facts in separate compartments of his brain, while he schooled himself to a relentless calm. And presently he turned again to the policeman.

"Where's the station?" he asked. "They must have an independent telegraph there."

"The station, sir? That'll be a little way oover the bridge. But you woon't foind anyone there at this toime, sir—"

"We don't want anyone," said the Saint. "Come on!"

He had mastered himself again completely, and he felt that nothing else that might happen before the dawn could possibly shake him from the glacial discipline that he had locked upon his passion. And, with the same frozen restraint of emotion, he understood that the trip to the station was probably a waste of time, but it had to be tried . . .

The crowd of villagers was still gathered outside the shop, and the Saint strode through them without looking to right or left. And he remembered what he had read about the place before he came there— its reputed population of 3,128, its pleasure grounds, its attractions as a watering-place—and at that moment he would cheerfully have murdered the author of that criminal agglomeration of trout-spawn and frog-bladder. For any glories that Saltham might once have claimed had long since departed from it: it was now nothing but a forgotten seaside village, shorn of the most elementary amenities of civilization. And yet, unless a miracle happened history would remember it as history remembers Sarajevo . . .

The policeman walked beside him, but Simon did not talk. Beneath that smooth crust of icy calm a raging wrath like white-hot lava seethed through the Saint's heart. And while he could have raged, he could as well have wept. For he was seeing all that Hermann's mission would mean if it succeeded, and that vision was a vision of the ruin of all that the Saint had sworn to do. And he thought of the waste—of the agony and blood, and tears, of the squandered lives, of the world's new hopes crushed down into the mud, and again of the faith in which Norman Kent had died . . . And something in the thought of that last superb spendthrift sacrifice choked the Saint's throat. For Norman was a link with the old careless days of debonair adventuring, and those days were very far away—the days when nothing had mattered but the fighting and the fun, the comradeship and the glamour and the high risk, the sufficiency of gay swashbuckling, the wine of battle and the fair full days of quiet. Those days had gone as if they had never been.

So the Saint came soberly to the station, and smashed another window for them to enter the station-master's office.

There was certainly a telegraph, and for five minutes the Saint tried to get a response. But he was without hope.

And presently he turned away, and put his head in his hands.

"It's no use," he said bitterly. "I suppose there isn't anyone listening at the other end."

The policeman made sympathetic noises.

"O' course, if you woon't tell me wot the trouble is—"

"It wouldn't help you. But I can tell you that I've got to get through to Scotland Yard before six-thirty—well before. If I don't, it means—war."

The policeman goggled. "Did you say war, sir?"

"I did. No more and no less . . . Are there any fast cars in this blasted village?"

"Noo sir—noon as Oi can think of. Noon wot you moight call farst."

"How far is it to Saxmundham?"

"'Bout twelve moile, sir, Oi should say. Oi've got a map 'ere, if you'd loike me to look it up."

Simon did not answer, and the constable groped in a pocket of his tunic and spilled an assortment of grubby papers on to the table.

In the silence Simon heard the ticking of a clock, and he slewed round and located it on the wall behind him. The hour it indicated sank slowly into his brain, and again he calculated. Two hours for twelve miles. Easy enough—he could probably get hold of a lorry, or something else on four wheels with an engine, that would scrape

through in an hour, and leave another hour to deal with the trouble
he was sure to meet in Saxmundham. For the bluff that could be put
over on a village cop wouldn't cut much ice with the bulls of a rising
town. And suppose the lorry broke down and left them stranded on the
road . . . Two lorries, then. Roger would have to follow in the second
in case of accidents.

The Saint stood up.

"Will you push off and try to find me a couple of cars?" he said.
"Anything that'll go. I've got another man with me—I'll have to go and
fetch him. I'll meet you—"

His voice trailed away.

For the constable was staring at him as if he were a ghost, and a
moment later he understood why. The constable had a sheet of paper in
his hand—it was one of the bundle that he had taken from his pocket,
but it was not a map—and he was looking from the paper to the Saint
with bulging eyes. And the Saint knew what that paper was, and his
right hand moved quietly to his hip pocket.

Yet his face betrayed nothing.

"What's the matter, officer?" he inquired curtly. "Aren't you well?"

Still staring, the policeman inhaled audibly. And then he spoke.
"Oi knew Oi'd seen your face befoor!"

"What the devil d'you mean?"

"Oi knoo wot Oi mean." The policeman put the paper back on the
table and thumped it triumphantly. "This is your phooto-graph, an' it
says as you're wanted for murder!"

Simon stood like a rock.

"My good man, you're talking through your hat," he said incisively.
"I've shown you my identity card—"

"Ay, that you 'ave. But that's just wot it says 'ere." The constable
snatched up the paper again. "You tell me wot this means: "'As
frequently represented 'imself to be a police officer:" An' if callin'

yourself a Secret Service agent ain't as good as callin' yourself a police officer, Oi'd loike to knoo wot's wot!"

"I don't know who you're mixing me up with—"

"Oi'm not mixin' you up with anyone. Oi knoo 'oo you are. An' you called me a blistered boob, didn't you? Tellin' me the tale loike that—the woorst tale ever Oi 'eard! Oi'll shoo you if Oi'm a blistered boob..."

The Saint stepped back and his hand came out of his pocket. After all, there was no crowd here to interfere with a straight fight.

"OK again, son," he drawled. "I'll promise to recommend you for promotion when I'm caught. You're a smart lad... But you won't catch me..."

The Saint was on his toes, his hands rising, with a little smile on his lips and a twinkle of laughter in his eyes. And suddenly the policeman must have realized that perhaps after all he had been a blistered boob— that he ought to have kept his discovery to himself until he could usefully reveal it. For the Saint didn't look an easy man to arrest at that moment...

And, suddenly, the policeman yelled—once.

Then the Saint's fists lashed into his jaw, left and right, with two crisp smacks like a kiss-cannon of magnified billiard balls, and he went down like a log.

"And that's that," murmured the Saint grimly.

He reached the window in three strides, and stood there, listening. And out of the gloom there came to him the sound of hoarse voices and hurrying men.

"Well, well, well," thought the Saint, with characteristic gentleness, and understood that a rapid exit was the next thing for him. If only the cop hadn't managed to uncork that stentorian bellow... But it was too late to think about that—much too late to sit down and indulge in vain lamentations for the bluff that might have been put over on the villagers while the cop lay gagged and bound in the station-master's office, if only the cop had passed out with his mouth shut. "It's a great little evening," thought the Saint, as he slipped over the sill.

He disappeared into the shadows down the platform like a prowling cat a moment before the leading pair of boots came pelting over the concrete. At the end of the platform he found a board fence, and he was astride it when a fresh out-cry arose from behind him. Still smiling abstractedly, he lowered himself on to a patch of grass beside the road. The road itself was deserted—evidently all the men who had followed them to the station had rushed in to discover the reason for the noise—and no one challenged the Saint as he walked swiftly and silently down the dark street. And long before the first feeble apology for a hue and cry arose behind him he was flitting soundlessly up the cliff road, and he had no fear that he would be found.

4

It was exactly half-past four when he closed the door of Marius's library behind him and faced six very silent people. But one of them found quite an ordinary thing to say.

"Thank the Lord," said Roger Conway.

He pointed to the open window, and the Saint nodded.

"You heard?"

"Quite enough of it."

The Saint lighted a cigarette with a steady hand.

"There was a little excitement," he said quietly.

Sonia Delmar was looking at him steadfastly, and there was a shining pity in her eyes. "You didn't get through," she said.

It was a plain statement—a statement of what they all knew without being told. And Simon shook his head slowly.

"I didn't. The telephone line's down between here and Saxmundham, and I couldn't get any answer from the station telegraph. Angel Face knew about the telephone—that's one reason why he heaved his own at me."

"And they spotted you in the village?"

"Later. I had to break into the post office—the dames in charge were away—but I got away with that. Told the village cop I was a secret agent. He swallowed that at first, and actually helped me to break into the station. And then he got out a map to find out how far it was to Saxmundham, and pulled out his Police News with my photograph in it at the same time. I laid him out, of course, but I wasn't quite quick enough. Otherwise I might have got something to take us into Saxmundham—I was just fixing that when the cop tried to earn his medal."

"You might have told him the truth," Roger ventured.

He expected a storm, but the Saint's answer was perfectly calm.

"I couldn't risk it, old dear. You see, I'd started off with a lie, and then I'd called him a blistered boob when I was playing the Secret Service gag—and I'd sized up my man. I reckon I'd have had one chance in a thousand of convincing him. He was as keen as knives to get his own back, and his kind of head can only hold one idea at a time. And if I had convinced him, it'd have taken hours, and we'd still have had to get through to Saxmundham, and if I'd failed—"

He left the sentence unfinished. There was no need to finish it. And Roger bit his lip.

"Even now," said Roger, "we might as well be marooned on a desert island."

Sonia Delmar spoke again.

"That ambulance," she said. "The one they brought me here in—"

It was Marius who answered, malevolently, from his corner.

"The ambulance has gone, my dear young lady. It returned to London immediately afterwards."

In a dead silence the Saint turned.

"Then I hope you'll go on enjoying your triumph, Angel Face," he said, and there was a ruthless devil in his voice. "Because I swear to you, Rayt Marius, that it's the last you will ever enjoy. Others have killed, but you have sold the bodies and souls of men. The world is poisoned with every breath you breathe . . . And I've changed my mind about giving you a fighting chance."

The Saint was resting against the door; he had not moved from it since he came in. He rested there quite slackly, quite lazily, but now his gun was in his hand, and he was carefully thumbing down the safety catch. And Roger Conway, who knew what the Saint was going to do, strove to speak casually.

"I suppose," remarked Roger Conway casually, "you could hardly run the distance in the time. You used to be pretty useful—"

The Saint shook his head.

"I'm afraid it's a bit too much," he answered. "It isn't as if I could collapse artistically at the finish . . No, old Roger, I can't do it. Unless I could grow a pair of wings—"

"Wings?"

It was Sonia Delmar who repeated the word—who almost shouted it—clutching the Saint's sleeve with hands that trembled.

But Simon Templar had already started up, and a great light was breaking in his eyes. "God's mercy!" he cried, with a passionate sincerity ringing through the strangeness of his oath. "You've said it, Sonia! And I said it . . . We'd forgotten Angel Face's aeroplane!"

CHAPTER FOURTEEN:
HOW ROGER CONWAY WAS LEFT
ALONE AND SIMON TEMPLAR
WENT TO HIS REWARD

1

The Saint's gun was back in his pocket; there was a splendid laughter in his eyes, and a more splendid laughter in his heart. And it was with the same laughter that he turned again to Marius.

"After all, Angel Face," he said, "we shall have our fight!"

And Marius did not answer.

"But not now. Saint!" Roger protested in an agony, and Simon swung round with another laugh and a flourish to go with it.

"Certainly not now, sweet Roger! That comes afterwards— with the port and cigars. What we're going to do now is jump for that blessed avian."

"But where can we land? It must be a hundred miles to Croydon in a straight line. That'll take over an hour—after we've got going—and there's sure to be trouble at the other end—"

"We don't land, my cherub. At least, not till it's all over. I tell you, I've got this job absolutely taped. I'm there!"

The Saint's cigarette went spinning across the room and burst in fiery stars against the opposite wall. And he drew Roger and the girl towards him, with a hand on each of their shoulders.

"Now see here. Roger, you'll come with me, and help me locate and start up the kite. Sonia, I want you to scrounge round and find a couple of helmets and a couple of pairs of goggles. Angel Face's outfit is bound to be around the house somewhere, and he's probably got some spares. After that, find me another nice long coil of rope—I'll bet they've got plenty—and your job's done. Lessing"—he looked across at the millionaire, who had risen to his feet at last—"it's about time you did something for your life. You find some stray bits of string, without cutting into the beautiful piece that Sonia's going to find for me, and amuse yourself splicing large and solid chairs on to Freeman, Hardy, and Willis over in the corner. Then they'll be properly settled to wait here till I come back for them. Is that all clear?"

A chorus of affirmatives answered him. "Then we'll go," said the Saint.

And he went, but he knew that all that he had ordered would be done. The new magnificent vitality that had come to him, the dazzling daredevil delight, was summed up and blazoned to them all in the gay smile with which he left them; it swept them up, inspired them, kindled within them the flame of his own superb rapture; he knew that his spirit stayed with them, to spur them on. Even Lessing . . .

And Roger . . .

And Roger said awkwardly as they turned the corner of the house and went swiftly over the dark grassland, "Sonia told me more about that cruise while you were away, Saint."

"Did she now?"

"I'm sorry I behaved like I did, old boy."

Simon chuckled.

"Did you think I'd stolen her from you, Roger?"

"Do you want to ?" Roger asked evenly.

They moved a little way in silence.

Then the Saint said, "You see, there's always Pat"

"Yes."

"I'll tell you something. I think, when she first met me, Sonia fell. I know I did—God help me—in a kind of way. I still think she's—just great. There's no other word for her. But then, there's no other word for Pat."

"No."

"More than once, it did occur to me—but what's the use? There are all kinds of people in this wall-eyed world, and especially all kinds of women. They're just made different ways, and you can't alter it. I suppose you'll call that trite! But I give you my word, Roger, I had to go on that cruise last night before I really understood the saying. And so did Sonia. But I got more out of it than she did, because it was the sequel that was so frightfully funny, and I don't think she'll ever see the joke. I don't think you will, either, and that's another reason why . . ."

"What was the joke?" Roger asked.

"When we met Hermann," said the Saint, "and Hermann pointed a gun at me, Sonia also had a gun. And Sonia didn't shoot. Pat wouldn't have missed that chance." He stopped, and raised the lantern he carried. "And that's our kite, isn't it?" he said.

A little way ahead of them loomed up the squat black shape of a small hangar. They reached it in a few more strides, and the Saint pulled back the sliding doors. And the aeroplane was there—a Gipsy Moth in silver and gold, with its wings demurely folded. "Isn't this our evening?" drawled the Saint.

Roger said cautiously, "So long as there's enough juice . . ."

"We'll see," said the Saint, and he was already peering at the gauge. His murmur of satisfaction rang hollowly between the corrugated iron walls. "Ten gallons . . . It's good enough!"

They wheeled the machine out together, and the Saint set up the wings. Then he hustled Roger into the cockpit and took hold of the propeller.

"Switch off—suck in!"

The screw went clicking round; then—

"Contact!"

"Contact!"

The engine coughed once, and then the propeller vibrated back to stillness. Again the Saint bent his back, and this time the engine stuttered round a couple of revolutions before it stopped again.

"It's going to be an easy start," said the Saint. "Half a sec. while I see if they've got any blocks."

He vanished into the hangar, and returned in a moment with a couple of large wooden wedges that trailed cords behind them. These he fixed under the wheels, laying out the cords in the line of the wings, then he went back to the propeller.

"We ought to do it this time. Suck in again!"

Half a dozen brisk winds and he was ready.

"Contact!"

"Contact!"

A heaving jerk at the screw . . . The engine gasped, stammered, hesitated, picked up with a loud roar . . .

"Hot dog!" said the Saint.

He sprinted round the wing and leapt to the side, with one foot in the stirrup and a long arm reaching over to the throttle.

"Stick well back, Roger . . . That's the ticket!"

The snarl of the engine swelled furiously; a gale of wind buffeted the Saint's face, and twitched his coat half away from his shoulders. For a while he hung on, holding the throttle open, while the bellow of the engine battered his ears, and the machine strained and shivered where it stood; then he throttled back, and put his lips to Roger's ear.

"Hold on, son. I'll send Sonia out to you. Switch off the engine if she tries to run away."

Roger nodded, and the Saint sprang down and disappeared. In a few moments he was back at the house, with the mutter of the engine scattered through the dark behind him, and Sonia Delmar was waiting for him on the door-step.

"I've got all the things you wanted," she said. Simon glanced once at her burdens.

"That's splendid." He touched her hand. "Roger's out there, old dear. Would you like to take those effects out to him?"

"Sure."

"Right. Follow the noise, and don't run into the prop. Where's Ike?"

"He's nearly finished."

"OK. I'll bring him along."

With a smile he left her, and went on into the library. Lessing was just rising from his knees; a glance showed Simon that Marius, the Boche, and the Bowery Boy had been dealt with as per invoice.

"All clear, Ike?" murmured the Saint, and Lessing nodded.

"I don't think they'll get away, though I'm not an expert at this game."

"It looks good to me—for an amateur. Now, will you filter out into the hall? I'll be with you in one moment."

The millionaire went out submissively, and Simon turned to Marius for the last time. Through the open window came a steady distant drone, and Marius must have heard and understood it, but his face was utterly inscrutable.

"So," said the Saint softly, "I have beaten you again, Angel Face."

The giant looked at him with empty eyes.

"I am never beaten, Templar," he said.

"But you are beaten this time," said the Saint. Tomorrow morning I shall come back, and we shall settle our account. And, in case I fail, I shall bring the police with me. They will be very interested to hear

273

all the things I shall have to tell them. The private plotting of wars for gain may not be punishable by any laws, but men are hanged for high treason. Even now, I'm not sure that I wouldn't rather have you hanged. There's something very definite and unromantic about hanging. But I'll decide that before I return . . . I leave you to meditate on your victory."

And Simon Templar turned on his heel and went out, closing and locking the door behind him.

Sir Isaac Lessing stood in the hall. He was still deathly pale, but there was a strange kind of courage in the set of his lips, and the levelling of the eyes with which he faced the Saint—the strangest of all kinds of courage.

"I believe I owe you my life, Mr Templar," he said steadily, but the Saint's nod was curt.

"You're welcome."

"I'm not used to these things," Lessing said, "and I find I'm not fitted for them. I suppose you can't help despising me. I can only say that I agree with you. And I should like to apologize."

For a long moment the Saint looked at him, but Lessing met the clear blue gaze without flinching. And then Simon gripped the millionaire's arm.

"The others are waiting for us," he said. "I'll talk to you as we go."

They passed out of the door, and the Saint, glancing back, saw a man huddled in one corner of the hall, very still. By the lodge gates, a little while before, he had seen another man, just as still. And, later, he told Roger Conway that those two men were dead. "You want to be careful how you bash folks with the blunt end of a gat," said the Saint. "It's so dreadfully easy to stave in their skulls." But he never told Roger what he said to Sir Isaac Lessing in the small hours of that morning as they walked across the landing field under the stars.

2

"And so we leave you," said the Saint.

He had been busy for a short time performing some obscure operation with the rope that Sonia Delmar had brought, but now he came round the aeroplane into the light of the lantern, buckling the strap of his helmet. Lessing waited a little way apart, but Simon called him, and he came up and joined the group.

"We'll meet you in London," said the Saint. "As soon as we're off you'd better take Sonia down to the station and wait there for the first train. I don't think you'll have any trouble, but if you do it shouldn't be difficult to deal with it. There's nothing you can be held for. But for God's sake don't say anything about Angel Face or this house—I'd as soon trust that village cop to look after Angel Face as I'd leave my favourite white mouse under the charge of a hungry cat. When you get to town I expect you'll want some sleep, but you'll find us in Upper Berkeley Mews this evening. Sonia knows the place."

Lessing nodded.

"Good luck," he said, and held out his hand. Simon crushed it in a clasp of steel.

He moved away, held up his handkerchief for a moment to check the wind, and went to clear the chocks from under the wheels. Then he climbed into the front cockpit and plugged his telephones into the rubber connection. His voice boomed through the speaking tube.

"All set, Roger?"

"All set."

The Saint looked back.

He saw Roger catch the girl's hand to his lips and then she tore herself away. And with that last glimpse of her, the Saint settled his goggles over his eyes and pushed the stick forwards, and the tumult of the engine rose to a howl as he threw open the throttle and they began to jolt forwards over the grass.

Not quite so damned easy, taking off on a dark night, with the Lord knew what at the end of the run . . . But he kept the tail up grimly until he had got his full flying speed, and then eased the stick back as quickly as he dared . . . The bumping lessened, ceased altogether; they rushed smoothly through the air . . . Looking over the side, he saw a black feather of tree-top slip by six feet below, and grinned his relief. Turning steeply to the west, he saw a tiny speck of light in the darkness beyond his wing-tip. The lantern . . . And then the machine came level again, and went racing through the night in a gentle climb.

The stinging swiftness of the upper air was new life to him. A little while ago he had been weary to death, though no one had known, but now he felt shoutingly fit for the adventure of his life. It might have been because of the fresh hope he had found when there had seemed to be no hope . . . For he had his chance, and, if human daring and skill and sinew counted for anything, he would not fail. And so the work would be done, and life would go on, and there would be other things to see and new songs to sing. Battle, murder, and sudden death, he had had them all—full measure, pressed down, running over.

And he had loved them for their own sake . . . And his follies he had had, temptations, nonsense, fool's paradise and fool's hell, and those also had gone over. And now a vow had been fulfilled, and much good done, and a great task was near its end, but there must be other things.

> *"For the song and the sword and the pipes of Pan*
> *Are birthrights sold to a usurer,*
> *But I am the last lone highwayman,*
> *And I am the last adventurer."*

Not even all that he had done was a destiny: there must always be other things. So long as the earth turned for the marching seasons, and the stars hung in the sky, for so long there would be other things. There was neither climax nor anti-climax: a full life had no place for such trivial theatricalities. A full life was made up of all that life had to offer; it was complete, taking everything without fear and giving everything without favour, and wherever it ended it would always be whole. So it would go on. To fight and kill one day, to rescue the next; to be rich one day, and to be a beggar the next; to sin one day, and to do something heroic the next —so might a man's sins be forgiven. And there was so much that he had not done. He hadn't walked in the gardens of Monte Carlo, immaculate in evening dress, and he hadn't tramped from one end of Europe to the other in the oldest clothes he could find. He hadn't been a beach-comber on a South Sea island, or built a house with his own hands, or read the lessons in a church, or been to Timbuktu, or been married, or cheated at cards, or learned to talk Chinese, or shot a sitting rabbit, or driven a Ford, or . . . Hell! Was there ever an end? And everything that a man could do must enrich him in some way, and for everything that he did not do his life must be forever poorer . . .

So, as the aeroplane fled westwards across the sky, and the sky behind it began to pale with the promise of dawn, the Saint found a strange peace of heart, and he laughed . . .

His course was set unerringly. In the old days there had been hardly an inch of England over which he had not flown, and he had no need of maps. As the silver in the sky spread wanly up the heavens, the country beneath him was slowly lighted for his eyes, and he began to school Roger in a difficult task.

"You have handled the controls before, haven't you, old dear?" he remarked coolly, and an unenthusiastic reply came back to him.

"Only for a little while."

"Then you've got about half an hour to learn to handle them as if you'd been born in the air!"

Roger Conway said things—naughty and irrelevant things, which do not belong here. And the Saint smiled.

"Come on," he said. "Let's see you do a gentle turn."

After a pause, the machine heeled over drunkenly . . .

"Verminous," said the Saint scathingly. "You're too rough on that rudder. Try to imagine that you're not riding a bicycle. And don't use the stick as if you were stirring porridge . . . Now we'll do one together." They did. "And now one to the left . . ."

For ten minutes the instruction went on.

"I guess you ought to be fairly safe on that," said the Saint at the end of that time. "Keep the turns gentle, and you won't hurt yourself. I'm sorry I haven't time to tell you all about spins, so if you get into one I'm afraid you'll just have to die. Now we'll take the glide."

They took the glide.

Then Roger was saying, unhappily, "What's the idea of all this, Saint?"

"Sorry," said the Saint, "but I'm afraid you'll be in sole charge before long. I'm going to be busy."

He explained why, and Roger's gasp of horror came clearly through the telephones. "But how the hell am I going to get down, Saint?"

"Crash in the Thames," answered Simon succinctly. "Glide down to a nice quiet spot, just as you've been taught, undo your safety belt, flatten out gently when you're near the water, and pray. It's not our aeroplane, anyway."

"It's my life," said Roger gloomily.

"You won't hurt yourself, sonny boy. Now, wake up and try your hand at this contour chasing . . ."

And the nose of the machine went down, with a sudden scream of wires. The ground, luminous now with the cold pallor of the sky before sunrise, heaved up deliriously to meet them. Roger's head sang with a rush of wind, and he seemed to have left his stomach about a thousand feet behind . . . Then the stick stroked back between his legs, his stomach flopped nauseatingly down towards his seat, and he felt slightly sick . . .

"Is it always as bad as that?" he inquired faintly.

"Not if you don't come down so fast," said the Saint cheerfully. "That was just to save time . . . Now, you simply must get used to this low flying. It's only a matter of keeping your head and going light on the controls." The aeroplane shot between two trees, with approximately six inches to spare beyond either wing, and a flock of sheep stampeded under their wheels. "You're flying her, Roger! Let's skim this next hedge . . . No, you're too high. I said skim, not skyrocket." The stick went forwards a trifle. "That's better . . . Now miss this fence by about two feet . . . No, that was nearer ten feet. Try to do better at the next, but don't go to the other extreme, and take the undercarriage off . . . That's more like it! You were only about four feet up that time. If you can get that distance fixed in your eye, you'll be absolutely all right. Now do the same thing again . . . Good! Now up a bit for these trees. Try to miss them by the same distance—it'll be good practice for you . . ."

And Roger tried. He tried as he had never before tried anything in his life, for he knew how much depended on him. And the Saint urged him on, speaking all the time in the same tone of quiet encouragement, grimly trying to crowd a month's instruction into a few minutes. And somehow he achieved results. Roger was getting the idea; he was getting that most essential thing, the feel of the machine, and he had started off with the greatest of all blessings—a cool head and an instinctive judgement. It was much later when he found a patch of grey hair on each of his temples . . .

And so for the rest of that flight, they worked on together, with the Saint glancing from time to time at his watch, yet never varying the patient steadiness of his voice.

And then the time came when the Saint said that the instruction must be over, hit or miss, and he took over the controls again. They soared up in a swift climb, and, as the fields fell away beneath them, a shaft of light from the shy rim of the sun caught them like a fantastic spotlight, and the aeroplane was turned to a hurtling jewel of silver and gold in the translucent gulf of the sky.

3

"Down there, on your right!" cried the Saint, and Roger looked over where the Saint's arm pointed.

He saw the fields laid out underneath them like a huge unrolled map. The trees and little houses were like the toys that children play with, building their villages on a nursery floor. And over that grotesque vision of a puny world seen as an idle god might see it, a criss-cross of roads and lanes sprawled like a sparse muddle of strings, and a railway line was like a knife-cut across the icing of a cake, and down the railway line puffed the tiniest of toy trains.

The aeroplane swung over in a steep bank, and the map seemed to slide up the sky until it stood like a wall at their wing-tip, and the Saint spoke again.

"Hermann's about twenty miles away, but that doesn't give us much time at seventy miles an hour. So you've got to get it over quickly, Roger. If you can do your stuff as you were doing it just now, there's simply nothing can go wrong. Don't get excited, and just be a wee bit careful not to stall when my weight comes off. I'm not quite sure what the effect will be."

"And suppose—suppose you don't bring it off?" They were flying to meet the toy train now.

"If I miss, Roger, the only thing I can ask you to do is to try to land farther up the line. You'll crash, of course, but if you turn your petrol off first you may live to tell the tale. But whether you try it or not is up to you."

"I'll try it, Saint, if I have to."

"Good scout." They had passed over the train, and then again they turned steeply, and went in pursuit.

And the Saint's calm voice came to Roger's ears with a hint of reckless laughter somewhere in its calm.

"You've got her, old Roger. I'm just going to get out. So long, old dear, and the best of luck."

"Good luck, Simon."

And Roger Conway took over the controls.

And then he saw the thing that he will never forget. He saw the Saint climb out of the cockpit in front of him, and saw him stagger on the wing as the wind caught him and all but tore him from his precarious hold. And then the Saint had hold of a strut with one hand, and the rope that he had fixed with the other, and he was backing towards the leading edge of the wing. Roger saw him smile, the old incomparable Saintly smile . . . And then the Saint was on his knees; then his legs had disappeared from view; then there was only his head and shoulders and two hands . . . one hand . . . And the Saint was gone.

Roger put the stick gently forwards.

He looked back over the side as he did so, in a kind of sick terror that he would see a foolish-spread-eagled shape dwindling down into the unrolled map four thousand feet below, but he saw nothing. And then he had eyes only for the train.

Hit or miss . . .

And Simon Templar also watched the train.

He dangled at the end of his rope, like a spider on a thread, ten feet below the silver and gold fuselage. One foot rested in a loop that he had knotted for himself before they started; his hands were locked upon the rope itself. And the train was coming nearer.

The wind lashed him with invisible whips, billowing his coat, fighting him with savage flailing fingers. It was an effort to breathe; to hold on at all was a battle. And he was supposed to be resting there. He had deliberately taught Roger to fly low, much lower than was necessary, because that extreme was far safer than the possibility of being trailed along twenty feet above the carriage roofs. When the time came he would slip down the rope, hang by his arms, and let go as soon as he had the chance.

And that time was not far distant. Roger was diving rather steeply, with his engine full on . . . But the train was also moving . . . At two hundred feet the Saint guessed that they were overtaking the train at about twenty miles an hour. He ought to have told Roger about that . . . But then Roger must have seen the mistake also, for he throttled the engine down a trifle, and they lost speed. And they were drifting lower . . .

With a brief prayer, the Saint twitched his foot out of the stirrup and went down the rope hand over hand.

"Glory!" thought the Saint. "If the fool stalls—if he tries to cut his speed down by bringing the stick back—"

But they weren't stalling. They were keeping their height for a moment; then they dipped straightly, gaining on the train at about fifteen miles an hour . . . no, ten . . . And the hindmost carriage slipped under the Saint's feet—a dozen feet under them.

There were only three coaches on the train.

But they were dropping quickly now—Roger was contour-chasing like an ace! He wasn't dead centre, though . . . A shade to one side . . . "Just a touch of left rudder!" cried the Saint helplessly, for one of his feet had scraped the outside edge of a carriage roof, and they were still going lower . . . And then, somehow, it happened just as if Roger could have heard him: the Saint was clear over the roof of the leading coach, and his knees and arms were bent to keep his feet off it . . .

And he let go.

The train seemed to tear away from under him; his left hand crashed into a projection, and went numb, and the roof became red-hot and scorched his legs. He felt himself slithering towards the side, and flung out his sound right hand blindly . . . He caught something like a handle . . . held on . . . and the slipping stopped with a jar that sent a twinge of agony stabbing through his shoulder.

He lay there gasping, dumbly bewildered that he should still be alive. For a full minute . . .

And then the meaning of it filtered into his understanding, and he laughed softly, absurdly, a laughter queerly close to tears.

For the work was done.

Slowly, in a breathless wonder, he turned his head. The aeroplane was turning, coming back towards him, alongside the train, low down. And a face looked out, helmeted, with its big round goggles masking all expression and giving it the appearance of some macabre gargoyle, but all that could be seen of the face was as white as the morning sky.

Simon waved his injured hand, and, as the aeroplane swept by in a droning thunder of noise, the snowy flutter of a handkerchief broke out against its silver and gold. And so the aeroplane passed, rising slowly as it went towards the north, with the sunrise striking it like a banner unfurled.

And five minutes later, in a strange and monstrous contrast to the flamboyant plumage of the great metal bird that was swinging smoothly round into the dawn, a strained and tatterdemalion figure came reeling over the tender of the swaying locomotive, and the two men in the cab, who had been watching him from the beginning, were there to catch him as he fell into their arms.

"You come outta that airypline?" blurted one of them dazedly, and Simon Templar nodded.

He put up a filthy hand and smeared the blood out of his eyes.

"I came to tell you to stop the train," he said. "There are two bombs on the line."

4

The Saint rested where they had laid him down. He had never known what it was to be so utterly weary. All his strength seemed to have ebbed out of him, now that it had served for the supreme effort. He felt that he had not slept for a thousand years . . .

All round him there was noise. He heard the hoarse roar of escaping steam, the whine of brakes, the fading clatter of movement, the jolt and hiss of the stop. In the sudden silence he heard the far, steady drone of the aeroplane filling the sky. Then there were voices, running feet, questions and answers mingling in an indecipherable murmur. Someone shook him by the shoulder, but at that moment he felt too tired to rouse, and the man moved away.

And then, presently, he was shaken again, more insistently. A cool wet cloth wiped his face, and he heard a startled exclamation. The aeroplane seemed to have gone, though he had not heard its humming die away: he must have passed out altogether for a few seconds. Then a glass was pressed to his lips; he gulped and spluttered as the neat spirit rawed his throat. And he opened his eyes.

"I'm all right," he muttered.

All he saw at first was a pair of boots. Large boots. And his lips twisted with a rueful humour. Then he looked up and saw the square face and the bowler hat of the man whose arm was around his shoulders.

"Bombs, old dear," said the Saint. "They've got the niftiest little electric firing device attached—you lay it over the line, and it blows up the balloon when the front wheels of the train go over it. That's my dying speech. Now it's your turn."

The man in the bowler hat nodded.

"We've already found them. You only stopped us with about a hundred yards to spare." He was looking at the Saint with a kind of wry regret. "And I know you," he said.

Simon smiled crookedly.

"What a thing is fame!" he sighed. "I know you, too, Detective-Inspector Carn. How's trade? I shall come quietly this time, anyway—I couldn't run a yard."

The detective's lips twitched a trifle grimly. He glanced over his shoulder. "I think the King is waiting to speak to you," he said.

CHAPTER FIFTEEN:

HOW SIMON TEMPLAR
PUT DOWN A BOOK

1

It was late in a fair September afternoon when Roger Conway turned into Upper Berkeley Mews and admitted himself with his own key.

He found the Saint sitting in an armchair by the open window with a book on his knee, and was somehow surprised.

"What are you doing here?" he demanded, and Simon rose with a smile.

"I have slept," he murmured. "And so have you, from all accounts."

Roger spun his peaked cap across the room.

"I have," he said. "I believe the order for my release came through about lunch-time, but they thought it would be a shame to wake me."

The Saint inspected him critically. Roger's livery covered him uncomfortably. It looked as if it had shrunk. It had shrunk.

"Jolly looking clothes, those are," Simon remarked. "Is it the new fashion? I'd be afraid of catching cold in the elbows, you know. Besides, the pants don't look safe to sit down in."

Roger returned the survey insultingly.

"How much are you expecting to get on that face in part exchange?" he inquired, and suddenly the Saint laughed.

"Well, you knock-kneed bit of moth-eaten gorgonzola!"

"Well, you cross-eyed son of a flea-bitten hobo!"

And all at once their hands met in an iron grasp.

"Still," said the Saint presently, "you don't look your best in that outfit, and I guess you'll feel better when you've had a shave. Some kind soul gave me a ring to say you were on your way, and I've turned the bath on for you and laid out your other suit. Push on, old bacillus, and I'll sing to you when you come back."

"I shall not come back for years," said Roger delicately.

The Saint grinned.

He sat down again as Roger departed and took up his book again, and traced a complicated arabesque in the corner of a page thoughtfully. Then he wrote a few more lines, and put away his fountain pen. He lighted a cigarette, and gazed at a picture on the other side of the room: he was still there when Roger returned.

And Roger said what he had meant to say before.

"I was thinking," Roger said, "you'd have gone after Angel Face."

Simon turned the pages of his book.

"And so was I," he said. "But the reason why I haven't is recorded here. This is the tome in which I dutifully make notes of our efforts for the benefit of an author bloke I know, who has sworn to make a blood-and-thunder classic out of us one day. This entry is very tabloid."

"What is it?"

"It just says—'Hermann.'"

And the Saint, looking up, saw Roger's face, and laughed softly.

"In the general excitement," he said gently, "we forgot dear Hermann. And Hermann was ordered to go straight back as soon as he'd parked his bombs. I expect he has. Anyway, I haven't heard that he's been caught. There's still a chance, of course . . . Roger, you may wonder what's happened to me, but I rang up our old friend Chief Inspector Teal and told him all about Saltham, and he went off as fast as a police car could take him. It remains to be seen whether he arrived in time . . . The Crown Prince left England last night, but they've collected Heinrich. I'm afraid Ike will have to get a new staff of servants, though. His old ones are dead beyond repair . . . I think that's all the dope."

"It doesn't seem to worry you," said Roger.

"Why should it?" said the Saint a little tiredly. "We've done our job. Angel Face is smashed, whatever happens. He'll never be a danger to the world again. And if he's caught he'll be hanged, which will do him a lot of good. On the other hand, if he gets away, and we're destined to have another round—that is as the Lord may provide."

"And Norman?"

The Saint smiled, a quiet little smile.

"There was a letter from Pat this morning," he said. "Posted at Suez. They're going on down the East Coast of Africa, and they expect to get round to Madeira in the spring. And I'm going to do something that I think Norman would have wanted far more than vengeance. I'm going adventuring across Europe, and at the end of it I shall find my lady."

Roger moved away, and glanced at the telephone. "Have you heard from Sonia?" he asked.

"She called up," said the Saint. "I told her to come right round and bring papa. They should be here any minute now."

Conway picked up the *Bystander* and put it down again.

He said, "Did you mean everything you said last night—this morning?"

Simon stared out of the window.

"Every word," he said.

He said, "You see, old Roger, some queer things happen in this life of ours. You cut adrift from all ordinary rules, and then, sometimes, when you'd sell your soul for a rule, you're all at sea. And when that happens to a man he's surely damned, bar the grace of Heaven, because I only know one thing worse than swallowing every commandment that other people lay down for you, and that's having no commandments but those you lay down for yourself. None of which abstruse philosophy you will understand . . . But I'll tell you, Roger, by way of a fact, that everything life gives you has to be paid for; also that where your life leads you, there will your heart be also. Selah. Autographed copies of that speech, on vellum, may be obtained on the instalment plan at all public houses and speakeasies—one pound down, and the rest up a gum-tree . . ."

A car drove down the mews and stopped by the door. But Roger Conway was still looking at the Saint, and Roger was understanding, with a strange wild certainty, that perhaps after all he had never known the Saint, and perhaps he would never know him.

The Saint closed his book. He laid it down on the table beside him, and turned to meet Roger's eyes.

"'For all the Saints who from their labours rest,'" he said. "Sonia has arrived, my Roger."

And he stood up, with the swift careless laugh that Roger knew, and his hand fell on Roger's shoulder, and so they went out together into the sunlight.

PUBLICATION
HISTORY

The Avenging Saint was the fourth Saint book to be published and the second, after *Meet—the Tiger!*, to be written as an original novel rather than being based on short stories already seen in the paper *The Thriller*. It was first published by Hodder & Stoughton in October 1930 with an American hardback appearing a year later from the Doubleday Crime Club. By 1941 Hodder was on a sixteenth impression, suggesting either that they were quite poor at forecasting sales figures or that the Saint books were selling substantially beyond their expectations. Since publishers who can't predict sales tend not to stay in business for too long, we'd have to suggest it's the latter.

Charteris dedicated the book to his agent at the time, Raymond Savage. Savage was his first literary agent, and their association dated back to Charteris's contract with Ward Lock, when Charteris was no doubt happy to be sharing an agent with T.E. Lawrence (of Arabia fame). However, within a year or so of the publication of *The Avenging Saint*, Charteris would move on to AP Watt & Son. The precise reasons for this remain hidden in the mists of time, though there was talk later about Savage's loyalty and honesty towards his young client. Savage passed away in 1964.

Opening the book with your hero singing Gilbert and Sullivan's *The Yeomen of the Guard* is an interesting technique and not something you'd associate with other more modern heroes. But then the Saint and Leslie Charteris were never one for convention, and the song seems a suitable fit alongside their poetic talents.

As with the previous Saint adventures, foreign editions soon appeared: Kulturelle Verlagsgesellschaft christened the book *Braut Wider Willen* (the literal translation of which is the rather splendid "Bride Aversion") and published the first German version in 1934, while a Hungarian translation, *A szoke bosszu*, appeared in 1935. Norwegians had to wait until 1939 to read *St. Simon spiller höit spill* (which translates literally as "St Simon Playing Loud Games") when it was published by Gylendal Norsk Forlag; their Finnish cousins had to wait until 1970 to read *Pyhimys pitaa sanansa*. A Swedish edition, *Helgonet hejdar världskrig*, was published by Skoglunds in 1936 and reprinted several times over the years. A Swedish audio book, read by Leif Liljeroth, was released in 2003. The most recent reprint was the July 1989 American paperback published by International Polygonics.

This novel is one of the few Saint stories that has never been adapted for any other medium.

ABOUT THE AUTHOR

*I'm mad enough to believe in romance. And I'm sick and
tired of this age—tired of the miserable little mildewed
things that people racked their brains about, and wrote
books about, and called life. I wanted something more
elementary and honest—battle, murder, sudden death, with
plenty of good beer and damsels in distress, and a complete
callousness about blipping the ungodly over the beezer. It
mayn't be life as we know it, but it ought to be.*

—*Leslie Charteris in a 1935 BBC radio interview*

Leslie Charteris was born Leslie Charles Bowyer-Yin in Singapore on
12 May 1907.

He was the son of a Chinese doctor and his English wife, who'd
met in London a few years earlier. Young Leslie found friends hard to
come by in colonial Singapore. The English children had been told not
to play with Eurasians, and the Chinese children had been told not to
play with Europeans. Leslie was caught in between and took refuge in
reading.

"I read a great many good books and enjoyed them because
nobody had told me that they were classics. I also read a great many
bad books which nobody told me not to read . . . I read a great many

popular scientific articles and acquired from them an astonishing amount of general knowledge before I discovered that this acquisition was supposed to be a chore."[1]

One of his favourite things to read was a magazine called *Chums*. "The Best and Brightest Paper for Boys" (if you believe the adverts) was a monthly paper full of swashbuckling adventure stories aimed at boys, encouraging them to be honourable and moral and perhaps even "upright citizens with furled umbrellas."[2] Undoubtedly these types of stories would influence his later work.

When his parents split up shortly after the end of World War I, Charteris accompanied his mother and brother back to England, where he was sent to Rossall School in Fleetwood, Lancashire. Rossall was then a very stereotypical English public school, and it struggled to cope with this multilingual mixed-race boy just into his teens who'd already seen more of the world than many of his peers would see in their lifetimes. He was an outsider.

He left Rossall in 1924. Keen to pursue a creative career, he decided to study art in Paris—after all, that was where the great artists went—but soon found that the life of a literally starving artist didn't appeal. He continued writing, firing off speculative stories to magazines, and it was the sale of a short story to *Windsor Magazine* that saved him from penury.

He returned to London in 1925, as his parents—particularly his father—wanted him to become a lawyer, and he was sent to study law at Cambridge University. In the mid-1920s, Cambridge was full of Bright Young Things—aristocrats and bohemians somewhat typified in the Evelyn Waugh novel *Vile Bodies*—and again the mixed-race Bowyer-Yin found that he didn't fit in. He was an outsider who preferred to make his own way in the world and wasn't one of the privileged upper class. It didn't help that he found his studies boring and decided it was more fun contemplating ways to circumvent the law. This inspired him to write a novel, and when publishers Ward Lock & Co. offered him a three-book deal on the strength of it, he abandoned his studies to pursue a writing career.

When his father learnt of this, he was not impressed, as he considered writers to be "rogues and vagabonds." Charteris would later recall that "I wanted to be a writer, he wanted me to become a lawyer. I was stubborn, he said I would end up in the gutter. So I left home. Later on, when I had a little success, we were reconciled by letter, but I never saw him again."[3]

X Esquire, his first novel, appeared in April 1927. The lead character, X Esquire, is a mysterious hero, hunting down and killing the businessmen trying to wipe out Britain by distributing quantities of free poisoned cigarettes. His second novel, *The White Rider*, was published the following spring, and in one memorable scene shows the hero chasing after his damsel in distress, only for him to overtake the villains, leap into their car . . . and promptly faint.

These two plot highlights may go some way to explaining Charteris's comment on *Meet—the Tiger!*, published in September 1928, that "it was only the third book I'd written, and the best, I would say, for it was that the first two were even worse."[4]

Twenty-one-year-old authors are naturally self-critical. Despite reasonably good reviews, the Saint didn't set the world on fire, and Charteris moved on to a new hero for his next book. This was *The Bandit*, an adventure story featuring Ramon Francisco De Castilla y Espronceda Manrique, published in the summer of 1929 after its serialisation in the *Empire News*, a now long-forgotten Sunday newspaper. But sales of *The Bandit* were less than impressive, and Charteris began to question his choice of career. It was all very well writing—but if nobody wants to read what you write, what's the point?

"I had to succeed, because before me loomed the only alternative, the dreadful penalty of failure . . . the routine office hours, the five-day week . . . the lethal assimilation into the ranks of honest, hard-working, conformist, God-fearing pillars of the community."⁵

However his fortunes—and the Saint's—were about to change. In late 1928, Leslie had met Monty Haydon, a London-based editor who was looking for writers to pen stories for his new paper, *The Thriller*— "The Paper with a Thousand Thrills." Charteris later recalled that "he said he was starting a new magazine, had read one of my books and would like some stories from me. I couldn't have been more grateful, both from the point of view of vanity and finance!"⁶

The paper launched in early 1929, and Leslie's first work, "The Story of a Dead Man," featuring Jimmy Traill, appeared in issue 4 (published on 2 March 1929). That was followed just over a month later with "The Secret of Beacon Inn," starring Rameses "Pip" Smith. At the same time, Leslie finished writing another non-Saint novel, *Daredevil*, which would be published in late 1929. Storm Arden was the hero; more notably, the book saw the first introduction of a Scotland Yard inspector by the name of Claud Eustace Teal.

The Saint returned in the thirteenth issue of *The Thriller*. The byline proclaimed that the tale was "A Thrilling Complete Story of the Underworld"; the title was "The Five Kings," and it actually featured Four Kings and a Joker. Simon Templar, of course, was the Joker.

Charteris spent the rest of 1929 telling the adventures of the Five Kings in five subsequent *The Thriller* stories. "It was very hard work, for the pay was lousy, but Monty Haydon was a brilliant and stimulating editor, full of ideas. While he didn't actually help shape the Saint as a character, he did suggest story lines. He would take me out to lunch and say, 'What are you going to write about next?' I'd often say I was damned if I knew. And Monty would say, 'Well, I was reading something the other day . . .' He had a fund of ideas and we would talk them over, and then I would go away and write a story. He was a great creative editor."⁷

Charteris would have one more attempt at writing about a hero other than Simon Templar, in three novelettes published in *The Thriller* in early 1930, but he swiftly returned to the Saint. This was partly due to his self-confessed laziness—he wanted to write more stories for *The Thriller* and other magazines, and creating a new hero for every story was hard work—but mainly due to feedback from Monty Haydon. It seemed people wanted to read more adventures of the Saint . . .

Charteris would contribute over forty stories to *The Thriller* throughout the 1930s. Shortly after their debut, he persuaded publisher Hodder & Stoughton that if he collected some of these stories and rewrote them a little, they could publish them as a Saint book. *Enter the Saint* was first published in August 1930, and the reaction was good enough for the publishers to bring out another collection. And another . . .

Of the twenty Saint books published in the 1930s, almost all have their origins in those magazine stories.

Why was the Saint so popular throughout the decade? Aside from the charm and ability of Charteris's storytelling, the stories, particularly those published in the first half of the '30s, are full of energy and joie de vivre. With economic depression rampant throughout the period, the public at large seemed to want some escapism.

And Simon Templar's appeal was wide-ranging: he wasn't an upper-class hero like so many of the period. With no obvious background and no attachment to the Old School Tie, no friends in high places who could provide a get-out-of-jail-free card, the Saint was uniquely classless. Not unlike his creator.

Throughout Leslie's formative years, his heritage had been an issue. In his early days in Singapore, during his time at school, at Cambridge University or even just in everyday life, he couldn't avoid the fact that for many people his mixed parentage was a problem. He would later tell a story of how he was chased up the road by a stick-waving typical

English gent who took offence to his daughter being escorted around town by a foreigner.

Like the Saint, he was an outsider. And although he had spent a significant portion of his formative years in England, he couldn't settle.

As a young boy he had read of an America "peopled largely by Indians, and characters in fringed buckskin jackets who fought nobly against them. I spent a great deal of time day-dreaming about a visit to this prodigious and exciting country."[8]

It was time to realise this wish. Charteris and his first wife, Pauline, whom he'd met in London when they were both teenagers and married in 1931, set sail for the States in late 1932; the Saint had already made his debut in America courtesy of the publisher Doubleday. Charteris and his wife found a New York still experiencing the tail end of Prohibition, and times were tough at first. Despite sales to *The American Magazine* and others, it wasn't until a chance meeting with writer turned Hollywood executive Bartlett McCormack in their favourite speakeasy that Charteris's career stepped up a gear.

Soon Charteris was in Hollywood, working on what would become the 1933 movie *Midnight Club*. However, Hollywood's treatment of writers wasn't to Charteris's taste, and he began to yearn for home. Within a few months, he returned to the UK and began writing more Saint stories for Monty Haydon and Bill McElroy.

He also rewrote a story he'd sketched out whilst in the States, a version of which had been published in *The American Magazine* in September 1934. This new novel, *The Saint in New York*, published in 1935, was a significant advance for the Saint and Leslie Charteris. Gone were the high jinks and the badinage. The youthful exuberance evident in the Saint's early adventures had evolved into something a little darker, a little more hard-boiled. It was the next stage in development for the author and his creation, and readers loved it. It became a bestseller on both sides of the Atlantic.

Having spent his formative years in places as far apart as Singapore and England, with substantial travel in between, it should be no surprise that Leslie had a serious case of wanderlust. With a bestseller under his belt, he now had the means to see more of the world.

Nineteen thirty-six found him in Tenerife, researching another Saint adventure alongside translating the biography of Juan Belmonte, a well-known Spanish matador. Estranged for several months, Leslie and Pauline divorced in 1937. The following year, Leslie married an American, Barbara Meyer, who'd accompanied him to Tenerife. In early 1938, Charteris and his new bride set off in a trailer of his own design and spent eighteen months travelling round America and Canada.

The Saint in New York had reminded Hollywood of Charteris's talents, and film rights to the novel were sold prior to publication in 1935. Although the proposed 1935 film production was rejected by the Hays Office for its violent content, RKO's eventual 1938 production persuaded Charteris to try his luck once more in Hollywood.

New opportunities had opened up, and throughout the 1940s the Saint appeared not only in books and movies but in a newspaper strip, a comic-book series, and on radio.

Anyone wishing to adapt the character in any medium found a stern taskmaster in Charteris. He was never completely satisfied, nor was he shy of showing his displeasure. He did, however, ensure that copyright in any Saint adventure belonged to him, even if scripted by another writer—a contractual obligation that he was to insist on throughout his career.

Charteris was soon spread thin, overseeing movies, comics, newspapers, and radio versions of his creation, and this, along with his self-proclaimed laziness, meant that Saint books were becoming fewer and further between. However, he still enjoyed his creation: in 1941 he indulged himself in a spot of fun by playing the Saint—complete with monocle and moustache—in a photo story in *Life* magazine.

In July 1944, he started collaborating under a pseudonym on Sherlock Holmes radio scripts, subsequently writing more adventures for Holmes than Conan Doyle. Not all his ventures were successful—a screenplay he was hired to write for Deanna Durbin, "Lady on a Train," took him a year and ultimately bore little resemblance to the finished film. In the mid-1940s, Charteris successfully sued RKO Pictures for unfair competition after they launched a new series of films starring George Sanders as a debonair crime fighter known as the Falcon. But he kept faith with his original character, and the Saint novels continued to adapt to the times. The transatlantic Saint evolved into something of a private operator, working for the mysterious Hamilton and becoming, not unlike his creator, a world traveller, finding that adventure would seek him out.

"I have never been able to see why a fictional character should not grow up, mature, and develop, the same as anyone else. The same, if you like, as his biographer. The only adequate reason is that—so far as I know—no other fictional character in modern times has survived a sufficient number of years for these changes to be clearly observable. I must confess that a lot of my own selfish pleasure in the Saint has been in watching him grow up."[9]

Charteris maintained his love of travel and was soon to be found sailing round the West Indies with his good friend Gregory Peck. His forays abroad gave him even more material, and he began to write true-crime articles, as well as an occasional column in *Gourmet* magazine.

By the early '50s, Charteris himself was feeling strained. He'd divorced his second wife in 1943 and got together with a New York radio and nightclub singer called Betty Bryant Borst, whom he married in late 1943. That relationship had fallen apart acrimoniously towards the end of the decade, and he roamed the globe restlessly, rarely in one place for longer than a couple of months. He continued to maintain a firm grip on the exploitation of the Saint in various media but was writing little himself. The Saint had become an industry, and Charteris couldn't keep up. He began thinking seriously about an early retirement.

Then in 1951 he met a young actress called Audrey Long when they became next-door neighbours in Hollywood. Within a year they had married, a union that was to last the rest of Leslie's life.

He attacked life with a new vitality. They travelled—Nassau was a favoured escape spot—and he wrote. He struck an agreement with *The New York Herald Tribune* for a Saint comic strip, which would appear daily and be written by Charteris himself. The strip ran for thirteen years, with Charteris sending in his handwritten story lines from wherever he happened to be, relying on mail services around the world to continue the Saint's adventures. New Saint books began to appear, and Charteris reached a height of productivity not seen since his days as a struggling author trying to establish himself. As Leslie and Audrey travelled, so did the Saint, visiting locations just after his creator had been there.

By 1953 the Saint had already enjoyed twenty-five years of success, and *The Saint Detective Magazine* was launched. Charteris had become adept at exploiting his creation to the full, mixing new stories with repackaged older stories, sometimes rewritten, sometimes mixed up in "new" anthologies, sometimes adapted from radio scripts previously written by other writers.

Charteris had been approached several times over the years for television rights in the Saint and had expended much time and effort during the 1950s trying to get the Saint on TV, even going so far as to write sample scripts himself, but it wasn't to be. He finally agreed a deal in autumn 1961 with English film producers Robert S. Baker and Monty Berman. The first episode of *The Saint* television series, starring Roger Moore, went into production in June 1962. The series was an immediate success, though Charteris himself had his reservations. It reached second place in the ratings, but he commented that "in that distinction it was topped by wrestling, which only suggested to me that the competition may not have been so hot; but producers are generally cast in a less modest mould." He resented the implication that the TV series had finally made a success of the Saint after twenty-five years of literary obscurity.

As long as the series lasted, Charteris was not shy about voicing his criticisms both in public and in a constant stream of memos to the producers. "Regular followers of the Saint saga . . . must have noticed that I am almost incapable of simply writing a story and shutting up."[10] Nor was he shy about exploiting this new market by agreeing to a series of tie-in novelisations ghosted by other writers, which he would then rewrite before publication.

Charteris mellowed as the series developed and found elements to praise too. He developed a close friendship with producer Robert S. Baker, which would last until Charteris's death.

In the early '60s, on one of their frequent trips to England, Leslie and Audrey bought a house in Surrey, which became their permanent base. He explored the possibility of a Saint musical and began writing some of it himself.

Charteris no longer needed to work. Now in his sixties, he supervised the Saint from a distance whilst continuing to travel and indulge himself. He and Audrey made seasonal excursions to Ireland and the south of France, where they had residences. He began to write poetry and devised a new universal sign language, Paleneo, based on notes and symbols he used in his diaries. Once Paleneo was released, he decided enough was enough and announced, again, his retirement. This time he meant it.

The Saint continued regardless—there was a long-running Swedish comic strip, and new novels with other writers doing the bulk of the work were complemented in the 1970s with Bob Baker's revival of the TV series, *Return of the Saint*.

Ill-health began to take its toll. By the early 1980s, although he continued a healthy correspondence with the outside world, Charteris felt unable to keep up with the collaborative Saint books and pulled the plug on them.

To entertain himself, Leslie took to "trying to beat the bookies in predicting the relative speed of horses," a hobby which resulted in several of his local betting shops refusing to take "predictions" from him, as he was too successful for their liking.

He still received requests to publish his work abroad but had become completely cynical about further attempts to revive the Saint. A new Saint magazine only lasted three issues, and two TV productions— *The Saint in Manhattan*, with Tom Selleck look-alike Andrew Clarke, and *The Saint*, with Simon Dutton—left him bitterly disappointed. "I fully expect this series to lay eggs everywhere . . . the only satisfaction I have is in looking at my bank balance."[11]

In the early 1990s, Hollywood producers Robert Evans and William J. Macdonald approached him and made a deal for the Saint to return to cinema screens. Charteris still took great care of the Saint's reputation and wrote an outline entitled *The Return of the Saint* in which an older Saint would meet the son he didn't know he had.

Much of his time in his last few years was taken up with the movie. Several scripts were submitted to him—each moving further and further away from his original concept—but the screenwriter from 1940s Hollywood was thoroughly disheartened by the Hollywood of the '90s: "There is still no plot, no real story, no characterisations, no personal interaction, nothing but endless frantic violence . . ." Besides, with producer Bill Macdonald hitting the headlines for the most un-Saintly reasons, he was to add, "How can Bill Macdonald concentrate on my Saint movie when he has Sharon Stone in his bed?"

The Crime Writers' Association of Great Britain presented Leslie with a Lifetime Achievement award in 1992 in a special ceremony at the

House of Lords. Never one for associations and awards, and although visibly unwell, Leslie accepted the award with grace and humour ("I am now only waiting to be carbon-dated," he joked). He suffered a slight stroke in his final weeks, which did not prevent him from dining out locally with family and friends, before he finally passed away at the age of 85 on 15 April 1993.

His death severed one of the final links with the classic thriller genre of the 1930s and 1940s, but he left behind a legacy of nearly one hundred books, countless short stories, and TV, film, radio, and comic-strip adaptations of his work which will endure for generations to come.

> *I was always sure that there was a solid place in escape literature for a rambunctious adventurer such as I dreamed up in my youth, who really believed in the old-fashioned romantic ideals and was prepared to lay everything on the line to bring them to life. A joyous exuberance that could not find its fulfilment in pinball machines and pot. I had what may now seem a mad desire to spread the belief that there were worse, and wickeder, nut cases than Don Quixote.*
>
> *Even now, half a century later, when I should be old enough to know better, I still cling to that belief. That there will always be a public for the old-style hero, who had a clear idea of justice, and a more than technical approach to love, and the ability to have some fun with his crusades.*[12]

---

1 *A Letter from the Saint*, 30 August 1946
2 "The Last Word," *The First Saint Omnibus*, Doubleday Crime Club, 1939
3 *The Straits Times*, 29 June 1958, page 9

4 Introduction by Charteris to the September 1980 paperback reprint of *Meet—the Tiger!* (Charter), the last ever print edition.

5 *The Saint: A Complete History,* by Burl Barer (McFarland, 1993)

6 PR material from the 1970s series *Return of the Saint*

7 From "Return of the Saint: Comprehensive Information" issued to help publicise the 1970s TV show

8 *A Letter from the Saint,* 26 July 1946

9 Introduction to "The Million Pound Day," in *The First Saint Omnibus*

10 *A Letter from the Saint,* 12 April 1946

11 Letter from LC to sometime Saint collaborator Peter Bloxsom, 2 August 1989

12 Introduction by Charteris to the September 1980 paperback reprint of *Meet—the Tiger!* (Charter).

WATCH FOR THE SIGN

OF THE SAINT!

THE SAINT CLUB

And so, my friends, dear bookworms, most noble fellow drinkers, frustrated burglars, affronted policemen, upright citizens with furled umbrellas and secret buccaneering dreams that seems to be very nearly all for now. It has been nice having you with us, and we hope you will come again, not once, but many times.

Only because of our great love for you, we would like to take this parting opportunity of mentioning one small matter which we have very much at heart . . .

—Leslie Charteris, *The First Saint Omnibus* (1939)

Leslie Charteris founded The Saint Club in 1936 with the aim of providing a constructive fanbase for Saint devotees. Before the War, it donated profits to a London hospital where, for several years, a Saint ward was maintained. With the nationalisation of hospitals, profits were, for many years, donated to the Arbour Youth Centre in Stepney, London.

In the twenty-first century, we've carried on this tradition but have also donated to the Red Cross and a number of different children's charities.

The club acts as a focal point for anyone interested in the adventures of Leslie Charteris and the work of Simon Templar, and offers merchandise that includes DVDs of the old TV series and various Saint-related publications, through to its own exclusive range of notepaper, pin badges, and polo shirts. All profits are donated to charity. The club also maintains two popular websites and supports many more Saint-related sites.

After Leslie Charteris's death, the club recruited three new vice-presidents—Roger Moore, Ian Ogilvy, and Simon Dutton have all pledged their support, whilst Audrey and Patricia Charteris have been retained as Saints-in-Chief. But some things do not change, for the back of the membership card still mischievously proclaims that . . .

> *The bearer of this card is probably a person of hideous*
> *antecedents and low moral character, and upon*
> *apprehension for any cause should be immediately released*
> *in order to save other prisoners from contamination.*

To join . . .

Membership costs £3.50 (or US$7) per year, or £30 (US$60) for life. Find us online at www.lesliecharteris.com for full details.

Made in the USA
Middletown, DE
21 October 2022